Once again Dylan James had stepped into Marissa's life and changed everything.

Only she wasn't some love-struck teenager any longer, and she wasn't about to make the same mistakes twice. After all, she didn't just have herself to look out for—she had Josh to think of now, too.

She needed time to think, time to try to figure out just what she was doing. She couldn't afford any mistakes—not this time. There was too much at stake. This time she wasn't worried about a broken heart, she was worried about Josh—her son.

Their son.

Dear Reader,

Happy Valentine's Day! And as a special gift to you, we're publishing the latest in *New York Times* bestseller Linda Howard's series featuring the Mackenzie family. Hero Zane Mackenzie, of *Mackenzie's Pleasure*, is every inch a man—and Barrie Lovejoy is just the woman to teach this rough, tough Navy SEAL what it means to love. There's nothing left to say but "Enjoy!"

Merline Lovelace concludes her "Code Name: Danger" miniseries with *Perfect Double*, the long-awaited romance between Maggie Sinclair and her boss at the OMEGA Agency, Adam Ridgeway. Then join Kylie Brant for *Guarding Raine*. This author established herself as a reader favorite with her very first book—and her latest continues the top-notch tradition. *Forever, Dad* is the newest from Maggie Shayne, and it's an exciting, suspenseful, *emotional* tour de force. For those of you with a hankering to get "Spellbound," there's Vella Munn's *The Man From Forever*, a story of love and passion that transcend time. Finally, Rebecca Daniels wraps up her "It Takes Two" duo with *Father Figure*, featuring the ever-popular secret baby plot line.

Pick up all six of these wonderful books—and come back next month for more, because here at Silhouette Intimate Moments we're dedicated to bringing you the best of today's romantic fiction. Enjoy!

Yours,

Leslie Wainger
Senior Editor and Editorial Coordinator

Please address questions and book requests to:
Silhouette Reader Service
U.S.: 3010 Walden Ave., P.O. Box 1325, Buffalo, NY 14269
Canadian: P.O. Box 609, Fort Erie, Ont. L2A 5X3

FATHER FIGURE

REBECCA DANIELS

Silhouette®
INTIMATE™ MOMENTS®

Published by Silhouette Books

America's Publisher of Contemporary Romance

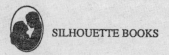

SILHOUETTE BOOKS

ISBN 0-373-07696-7

FATHER FIGURE

REBECCA DANIELS

will never forget the first time she read a Silhouette novel. "I was at my sister's house, sitting by the pool and trying without much success to get interested in the book I'd brought from home. Everything seemed to distract me—the kids splashing around, the sea gulls squawking, the dog barking. Finally, my sister plucked the book from my hands, told me she was going to give me something I wouldn't be able to put down and handed me my first Silhouette novel. Guess what? She was right! For that lazy afternoon by her pool, I will forever be grateful." That was years ago, and Rebecca has been writing romance novels ever since.

Born in the Midwest but raised in Southern California, she now resides in Northern California's San Joaquin Valley with her husband and two sons. She is a lifelong poet and song lyricist who enjoys early-morning walks, an occasional round of golf, scouring California's Mother Lode region for antiques and traveling.

TYVMFE! — For Lucy and Ethel

Also:
For Jonathan, Christian,
Mary, Maureen and Janis,
for listening, for holding on,
and for saving my life.

Prologue

"If you'd just let me explain—"

"Explain?" Dylan shouted, turning away and slamming the football he held onto the grass. The pigskin ball bounced high from the force of impact and spun wildly across the lawn. "What's there to explain? It worked—I fell for your little trick hook, line and sinker. So you can go now—get out of here. You and your sister have had your fun, you've gotten your laugh. Just leave me alone."

"Dylan, please," Marissa pleaded, taking a step forward and feeling more desperate, more frightened, than she'd ever been in her life. "Please just listen. It wasn't like that, it wasn't a joke."

"Then, what was it, Marissa?" Dylan demanded, spinning back around and glaring down at her. "What would you call letting me think all this time you were Mallory? What would you call it when one twin pretends to be the other?"

Marissa stared up at him. His strong, handsome face was streaked with anger, and his dark eyes shimmered bright with tears he wouldn't allow to fall. "I wanted to tell you—I would have—"

"Oh, really? When, *Marissa?* When would you have done that?" he demanded, his mouth twisting into an angry snarl. "Before you slept with me, or after?"

Marissa felt his words like a million little arrows straight through the heart. Mallory had warned she would be playing with fire, had pleaded with her to go to Dylan with the truth. Why hadn't she listened? Why hadn't she been smart this time?

She hadn't meant to hurt his feelings. She and her identical twin sister Mallory had been fooling people since the day they were born. She was used to being mistaken for Mallory, used to people who were unsure "which one" she was. It hadn't surprised her a bit that Dylan had thought she was Mallory when she'd pulled into the service station where he worked for the summer.

As head cheerleader for the football team, Mallory had been friends with all the players on the team—and of course that had included star quarterback Dylan James. After all, Mallory was the "popular" twin, the "fun" one—the one who cheered at all the football games and went to all the dances and parties. Marissa, on the other hand, had always been the "quiet" twin, the "shy" one—the "brainy" one who studied all the time and always made the honor roll. She'd often envied Mallory's outgoing nature and her ease with people, but never more so than on that hot summer morning at the service station. When Dylan had stepped up to the car and started talking to her, she'd actually wished at that moment she were Mallory.

She'd meant to correct him—she really had. It just had been so nice to actually have his attention for a while, and it seemed like such a harmless pretense. Mallory wouldn't have cared—she had no interest in Dylan. The uncanny connection the two of them shared—the "twin radar" that allowed them to know what the other was feeling—made her sure of that, just like it had made Mallory aware of the secret crush Marissa had always carried for Dylan. Only...somehow the pretending had gotten out of hand....

Suddenly he'd asked her for a date, and foolishly she'd accepted. She'd driven out of the service station telling herself it wasn't right, telling herself she would tell him the truth the minute she saw him again. Only he'd looked so handsome on her porch that night, and he'd looked at her with such dark, hungry eyes. Marissa found herself pretending again, found herself making believe and letting the charade continue—and letting one date lead to another, and then another, and then another....

Suddenly the summer months seemed to disappear. She and Dylan had become inseparable, spending every free moment together—alone and away from everyone else. Mallory had seen what was happening, and she'd pleaded with her to stop, but she'd hesitated, she'd been too afraid of losing Dylan for good.

How had things gotten so out of control? How could she have been so foolish? She knew time was running out. School would be starting soon, and the truth had to come out. She'd fallen in love with him, and he loved her, too. She wanted him to know it was *her* he loved—Marissa, not Mallory. She wanted to wait for the right moment, wanted a chance to explain.

But she'd waited too long. Word had gotten out, gossip had spread and he'd discovered the truth on his own. The whole football team knew the trick Marissa had played on him, and he would never forgive her now.

"Dylan, please, please, just listen," she cried, the tears spilling out of her eyes so quickly she could barely see any longer. She reached out, placing a hesitant hand on his arm. "I'm sorry. I'm so sorry. I love you. I love you."

"You *love* me?" Dylan snorted, snatching his arm away and stumbling back a step. "I don't even know who you are. I don't know anything about you."

"That's not true," she said, sobbing, taking an unsteady step toward him. "You know me. You know everything about me."

"I thought you were Mallory," he growled. "I thought I knew Mallory. I thought . . ." He squeezed his eyes tight, shaking his head. "I thought I'd fallen in love with Mallory."

"Dylan," Marissa cried when he turned and started across the yard. "Please, come back."

"Leave me alone," he said, stopping as he stalked across the grass and slowly turned around. "I was never interested in playing with the second string."

Chapter 1

Sixteen years later

Dylan took the granite steps leading up to the Amador County sheriff's office two at a time. It wasn't even ten yet, but already temperatures in Northern California's rustic little town of Jackson had started to climb. He swiped at the sweat forming along his brow, cursing beneath his breath. Summers in the Mother Lode could be miserably hot, and this was promising to be a cooker.

Loosening his tie from the collar of his wilted khaki shirt, he headed for the door marked Authorized Personnel Only. Pushing it open, he was greeted by a cooling blast of air, hitting him in the face and sending a welcoming gust of relief through his overheated system. He sailed down the narrow corridor toward the reception area, reaching up and wrestling the top button of his shirt free.

He hated getting to work late. He also hated wasting a good chunk of the morning in long, boring budget meetings with a board of supervisors more interested in reelection campaigns than providing leadership to their constituency, but this morning he'd had little choice. As sheriff, his attendance at the county's semiannual budget meeting was mandatory. However, one budget meeting was pretty much like the next—with him asking for enough money to hire five new deputies and with the board approving enough funds for one.

Sheriff Dylan James was too practical, too used to rolling up his sleeves and meeting problems head-on, to enjoy playing political games. But in a county where special interest and favoritism were as much a part of local government as gold mining was to the historical landscape, it was something he'd had to get accustomed to. At thirty-three, he found dealing with the "good old boys" no easier now than he had when he'd been a kid growing up on the wrong side of the tracks. Except now those "old boys" looked to him to keep the peace. One additional deputy wasn't going to ease the burden of his overworked staff, but when other departments were being cut, it was better than nothing.

Dylan smiled a little. Political savvy. Maybe he'd developed a little in spite of himself.

He stepped behind the desk sergeant and reached for the mail in his bin. He thumbed through the stack of letters and flyers, only vaguely aware of the cluster of people on the other side of the counter lined up to speak with the desk sergeant. He was too busy trying to decide which of the letters he had to answer first, and which ones he could bury until later.

"I'm back, Kim," he said to the pretty, blond female officer behind the counter, not bothering to look up from the letter in his hand. "Send down my messages, would you? And could you find me that report on overtime hours? I need to take a look at that."

"Sure thing, Sheriff," Kimberly Young said quickly. "Oh, and, Sheriff—"

"And get the D.A.'s office on the line, too, would you?" Dylan added, cutting her off. "I want to know what the hell happened to that warrant request we sent over."

"Will do," Kimberly said, nodding. "But—"

"And make sure they know we're waiting."

Exasperated, Kimberly purposefully reached out and caught him by the arm. *"Sheriff."*

Dylan looked up from the letter, surprised. "What is it?"

She leaned closer, lowering her voice. "There's someone waiting to see you."

Dylan made a face, checking the time on his wristwatch. "I'm running kind of late this morning. Have you any idea what it's about?"

"It's about Joshua Wakefield."

It wasn't the name that sent a cold jolt of surprise shooting down his spine, but rather the sound of the voice of the woman who said it. Looking up, he felt all the air empty out of his lungs and was jolted backward in time, back to when he'd been Jackson High School's star quarterback, and had thought he'd found the girl of his dreams.

"Marissa?"

"Hello, Dylan," Marissa said in that whispery voice that he'd heard a million times in his dreams—and in his nightmares. "It's been a long time."

Long time? Had she honestly said it had been a *long time?* It had been a lifetime.

"Yeah, I guess it has been," he said, keeping his voice bland and unemotional as only a seasoned cop could. But the fact was, seeing her had shaken him up. "How have you been?"

"Fine, thanks," she said, taking a deep breath. "And you?"

Actually, he felt a little like he'd just had a close encounter with a boxer's fist, but he simply shrugged. "Fine. Just fine."

For years he'd wondered what he would say, or what he would do, if he ever saw her again. Now, apparently, he would find out. Memories were coming back in a rush—painful, haunting memories he'd hoped would stay buried for good. He'd worked hard at forgetting her, forcing her out of his life and out of his head. But now, after what seemed like a lifetime away, Marissa Wakefield was back in both.

"You needed to see me about something?" he asked after a moment.

"Yes, yes, I did," she said with a small laugh, giving her head a little shake. "I can see that you're awfully busy. It's just that Josh's hearing is tomorrow, and I thought if you had a few minutes..." She let her words drift, primly tucking a strand of long blond hair behind an ear. "I don't mind waiting, really."

He wasn't exactly surprised. Marissa Wakefield's nephew had been a gigantic pain in the butt the last couple of years. Josh and his friends had been responsible for their own minor reign of terror in Amador County. Dylan had pulled them in on charges ranging from trespassing when they egged the mayor's house to joyriding in his mother's car. In the past, the Wakefields had always had someone around to bail them out, soothe the ruffled feathers and keep a tight lid on everything—but it was serious this time. Josh and his friends were facing a charge of arson, and they were all headed for juvenile hall.

Dylan looked at the woman who had once been his lover, and felt a tightness in his chest. They'd barely been much older than Josh and his buddies when they'd known each other back in school, and yet she'd hardly changed. Of course there was a maturity about her now, and a sophistication that hadn't been there before. But she had the same beauty, the same elegance and class.

And classy was exactly how she looked standing there in a sleek blue-green linen suit that matched the color of her eyes almost perfectly. Around her neck was a delicate gold necklace, a thin chain with a crescent-shaped cluster of stars forming the pendant. She looked so cool, so composed, as if the sweltering summer sun wouldn't dare overheat her.

She looked good all right, but Dylan knew better than most just how deceiving looks could be—especially when it came to Marissa Wakefield.

"Kim, hold all my calls," he said in a quiet voice. Turning back to Marissa, he gestured to the door at the end of the counter. "Come on back. Let's talk in my office."

"It was nice seeing you again, Kimberly." Marissa smiled at the young desk officer behind the counter. "Give my best to your family."

"I will, Marissa," Kimberly said, giving her a small wave. "Nice to see you, too."

Marissa stepped into the small corridor where Sheriff Dylan James stood waiting. She felt awkward and completely defenseless, a little like a lamb entering a lion's den. But she'd come too far to back out now. Josh's whole future was at stake, and for him she was willing to take on the whole pride.

She hadn't exactly given this a lot of thought—just showing up out of the blue. Josh's intrepid, but somewhat embattled, lawyer, Evan Brown, had thought an appeal to the judge by the county sheriff on Josh's behalf just might help against a district attorney who was hell-bent on seeing his client sentenced to the youth authority. And while she hadn't exactly welcomed the idea of seeing Dylan James again—especially to ask for his help—there was too much on the line to let a few reservations get in the way. So, without much thought or debate, she'd simply decided to come—just like that.

Normally Marissa Wakefield never did anything "just like that." She was too structured, too down-to-earth and too rooted in practicality and realism to make rash or impulsive decisions. She'd been rash and impulsive only once—sixteen years ago, as a matter of fact—and her life had never been the same since. And from that point on, she'd played it safe. Except this time it wasn't about her, it was about Josh, and when it came to him, she had a hard time playing it safe.

Marissa allowed Dylan to usher her down the narrow hall toward a large set of doors at the end. Nerves had her feeling clumsy and self-conscious. The simple act of putting one foot in front of the other took considerable concentration, and she found his polite hand at her elbow distracting. It was an innocent gesture, automatic and meaningless, really, but it made her terribly uncomfortable, and she didn't want him to feel her trembling.

"This way," Dylan said, reaching around her to pull open one of the heavy wooden doors.

Dropping his hold on her elbow, he gallantly stepped to one side to allow her to pass. But Marissa had taken only a few steps forward when her ankle buckled suddenly beneath her, throwing her off-balance and sending a painful cramp up her leg. She landed against Dylan's solid frame with a thud.

"Are you all right?" he asked quickly, his arms snapping up to steady her. "Have you hurt yourself?"

"No, I'm fine," she groaned, as much from humiliation as the pain. She could feel the heat rising in her cheeks, and she dared not look up at him. "I'm sorry. It's my ankle."

"Is it okay?" he asked, but then didn't wait for an answer. "Let's get you inside and off your feet."

"I'm fine, really," she insisted, protesting his efforts, but it was too late. His arm was already around her waist, and he was guiding her through the open doorway and across the hard gray carpet to one of the chairs in front of his desk.

"Maybe we should get someone down here, have a look at it," he said, kneeling down and gently slipping a hand around her ankle. "Just to be on the safe side."

"No, it's fine. *Really,*" she insisted again, fighting off a feeling of desperation. Her face was flaming now, and she found his hand around her ankle unnerving. Only the thin nylon of her stocking separated his skin from hers, and as far as she was concerned that wasn't nearly enough. She reached down, tactfully waving his hand and his concern aside. "It's nothing, really. I broke it a while back. The cast's only been off a few days—it's just still a little weak."

Dylan leaned back, releasing his hold and looking up at her. He'd felt a tremble when he'd touched her, a momentary stirring beneath the skin. It had surprised him, but what surprised him more was that he hadn't been able to tell if it had come from her—or him.

"You should probably take it easy," he advised, slowly rising to his feet and making his way around the desk. "Another fall could easily reinjure it."

"I know," she said with a sigh, making a play of twisting her ankle about as though working out a kink. With him farther away and his hands no longer touching her, she began to relax again. The heat in her cheeks had cooled, and she felt her composure return. "I've been doing some strengthening exercises, but obviously there's a ways to go. It's been very frustrating."

"You must have taken quite a spill."

Marissa straightened up, rolling her eyes and making light of the fall she'd taken that had left her ankle fractured in two places. "Well, let's just say it was enough so that if I don't see another set of crutches again for a while, I won't be upset."

She glanced around the office, spotting a small framed picture of Dylan in a battered Jackson High School football uniform, holding a muddied football triumphantly over his head.

Second string. She still remembered him calling her that. Those words had created a wound in her psyche that had taken years to heal. She'd given him her love, but all he'd really wanted was the most popular girl in school.

"This is nice," she said, gesturing with her hand around the office and pushing that unpleasant thought from her mind. "Looks like things have gone well for you."

"It's been okay," he mumbled with a nod as he gathered up the loose papers on his desk and stuffed them back into a file folder. He was suddenly self-conscious of the pictures and plaques that lined the walls, and the memorabilia that littered his desk and shelves. They revealed everything about him—his education, his friends, his interests, even his sense of humor. It was as though his whole life surrounded her, and he wasn't sure he was comfortable showing her so much. "Uh, could I get you something? A cup of coffee, maybe, some iced tea?"

"No, nothing, thanks," she said, thinking a dose of caffeine was just about the last thing her jumpy nerves needed.

"So, is Mallory back with you?" he asked, the slight tension at his jaw the only outward sign of discomfort. The subject of her identical twin wasn't exactly one he broached with enthusiasm.

"No. No, I just flew in yesterday myself," Marissa said, shaking her head and smiling just a little too broadly. "Actually, Mallory's been on her honeymoon. She got married a few weeks ago."

"No kidding? I hadn't heard," he said, settling back in his chair and resting his elbows on the arms.

"It all happened pretty fast," Marissa admitted.

"That's great. You'll have to congratulate her for me. Someone she met in D.C.?"

"Uh, no," she answered, wondering how it was he knew she'd lived there. "Actually, it was someone she met when she was visiting me in Arizona. Benjamin Graywolf. He's a lawyer—a tribal lawyer, actually. They live on the Navaho reservation.''

"Really?" His dark brow rose sightly. "Sounds interesting. I hope they'll be very happy."

"Oh, I think they will," Marissa said wistfully. She thought of Mallory and how beautiful her sister had looked on her wedding day. "Graywolf is a wonderful man, and he loves my sister very much."

"What about you?"

She looked up, surprised. "What about me?"

"Is there a husband somewhere?" Dylan was satisfied that the bland, unemotional tone of his voice betrayed none of the emotion churning around inside him. He'd made it a point not to think about her over the years, but sometimes that hadn't always been possible. Every once in a while something would happen and he would find himself remembering her—locked in time as a perpetual teenager—young, beautiful…and forever belonging to him. But it was a real woman who sat across from him now, a real woman who had left him behind and gone on with her life. Still, there was something inside of him that refused to let go and revolted at the thought of her with another man.

"No," Marissa said with a little laugh, shaking her head. "I'm not married."

"Kids?"

Kids. Marissa felt the knot in her stomach double twice in size. If he only knew. But then, she'd taken careful pains so that he never would.

Chapter 2

"No," she said quietly, feeling every muscle in her face betray her. "No children." She nervously twisted the strap of her purse and forced herself to smile. "But I remember hearing you'd gotten married. Stephanie Jacobs, wasn't it?" She also remembered crying for two days straight after Mallory had called to tell her the news.

"Yeah, Steph," he nodded, thinking how easily he'd put those four turbulent years with Stephanie behind him. "But that's been over a long time."

"I'm sorry," she mumbled. She'd known that, too.

He shrugged carelessly. "We're both better off, and thankfully there weren't any children involved."

He watched as she toyed with the handle of her purse, thinking the gesture seemed oddly out of place for someone so cool and collected. It was the kind of nervous fidgeting he expected from a suspect with something to hide. Did she have something to hide, or was she just remembering the trick she and her sister had played on him, the gag that had cut like a knife and turned his heart to stone?

Like every guy on the Jackson High football team, he'd wanted Mallory Wakefield. She'd been the most popular girl in school—rich, pretty—the one all his buddies pursued for a date. He could hardly believe it when she'd agreed to go out with him. But the Wakefield twins had faked a pass, they'd sent in a ringer, and he'd been left looking like a clown.

Of course, when his buddies on the team found out, they'd all thought it was hilarious. The brainy captain of the debate team had really managed to put the dumb jock in his place. And of course he'd done what he always did when things hurt him—he'd laughed, joked and covered up. He laughed right along with his friends—taking the ribbing with good nature, never showing his real feelings. But the truth was, he'd been devastated.

Dylan closed his eyes, feeling the embers of that old hurt sputter briefly into flame. It was history. He had more important things to worry about now and was too old to let things that had happened a lifetime ago bother him now.

He came forward slowly in his chair, careful to keep all trace of bitterness out of his voice. "I was sorry to hear about your brother, and Penny, too. That had to be rough for your family."

Marissa drew in a weary breath. Caleb's death two years ago from a car accident had left them all in shock—especially her nephew, Josh. He began skipping school, getting into trouble. Penny never really recovered from the loss either, and Josh's problems were more than she could handle. Three months ago, when she slammed her car into the side of a mountain, they all knew the accident wasn't really what killed her. She'd really died of grief.

But while the accident had ended Penny's pain, it had also left Josh alone—and in serious trouble. He was arrested for arson one short month after his mother's funeral.

"Yes, it's been difficult on everyone," she agreed in a quite voice. "Especially Josh."

"And that's why you're here," he said, linking his fingers together. "To talk about Josh."

She lifted her gaze, looking up at him. This was going to be more difficult than she'd thought. The slant of his brow, the angle of his cheekbone, the set of his chin, were all so endearingly familiar she felt a thick lump of emotion build in her throat. "Yes, to talk about Josh."

He reached down and picked up a pencil from his desk. "What can I do to help?"

She straightened up in her chair. "I'm petitioning the court for custody tomorrow."

Dylan's eyes widened. "Oh?"

"You sound surprised."

He sat back in the chair again. "I guess I am, a little. I'd just assumed...I don't know, I guess I thought he'd just live here with your folks—after all this is over, I mean."

"They aren't up to raising a teenager," she said, repeating the well-rehearsed speech she'd prepared for Dylan or anyone else who might ask about her motivation. "My dad will be eighty in a few months, my mom is seventy-three. This whole thing has taken its toll on them."

"But with you in Arizona, won't that be a problem with the courts?"

"I . . . I'm not living in Arizona any longer," she said in a quiet voice. "I'm back in Jackson. For good."

Dylan felt the chair beneath him shift. "You're going to live here?"

"I've taken a job at Sutter High, the continuation school."

The muscle in Dylan's jaw worked furiously. He knew the district's school for troubled teens all too well—having hauled in a number of the students at one time or another. "I didn't know you were a teacher. What grade?"

"I won't actually be teaching there," she explained. Those dark, probing eyes made her uneasy, as though he was able to see more than she wanted him to, more than she'd intended. "I've been hired as principal."

"I see," he said in that noncommittal way cops get so good at.

"We . . . the family, I mean, talked about it when I was here for Penny's funeral," she continued, doing her best to ignore his intense gaze. She glanced down at her lap but could still feel his eyes on her. "I would have filed the papers then, but there didn't seem to be any rush, and Evan— our lawyer—thought it would be better for the courts if I'd had some clear plans first—for relocating, and a job, things like that. Unfortunately I got waylaid by this stupid ankle injury, and things got held up." She paused then, and shook her head. "And then Josh got arrested."

His eyes narrowed again as he watched her. Raising a juvenile delinquent hardly seemed to fit into the Wakefield style, but then serving as principal to a school full of misfits and outcasts didn't, either. "And now you have second thoughts?"

Her head jerked up. "No, nothing like that. I want Josh with me, I want to do what I can to help him, give him some direction."

"And what does Josh want?"

She clasped her hands together, taking a deep breath. "The same thing—at least he did. Since the arrest, I haven't been able to talk to him. The jail wouldn't allow any long-distance telephone calls, and by the time my flight got in last night, I'd missed visiting hours. I'm headed out there next."

"Is that what you'd like me to do? Make arrangements at the jail for you?" he asked, feeling just a little deflated. Was her reason in coming that simple?

"Uh . . . no," she said, stopping him as he picked up the phone with a hand on his. "Actually, I was hoping to talk to you about the hearing tomorrow."

He looked at her pale, beautiful hand on his, and his mind flashed to another time, another place. "I'm not sure what I can do to help you with that. It's the D.A. you should be talking to, not me."

She moved her hand back to her lap, embarrassed by the impulsive move. "But that's the problem. The district attorney wants to put Josh in the juvenile authority. Evan said he's insisting on at least six months, maybe even a year." She leaned forward, forgetting everything at the moment except her concern for Josh. "Dylan, that's the last thing Josh needs right now. He needs someone in his corner, to watch out for him. He needs to be with me. I'll take the responsibility. I'll make sure he stays out of trouble." She paused, moistening her dry lips. "I was hoping you would help me convince the judge of that."

Dylan leaned back in his chair. "But you're forgetting he's committed a very serious crime."

"No, I'm not," she said, shaking her head. "I don't deny what he did was wrong. He's a kid with problems—serious problems—and I intend to see he gets counseling." She paused again, not wanting emotion to scatter her thoughts. "He needs love and understanding, not to be stuck in a cell somewhere and forgotten."

Dylan had to smile at her bleak description of the juvenile facility in nearby Ione. "Prescott is hardly a dungeon. It just looks like one. It's more like a military school. And it's close. You could visit him whenever you wanted."

Marissa reared her head up, not wanting to think of Josh behind bars. "It would be a mistake to send him there."

Something in her clipped, authoritarian tone had his hackles going up. He'd treated Josh Wakefield like any other kid who'd been brought in, and he owed her no explanations. He was the sheriff, and he'd been doing the job, enforcing the laws he'd been sworn to uphold. So how could those cool blue eyes of hers make him feel defensive? Why did he feel he wanted her to understand?

"It's discipline, and that's exactly what he needs," Dylan said in a tight, controlled voice. "Look, I know it might seem harsh to you, but you have to understand, this isn't the first time Josh has been in trouble. It's not up to me to decide if he stays in jail or not—only the judge can make that decision. But I have to tell you, with Josh's background of trouble, it's a pretty sure bet the court is going to want Josh to spend some time in custody on this."

Her head snapped up. "He's already been in custody. You've kept him in that holding facility for the last six weeks."

Dylan saw the fire in her eyes, the passion, and felt an old emotion stir. "It was Judge Kent's decision to deny bail." He paused a moment, tapping the pencil lightly against the edge of the desk. The casual gesture helped divert some of the emotion simmering just below the surface. "And like I said, this isn't the first time he—"

"I know this isn't the first time," Marissa snapped impatiently, cutting him off. "I don't need to be reminded of Josh's history. I know he's been in trouble before. But surely you understand that a lot has happened in his life in the last two years. For God's sake, doesn't he deserve some compassion? He's lost both his parents, his whole life has been turned upside down."

Dylan tossed the pencil back down onto the desk. "I'm aware of that, and I'm sure Evan Brown is going to make the court aware of it, too." He stopped, forcing himself to take slow, regular breaths. "But the fact remains that this isn't the first time Josh has been arrested. I've had that kid in here more times than I care to remember in the last two years." He stopped again, leaning forward in his chair. "Let's be honest, Josh has been given chance after chance to straighten out, to get his act together, and he's ignored

every one of them. The thing that's different this time is
that he's being charged with a serious crime. He upped the
ante this time, and I don't think the judge will be so willing to sweep it under the rug. He and his two buddies
knowingly destroyed public property—on the very campus
of the school you'll be working at, I might add. There was
a lot of damage done, and it's just lucky no one was hurt."

"But no one *was* hurt," she insisted, knowing everything he said was the truth, but hating the fact that it was
he who was saying it.

"But what about next time? Do we have to wait until
someone is?"

Marissa thought for a moment, working the handle of
her purse nervously. "But what if I promise there won't be
a next time?"

"Can you do that?" he asked skeptically.

"Yes," she said earnestly. "I think I can. It's important
for Josh to get his life together. I want him to know there's
someone in his corner, someone he can depend on, who
isn't going away, who's never going to leave him."

Dylan recognized the look of love and sincerity in her
eyes and almost felt himself believing. But dark, distant
memories had him remembering a time he'd seen that soft
look of hers before. She'd been lying to him then—was she
lying now, too?

Dylan took a deep breath. They might have been lovers,
but they were hardly old friends, and it wasn't fair to try
and second-guess the motives of a woman who was little
more than a stranger to him now.

"It isn't you who needs to promise," he said quietly.
"It's Josh." He stopped, searching for the right words. "I
know this might be hard for you to believe, but I like
Josh—I really do, and I think he's basically a good kid. But
he's got to learn to be accountable, he's got to start taking
responsibility for his actions."

Marissa's throat was thick with emotion. "But he's . . . he's just a boy, he's—"

"He's fifteen years old," he said, not waiting for her to finish. "Every time I've brought him in here, *every time,* there has been someone—Penny, or your father, or one of your family's friends on the city council or board of supervisors—someone to step in and make excuses, someone to smooth things over for him. Now you're here, and you're asking me to do the same thing. I'm sorry, I just don't think that's what Josh needs."

"Look, I'm not asking you to smooth over anything," she said in a voice that belied the flash of anger. She'd come to ask his help, not to pull strings and make excuses. "Or sweep anything under the rug. What Josh needs is stability in his life again. I'm just asking for a chance to give him that, to make a difference in one boy's life."

"Doing six months at juvy would make a difference, too."

"Well," Marissa said after a moment, taking a deep breath. "It's obvious we're not going to agree on this." She reached for her purse, slipping the long strap over her shoulder. "I appreciate you taking the time to see me."

He studied her for a moment, making no move to get up or usher her out. "You've changed a lot in sixteen years."

She stopped as she started to rise, settling back in the chair. His affable tone surprised her, and immediately her defenses were up. "Should I take that as a compliment or an insult, Sheriff?"

He laughed, giving her a shrug. "It's just I remember you were supposed to be the *quiet* one."

Yes, she'd been the quiet one, the one he hadn't bothered with, the one he'd overlooked—second string and second best. "Well, a lot has changed since we were kids." She hesitated only briefly, knowing it was dangerous ground she was treading. "And maybe you didn't know me quite as well as you thought."

''Or... maybe you just didn't let me,'' he muttered quietly.

Marissa stared at him, feeling the heat rise in her cheeks again. ''Regardless of what you may think, Sheriff, I'm committed to this, to Josh,'' she said pointedly, refusing to stray from her purpose in coming. ''To making a home for him and helping him get his life back on track.''

''And helping him out of a jail rap is your way of doing that?''

''No,'' she said, coming to her feet. ''By trying to spare him an ordeal that would only be destructive.''

Dylan rose slowly, rounding the desk. He followed her to the door, watching her as she moved. Despite the weak ankle, her strides were smooth and determined, like a model on a runway. If there was one thing a career in law enforcement had given him, it was an insight into people, and if this woman had ever had been a shrinking violet—content to live in the shadow of her sister—she sure as hell wasn't one now. This was a woman who knew what she wanted and wasn't afraid to go after it. And even without the past they shared, she was someone he would never overlook again.

He thought of her passionate defense of her nephew, how she had spoken with such fervor and intensity. Would she bring that passion to everything she did?

His gaze dropped to her long blond hair. It looked shiny and lush against her blue-green linen jacket. He could remember what it felt like to have it fall against his skin—soft and satiny, with the delicate scent of honeysuckle and sunshine. Was it just as silky as he remembered?

''I'll bet you'll make a great principal,'' he said as he reached around her and pulled open the door.

''Why? Because I want to keep my nephew out of jail?''

''No,'' he said, watching the light from the fixtures overhead flash golden in her hair. ''Because you seem to care a lot about kids—about what happens to them.''

"Well, it would be a little silly to work in a school if you didn't care, don't you think?"

"I guess," he admitted, taking a step closer and convinced he could smell a hint of honeysuckle. "Kind of ironic, though, don't you think? I mean, you care so much about kids, yet you don't have one of your own."

"You're making too much of it."

"Mallory, you didn't see how he looked at me."

Marissa heard her sister's snort over the line and could picture the face she made.

"You're acting paranoid," Mallory said. "I told you this would happen if you moved back there."

"I'm not paranoid," Marissa insisted, even though she suspected that was exactly what she was. "I just thought it was kind of strange the way he stared at me, that's all."

"He was probably staring at you because he thought you looked great, and he couldn't believe what a jerk he'd been back in high school."

Marissa had to laugh, knowing she could always rely on her sister to make her feel better. "Yeah, well apparently he wasn't so torn up that he felt he could put in a good word with the judge."

"Maybe not," Mallory admitted, sensing her sister's smile and smiling herself. "But the judge gave you what you wanted, anyway, so you didn't need an endorsement from the good sheriff."

"Yeah, I guess you're right." Marissa sighed, peering through the breakfast nook and into the living room to where Josh lay sprawled across the sofa watching television. He glanced up just then, giving her a crooked grin and making her heart swell with emotion. He belonged with her now, and she couldn't help smiling.

Marissa had waited a long time for this day. She could still remember how she had felt when the doctor had confirmed what she already knew in her heart to be true—that she was carrying Dylan's child. First she'd panicked, then there had been a litany of self-recriminations, and then reality had set in. She was going to have a baby.

Going to Dylan had been out of the question. He hated her. And as far as she was concerned, he'd given up all rights to their child when he'd called her the second string. But she'd still had to tell her parents, and plans would have to be made.

With Mallory's help, she'd gone to her parents. She didn't think she'd ever loved her parents more than on that afternoon when she'd told them she was pregnant. There was no screaming, no fits of rage, no stern lectures or senseless scolding. That wasn't their style. They hadn't even pressed her to name the child's father. They simply had sat her down and helped her work out a solution—together.

The plan had been simple. She would go to her Aunt Bernice's in Maryland, to finish out her senior year of high school and quietly have her baby, away from the prying eyes of all those in Amador County. She had insisted on keeping her baby—until her brother Caleb had come to see her.

Caleb and his wife Penny had desperately hoped for a family, and had been devastated when they'd learned they could have no children of their own. They had pleaded with her, pointing out that she was so young, and had years of education and hard work ahead of her. They could provide her child with the kind of home and security it would take her years to achieve. They promised her access to the child at any time, only it would have to be as his aunt, and not his mother.

In the end, she turned the baby over to them, though a part of her died on the day. Her baby—a perfect little boy. She had named him Joshua—meaning salvation, because he'd been hers. And over the years she'd kept up the charade—playing the role of the doting aunt. But never had she stopped thinking of Josh as her own.

And now he belonged to her again…legally. Judge Kent had granted her custody just as he had granted the plan she and Evan had proposed that spared Josh the ten-month jail sentence the district attorney had been seeking. He was going to allow Josh and the other two boys arrested with him to work off their sentences by agreeing to maintain their attendance at the continuation school—starting with the summer school session—and to work afternoons to rebuild the toolshed they'd destroyed. All in all, her day in court had truly been a wonderful one.

"Of course I'm right," Mallory said, sounding uplifting and enthusiastic. "And with the hearing out of the way, you and Josh can concentrate on getting on with your lives and not have to worry about seeing Dylan any longer."

"Oh…about that," Marissa groaned, feeling some of her enthusiasm fade.

"What?" Mallory demanded, feeling her sister's disheartened spirit despite the sixteen hundred miles between them. "What haven't you told me?"

"Nothing, really," Marissa twisted the spiral telephone cord around her finger, remembering the look on Dylan's face when the judge read the sentence. "Just that when the judge agreed to let Josh and the other boys work off their sentence, the district attorney requested that a series of random checks be made on their progress—to be sure they make it to class, that the work on the shed is actually getting done—things like that."

"So?" Mallory prompted when her sister hesitated.

"So the judge granted the D.A.'s request."

"So what does that mean?"

"It means he's asked the good sheriff to stop from time to time to check on Josh's progress, and if Dylan finds that Josh isn't fulfilling his obligation, he can take him back into custody and send him to the youth authority."

"Oh," Mallory said glumly. "Which means Dylan James is smack-dab in the middle of your life again. You know, maybe this wasn't such a good idea, you moving back to Jackson—seeing him all the time.''

"How can you say that? Mallory, I've got my son. Don't you realize in my whole life, I never thought that would happen?''

"But at what cost? You don't think seeing Dylan over and over again won't hurt. You forget, I *know* what you felt for him. I remember what it did to you to lose him.''

Marissa closed her eyes. She remembered, too. "I've got Josh back, that's all that's important.''

"Is that Auntie Mal?''

Marissa jumped violently at the sound of Josh's voice behind her. She turned around, feeling the guilt spread across her face like a flashing neon sign. "Uh . . . yes, yes it is. She—uh—she called to see how things went in court today.''

"Can I talk to her?''

She searched his face, looking for any sign that he might have overheard any of their conversation, but his young handsome face looked innocent and sweet. Unaware until that moment that she was holding her breath, she slowly let it out. Maybe Mallory was right, maybe she was just a little bit paranoid.

"Sure honey, sure,'' she said, handing him the phone.

"Hi, Auntie Mal,'' he said, bringing the phone to his ear. "How does it feel to have a nephew who's not a jailbird any longer?''

Marissa watched her son as he talked and felt her heart swell. She took his teasing and flashes of humor as a good sign. The six weeks he'd spent at the juvenile holding facility at the Amador County jail had left him frightened, and very angry with life—and he still struggled with the loss of Penny. Of course, he'd done his best to put up a tough exterior—joking and acting like he didn't care—but she'd seen the look on his face when the judge had released him into her custody. He'd been tremendously relieved.

She walked across the kitchen, gazing out the window above the sink. But she didn't see the foothills in the distance. She thought of Dylan. Josh was so much like him, so much like the dashing high school quarterback she'd known all those years ago.

She thought of the man she'd seen in the courtroom today. He'd remained in the background of the proceedings, acknowledging her presence with only the slightest of nods. But she'd been aware of him just the same. He was different now. His shoulders were still as broad and straight as they'd been on the football field, but there was a harshness to his features now, a harshness in his face that hadn't been there before.

She pictured the stern set of his jaw, the lean cheeks, the cold, dark eyes. The beautiful boy had grown into a handsome man, but the life he'd seen was there on his face. And that is how he'd looked at her—hard, dispassionate and angry. Was there any of the boy left inside the man?

She glanced back across the small kitchen to Josh as he talked on the phone. His profile, the set of his shoulders, the slant of his eyes, were all so familiar. The physical resemblance between father and son was striking—so striking it made her uneasy. What did Dylan see when he looked at Josh? How long would it be before he looked at his son and recognized himself?

Chapter 3

"She wants to talk to you again."

Marissa gave her head a shake, forcing her thoughts aside, and reached for the phone.

"Hi," she said into the receiver, her voice sounding distant even to her own ears. She smiled as she watched Josh grab a bag of the cheddar-flavored popcorn they both loved, and amble back into the living room to collapse onto the sofa again. "So, what do you think?"

"I think what I always have—that he's a great kid," Mallory said without hesitation. "And that he sounds remarkably wonderful considering everything he's been through. And that the two you are lucky to have each other."

"I think you're right about that, big sister," Marissa said with a smile, referring to the seven minutes that separated their births. "I'm just glad he's out of that awful holding facility. It was such a terrible place."

"Well, it sounds like he's pretty relieved about that, too."

Marissa was quiet for a moment, emotion squeezing her throat tight. "Tell me I can do this, Mallory. Tell me I can help him. I can figure out a way to keep him out of places like that forever."

Mallory felt her sister's fears and insecurities, and understood them. Marissa wasn't really uncertain or unsure, just in desperate need of bolstering and assurance. "Are you kidding—you? Of course you can. You're the 'smart' one, remember? You can figure out anything," Mallory said, playing the role of cheerleader again. "And look at it this way. You've made it through the worst part. You got your son, and you've faced Dylan James and survived. The rest is smooth sailing."

Marissa had to smile, her sister's encouraging words doing what they were meant to—make her feel better. Gradually their conversation moved on to other things—their parents, old friends and Mallory's new husband, Benjamin Graywolf. There was no need for "twin radar" for Marissa to feel her sister's happiness—it virtually traveled through the telephone lines on its own. She listened as Mallory caught her up on her life as a newlywed and couldn't quite help feeling just a small pang of envy. Did the kind of love that Graywolf and Mallory shared happen only once in a lifetime?

After hanging up the phone, Marissa walked back to the window and glanced outside again. She'd loved Dylan once the way Mallory loved her husband. Had that been her once-in-a-lifetime chance? Had she lost her only chance at happiness when she lost him?

"Second thoughts?"

She spun around, startled. Josh's voice had sounded so much like Dylan's just then it had gooseflesh rising on her arms. "Remind me to tie a bell around your neck so I'll know when you're coming up behind me."

Josh smiled. "Sorry, I wasn't trying to startle you. Honest." The smile slowly faded from his face. "You looked so sad just now. I thought maybe..." He shrugged as his words drifted.

At fifteen, he stood as tall as she, and the frightened look on his face tore at her heart. "For better or for worse, you're mine now, so don't be trying to wiggle out of it, you got that?" she said, reaching out and giving him a hug. She pulled back and looked into his dark eyes—eyes that were so much like his father's. "And just in case I haven't mentioned it, I've never been happier in my life."

Marissa thought she saw the hint of tears in his eyes when he reached out and hugged her again, but she couldn't be sure. When he'd pulled away, his dark eyes shone dry and clear. Still, she knew the emotions were there, and understood how awkward he was with them.

With an embarrassed grin, he stepped back and held up the half-eaten bag of cheese popcorn, and wiggled his orange-stained fingers at her. "I saved you some, and a movie's just starting on the tube. Wanna watch?"

Marissa's heart swelled in her chest. "I'm right behind you."

"You sure you want to do that?"

Dylan glanced up from the coffee urn, confused. "Do what?"

"The coffee," Kimberly explained, gesturing to the mug he was filling to the brim. "It's been brewing all day. It will practically be lethal by now. I take it you don't plan on sleeping tonight."

Dylan shrugged carelessly and finished filling his cup. "So I'll take an extra patrol."

Kimberly's big blue eyes narrowed. "What's got you in such a mood?"

"A mood?" Dylan taunted, sipping the caustic black liquid and wincing. "Am I in a mood?"

"Never mind," Kimberly muttered, turning back to the report she was typing. She recognized the tone, and knew to back off. She'd worked for Sheriff James long enough to know that when he was in a good mood, she could joke and tease with him, but when he wasn't... well, when he wasn't it was best to just stay out of his way.

"No, no, no," Dylan insisted, walking to her desk and glowering down at her. "When one of my people says I'm in a...*mood,* I listen." Leaning forward, he bent close, wondering if he'd ever noticed her blue eyes before. "Just what kind of *mood* do you think I'm in?"

Kimberly stopped typing and swiveled her chair in his direction. She hated it when he got like this, and he'd been like this ever since Marissa Wakefield had come to see him. "Look, Sheriff, I don't want to start anything. I just thought you came back from court a little...upset. That's all."

"Upset?" Dylan cracked, laughing sarcastically. He toasted her with his coffee mug, taking another sip of his coffee and liking the brilliant bitterness. "Why should I be upset? I thought I was perfectly calm."

"Yeah, calm," Kimberly muttered almost to herself. Like a calm before the storm.

"Oh, I admit sitting in the courtroom and watching a gullible, unreasonable old judge toss away a kid's only chance to straighten out his life did get me a little annoyed."

"Don't tell me," Kimberly moaned. "They let Josh Wakefield go again?"

"You got it in one," Dylan said cynically, shaking his head.

"How could he do that?"

Dylan leaned against her desk and set his coffee mug down. "I don't know, but he did."

"You mean he just...let him go? Scot-free, just like that?"

"Oh, no," he said, remembering Marissa in the courtroom and the look that passed between her and her nephew when Judge Kent handed down his sentence. "He gave Josh and the other two picked up with him each ten months' probation, made their attendance in summer school classes at Sutter High a condition of probation, and demanded restitution by ordering them to work with one of the industrial arts instructors to rebuild the shed they torched."

"And Ron Cox agreed to this?"

Dylan cracked a little half smile, thinking about the heated exchanges that had gone on between Amador County's hotshot district attorney and the normally sedate Evan Brown. "Are you kidding? He hit the roof. The reason he wanted me there in the first place was to recommend to Judge Kent these kids do some time in custody." He laughed, loud and humorlessly. "For all the good it did. He never got the chance to call me to testify."

"Why not, what happened?"

He turned and glared down at her. "What happened? Marissa Wakefield happened, that's what."

"I don't understand."

"The judge. She got to the judge," he snorted, tossing his hands in the air. "She came here yesterday trying to get to me, and when that didn't help, she went straight to him. I tell you, she had Kent wrapped right around her little finger. By the time he took the bench, he was ready to give her anything she asked for—no time, restitution and legal custody."

Kimberly shook her head. "Ron must have been fit to be tied."

Dylan laughed. "Yeah, you could say that. All he could get the judge to do was require us to keep a regular check on the three."

"And if they aren't doing what they're supposed to?"

Dylan shrugged. "Then we lock them up."

Kimberly digested all this for a moment, then looked up at him. "You said something about legal custody?"

"Yeah." Dylan nodded and reached for the coffee again. "Marissa petitioned the court for custody. She's his legal guardian now."

"Wow," Kimberly murmured, taking it all in. "How come nothing this good ever happens when I have to be in court?"

Dylan swallowed another slug of coffee. Caffeine raced through his system, wild and furious, and thoughts sped crazily through his mind. He thought of how Marissa had looked standing there before the judge—her long, luscious hair styled back into a sedate bun, delicate tortoiseshell-framed glasses perched primly on her nose, and her figure hidden beneath a conservative suit. She'd looked like every man's fantasy schoolmarm—prim and proper on the outside, but smoldering with sensuality beneath the surface. He hardly blamed Judge Kent for his decision. He'd probably would have given her everything she'd wanted, too.

"It was pathetic," he muttered, almost to himself. "She had him eating out of her hand."

"Well," Kimberly said with a thoughtful sigh. "No matter what, she sure is gorgeous. But you know, when she showed up here the other morning, I wasn't sure who she was—you know, which twin—Marissa or Mallory."

Pulled abruptly from his thoughts, Dylan looked down at her. "What do you know about them?"

"What do you mean what do I know *about* them," Kimberly retorted. "I *know* them—or used to, anyway."

Dylan felt a burning in his stomach. Did she know he'd fallen in love with her? Did she know they'd played him for a fool? "How?"

"Sheriff," she said deliberately, giving him a look. "Jackson is a small town. Everybody knew the Wakefield twins."

Dylan felt a surge through his system, a combination of emotion and the side effect of the near-lethal dose of caffeine he'd just ingested. "But they're older than you."

"Not that much," Kimberly reminded him. "A couple of years, maybe. Besides, they were Jill's friends. You remember Jill, don't you, my oldest sister? I called and told her Marissa had been in the other day. Marissa used to come over and help Jill take care of us when my mom got so sick. And believe me, with eight kids in the family, poor Jill needed all the help she could get." Kimberly's expression grew wistful. "And afterward, after Mom died, she would spell Jill from time to time, so Jill could go out and have some fun once in a while. She and Dom were dating then and wanted to spend time together. I remember loving it when Marissa would come. She was the only one who could handle Kevin. He was about six then and really turned into a handful after Mom died. But I swear, Marissa really had a way with him. We all missed her when she moved away." Kimberly gave her head a little shake. "Anyway, that's how I know the twins. Are they both back?"

"No," Dylan said tersely, trying to shake the image of Marissa comforting a frightened child, trying to rid himself of the image of her in his head. "Just Marissa."

"For good, you mean?"

"She's principal over at Sutter," he said by way of explanation.

"No fooling? My nephew goes there," Kimberly said, surprised. "She still goes by Wakefield, and there wasn't a ring on her finger. I take it she's not married."

"No husband, no kids," Dylan muttered, wondering what drove a woman like her to devote her life to other people's kids instead of her own.

"Interesting." Kimberly turned back to her typing. "Well, she was always great with kids, so maybe she's just what Josh needs."

"Yeah, maybe," Dylan mumbled, picking up his coffee cup and refilling it again. He'd just turned and started down the corridor for his office when Kimberly stopped him again.

"Why'd she come to you for a favor?"

Dylan stopped, having asked himself that same question. "We used to be . . . uh, friends?"

Kimberly nodded, and watched as he made his way down the corridor. When he'd disappeared into his office, she stopped typing and reached for the telephone. "Jill?" she said after a moment. "You'll never guess what I found out."

Dylan pulled the rugged four-wheel drive patrol vehicle to a stop, listening to the engine groan and creak as it cooled in the night air. It was well past midnight, but the streets still radiated warmth from the harsh heat of the day, and the gentle breeze through the open windows of the Jeep did little to cool his overheated skin. He knew he should be home trying to get some sleep instead of aimlessly driving the streets of Jackson, but Kimberly had been right. The coffee had been toxic. Despite the long day he'd put in, despite his scratchy eyes and sore muscles, despite his tired mind and languid spirit, he was wide-awake.

He glanced across the street to the row of luxury condominiums that lined the quiet drive. But he didn't see the well-manicured lawns or neatly trimmed hedges. Instead, his eyes had homed in on one particular unit, one specific address that had grabbed his attention despite the fact that the row of homes all looked exactly the same. It was probably his imagination, but like the occupant who inhabited it, Marissa Wakefield's condominium seemed to stand out.

He leaned back in the seat, staring up at the darkened windows of her condo and wondering just what the hell he was doing there. He'd cruised down the street several times, telling himself he was just checking up, telling himself he was simply doing his duty, but he'd just been fooling himself.

Dylan closed his eyes, rubbing at them, wishing he could just fall asleep and stop thinking about all of this—stop thinking about her. He'd almost wished a call would come through on his police radio to distract him, but it seemed that a rash of *lawfulness* had broken out on the streets of Jackson. It was a quiet night. He'd turned the sound low on his radio, just barely aware of its infrequent bursts, and his mind kept drifting . . . to Marissa, always to Marissa.

Why couldn't she have stayed away? Why did she have to come back and stir up all the old memories again? He'd told himself a million times in the last two days what had happened between them just wasn't important, that time had long ago healed the wounds, and the hurt feelings simply didn't matter anymore. He'd rationalized and analyzed, reasoned and justified—but he couldn't get her out of his head.

Sixteen years ago, he'd worked hard to convince everyone that what she'd done to him was just a joke, no big deal. He'd worked so hard, and been so convincing, that he'd begun to believe it himself. But the fact of the matter was, it hadn't been a joke—not to him, anyway. He'd fallen in love that summer with the woman he'd spent time with, the woman he'd held, the woman he'd made love to. It hadn't mattered who she was, or what her name had been; it was the *woman* he had loved, the *woman* he had wanted. What had hurt was that she'd lied to him.

A car turned onto the dark street, its lights cutting through the darkness and illuminating the inside of the Jeep. Dylan sat up, squinting against the glare, and followed the car's slow path as it passed him and headed toward a driveway down the block. He settled back into the seat again, gazing up into the night sky, swearing under his breath. Why was he torturing himself with all this now? Why didn't he just forget once and for all?

But he already knew why. Marissa Wakefield had walked into his office, and his life and emotions had been in an uproar ever since. He might have buried the past, he might have been able to hide the pain—pave it over, lock it away, cloak it behind a mask of indifference, but he'd never actually dealt with it.

He turned and stared up at the windows of her apartment again, a rush of emotion spreading through his system like the caffeine had done earlier. He'd never really coped with the hurt; he'd just stuck it away and hoped it would just disappear.

Only it didn't disappear. It had come back the moment he saw her again, and he was going to have to find some way of coping with Marissa and the memories. He'd do his best to avoid her, but that wasn't going to be easy with the judge expecting him to monitor Josh's progress. But even without that, Kimberly had been right when she'd said Jackson was a small town. It was unreasonable to think he wouldn't run into her. And it wasn't exactly reasonable to camp out in front of her house for no apparent reason, either.

Suddenly a light snapped on, filling one of the dark windows he'd been watching with a soft yellow glow. Startled, he bolted upright, knocking his knee harshly against a sharp edge of the rifle rack mounted to the dash. But Dylan was only vaguely aware of the pain radiating from his kneecap. He was too absorbed in watching the shadowy figure that moved behind the curtains. Straining against the steering wheel, he leaned forward, the breath catching in his throat.

It was her. Even with the muted background and the distortions caused by the folds of fabric, he would have recognized her delicately curved silhouette anywhere. He watched as her shadow drifted back and forth along the window, feeling the slow, steady rhythm of his heart begin to pulse wildly at his neck and throat. He'd been on countless stakeouts, had spent many a night keeping a suspect under surveillance. There was always that rush of excitement, that glorious burst of exhilaration, when something finally happened after long hours of waiting.

But this was nothing like that. He wasn't a cop on a stakeout. He was a man, watching a woman—a woman not only forbidden by the past, but by circumstance. A woman he had to forget.

He watched her glide through the room—smooth, graceful motions. He found himself captivated, and for the first time in two days, he forgot about the past and the memories that hurt.

He'd been so caught up in her image, so hypnotized by the movements, that when she suddenly reached out and pulled the curtain aside, it caught him by surprise. There she was, standing at the window, staring out into the night.

He leaned back against the seat, his breath strangled in his throat. Given the darkness of the night and the shadows of the street, it was impossible to think that she could see him, but still he felt embarrassed—exposed like a voyeur caught in the act.

In the quiet darkness of the night, she looked more like an illusion than a flesh-and-blood woman. He watched as she reached up and unhooked the latch, sliding the window wide to one side. As she stood behind the finely woven mesh screen, her long hair fell loose and unchecked down her shoulders—a stark contrast to the confining bun that had restrained it in court. Something glinted bright at her neck, catching the light from the moon or the street lamp, and he remembered the delicate necklace she wore— the fine gold chain with a pendant formed by a cluster of stars. Her satiny nightgown shone luminescent in the moonlight, reflecting off the soft curves of her body and causing his heart to thud loudly in his chest. The night breeze through the open window caught the delicate fabric, pressing it tight against her body.

Dylan felt his own body come alive, felt heat flood his system and his mouth go as dry as sand. Desire engulfed him with such violence, such a vengeance, it had the air stalling in his lungs and the blood slowly draining from his limbs.

The radio on the dashboard crackled to life, its muted burst causing him to jump violently. Even though it had been little more than a muffled crack, in the quiet of the Jeep it had sounded as loud as an air-raid siren.

He quickly looked around, disoriented and confused. His breathing was labored, and his shirt and forehead were awash with sweat. What the hell had he been thinking? How could he have allowed himself to be caught so off guard? If this had been a stakeout, he would have been dead by now.

He glanced back up at the window, which was black now. No sign of light, and no sign of her.

Dylan straightened up in the seat, running an impatient arm across his brow. He was burning up, the night feeling still and sultry to him now. He took a deep breath, cursing to himself and trying without much success to bring his heart rate back to normal.

He reached for the key, twisted it and brought the engine to life. Slipping the car into gear, he switched on his lights and pulled away from the curb. As he passed the condo, he glanced up at the window, picturing her as she'd looked just moments before, and another rustle of desire had him shifting uneasily in the seat. He never should have looked, then he wouldn't have to know that her smooth skin glowed white in the moonlight, that her warm, honey-silk hair was tousled and loose.

He steered the car around a corner, picking up speed as he went. Maybe his real problem wasn't the past at all, maybe it wasn't having to cope with what had happened, but rather it was what his mind was imagining right now. Maybe his problem was a woman who could make him want her even when he didn't want to.

Chapter 4

"Karen, do you know where—" Marissa stepped out of her office and skittered to a dead stop. She stared up at Dylan and blinked, her eyes growing wide with surprise. "Sheriff. What are you doing here?"

"I was on my way in to see you," he said, frowning that she hadn't used his given name. She looked very strait-laced and proper with her hair gathered back in a bun again—neat, tidy and without so much as a strand out of place—and the cotton blouse with the little lace-trimmed stand-up collar looked very pristine and modest. But his mind flashed to the picture of her standing at the window—the flimsy nightgown clinging to her body and her hair loose and sleep-tossed. "Your secretary wasn't at her desk."

"No, I guess she's not," Marissa mumbled, glancing down at the empty desk beside her and vaguely remembering Karen saying something about a doctor's appointment. She turned back to Dylan, feeling the pulse at her neck begin to throb against the collar of her blouse.

It had been almost two weeks since Josh's hearing—two of the most hectic and most wonderful weeks of her life. Both she and Josh had started school. Josh had begun summer school classes, and she'd started in her position as principal. They were both putting in long hours and adjusting to new routines. Under the guidance of Sutter High's computer and industrial arts teacher Rick Mathers, ground had been broken and construction on the new toolshed had begun. Their days had become long and exhausting, and Marissa couldn't remember a time in her life when she'd worked as hard, or had been so happy. Josh was with her. After so many years apart, she and her son were finally a family.

"Did we have an appointment?" she asked pleasantly, knowing very well they did not. An appointment with him was hardly something she would forget.

Dylan shook his head. "No, I just came by to check up."

"On Josh, or me?" she asked stiffly, her smile turning brittle.

"Well, I guess that depends," he said dryly, giving her a sly look. "Have you done something I should know about?"

His humor only made her smile grow more rigid. Josh teased with the same slow smile, the same playful gleam in his eyes, and the reminder was surprisingly painful. They were so much alike—father and son—and the older Josh got, the more the resemblance seemed to grow. It was as though she lived with a time bomb, and each day she wondered just how much longer it would be before everything exploded and someone noticed.

Was Mallory right? Was she becoming paranoid? Or was it just that the truth had become such a heavy burden to bear—a lonely burden, an albatross she struggled with for the sake of her son?

"So, where did you want to start?" she asked abruptly, ignoring his humor and getting right to the point. She glanced up at the clock on the wall, running schedules in her mind. "Classes are over for the morning, but lunch should just be ending. All three boys will be reporting out at the construction site in a few minutes. Would you like me to take you there, or was there something you wanted to see me about?"

Dylan's eyes narrowed, and he felt the chill from her blue eyes in every pore of his skin, every layer of muscle. She was all business—no more friendly smiles, no more idle chitchat or polite greetings. Apparently the lady had decided there was nothing more he could do for her, no special favor he could grant, and she'd established the ground rules accordingly.

He clenched his teeth together, working his jaw hard and telling himself it wasn't disappointment he felt, but relief. After all, wasn't that what he wanted, to keep it strictly business between them? Wasn't he more comfortable with that? She'd been on his mind too much lately, in a way that had nothing to do with random security checks and devotion to duty, and the image of her standing at her bedroom window was one he'd just as soon forget. He understood the importance of keeping things in perspective, and it would be strictly business between them because it *was* strictly business between them.

"Actually, I'd like to see the registration forms and progress reports for all three boys," he said, his voice all business now. "And maybe I could get some photocopies of those for the judge?"

"Sure," she said, turning to the large filing cabinet along the back wall. "Why don't you go into my office and sit down? I'll grab what you need and be right in."

Dylan nodded, moving past the open door marked Principal. He looked about the small cubical, surprised by the unadorned walls and sedate-looking furniture. It wasn't what he'd imagined Marissa Wakefield would have for herself. The tiny office appeared functional enough with its uncluttered shelves and neatly stacked files, but he'd pictured her amid more lavish surroundings. After all, she was a Wakefield, and for almost three generations, the Wakefields had been setting the standard for opulence and elegance in the Mother Lode. Their imposing family home had been a fixture in the community for nearly a century, and Marissa's practical and efficient little office hardly seemed to fit the standards.

He spotted a small potted African violet on the windowsill, looking slightly limp with sunburned leaves and faded blossoms, and two small framed pictures on her desk—one of a baby-faced Josh that looked like it had been taken about ten years ago, and the other of Mallory with a man he assumed to be her new husband—a tall Indian with a massive frame and incredibly long black hair.

Dylan noticed that the jacket that matched her skirt was hanging neatly from a hanger, and that on the credenza was a half-filled coffee mug with Meecher Teecher—I'm Miss Wakefield printed across it in bold red letters. Other than those personal items, it appeared at first glance that the small office revealed little about her. And yet, as he surveyed it with a cop's eye, he noted that the plain, unadorned room said more about the woman than perhaps she'd intended—and what he saw surprised him.

Not that he should have been, he reminded himself as his gaze slowly prowled the room once again. It wasn't the first time in the last two weeks the woman had surprised him. She'd surprised him by moving back to Jackson, by wanting custody of her troubled adopted nephew, and by choosing to live in the comfortable condominium instead of the family's sprawling hillside estate. It all seemed to point to one thing—Marissa Wakefield was a person in her own right, independent of her family and her twin.

"Here we are," she said, breezing into the office with two folders in her hand. She gestured to the straight-back chair beside her desk. "Have a seat," she said, slipping past him and sitting in her chair. She laid two long manila folders on the desk, then turned and opened a file drawer in the credenza behind her. "Those are Skip Carver's and Randy O'Riley's records. I had Karen file Josh's records here in my private files so they'd be handy."

"Anticipating trouble?" Dylan asked dryly, walking to the desk and picking up the folders she'd set out for him. He had to admit she looked comfortable in her role as principal. He realized the woman didn't need a plush office and opulent decor. Just sitting there, she lent her own air of elegance and style to the austere surroundings.

"No," she said purposefully, looking up at him and scowling. "For convenience." She pulled another file from her drawer and offered it to him. "Here's Josh's records. Just let me know what you want copies of."

Dylan sat down on the chair beside her desk, aware of an odd sensation of déjà vu. How many times as a kid had he been sent to the principal's office and had the riot act read to him? What a pain in the butt he must have been—cocky and insolent—not unlike Josh Wakefield and his friends.

Dylan peered over the top of the folder and watched Marissa as she absently fingered a paper clip on the blotter in front of her. What would it be like to have the prim and proper Miss Wakefield read the riot act? She might look cool and calm, but he suspected she could get fired up when she wanted, and she'd be a force to be reckoned with then. He could picture her—with eyes alive with fire and her body teeming with righteous indignation. It would be something to see, all right—almost worth getting into trouble for.

He glanced back at the papers in the folder, occasionally pulling out the documents he thought might be of interest to the judge, but his mind wasn't on registration forms and progress reports. He was thinking about seeing Miss Wakefield all hot and bothered, about her blue-green eyes flashing bright, about the feel of her lips along his, and her chest rising and falling wildly with emotion. He was thinking about reaching up and grabbing the tight bun at the base of her neck, slowly unfurling it and pulling the long strands of hair free. He thought of running his hands through its silky softness, of burying his face in its scented mass. He thought of drawing her into his arms, of feeling her body heat with passion, of laying her back across the sterile-looking desk and pulling that prim and proper business suit from her slender, beautiful body, of—

"Finding everything okay?"

Dylan jumped at the sound of her voice, tipping one folder and sending the contents drifting silently to the carpet. He felt a deep flush creeping up his neck, and he reached down to retrieve the papers, cursing under his breath.

What the hell was he doing? What happened to perspective? What happened to strictly business?

"Yeah, this is fine," he mumbled absently, stuffing the papers back into the files. He quickly finished looking through the first folder and opened another, determined to keep his mind on business. "So, things going okay?"

"Things are going just fine," Marissa said, leaning back in her chair. "Of course, the summer term is just beginning. It's too soon to chart any real progress. But I've alerted all the boys' teachers, and they'll keep me informed on their academic progress or any behavior problems that might come up."

"Attendance?" he asked, keeping his eyes riveted to the pages in front of him.

"Attendance has been fine," she announced proudly. "Perfect, in fact. Both in class and at the work site."

"Well, classes have just started," he grumbled, flipping quickly through the documents. He wanted to have this done with and get away from her and the effect she had on him.

Marissa's smile faded. "But I certainly don't anticipate any problems. I feel very hopeful."

"Hmm," he nodded, forcing himself to slow down and concentrate on the papers he was reviewing. Besides, he needed time to collect himself, to let the images in his head fade and disappear.

Marissa's frown deepened; she was annoyed by his obvious skepticism. "In fact, I have every confidence that all the boys will fulfill their obligation."

"Uh-huh," he said, slipping another document from the folder.

Marissa had the feeling he was only half listening, and bristled. She wasn't crazy about the idea of him coming around here poking his nose in her business, anyway, but then if he wasn't even going to have the decency to listen to her... She drew in a deep breath, raising her voice just a little. "And I think we're off to a good start."

"What?" he said, glancing up as though surprised to discover she'd said something. "Oh, a good start, well, yes..." He looked down at the folder again. "I guess it does appear that way."

Marissa frowned again. "*Appear* that way? You have doubts?"

"Not really," he mumbled.

"Then what *really* did you mean by that?"

The anger in her voice surprised him, and he looked up again. It wasn't that he hadn't been listening, exactly. It was just that keeping his mind on business had taken all his concentration. "Did I miss something here?"

She glared at him, completely frustrated. "What?"

He looked into her angry eyes, and shook his head helplessly. "Well, you're obviously upset about something. What's the problem?"

"The problem is I don't like the implications you're making."

"Implications?" he asked, his dark brows arching. "About what? What are we arguing about?"

Marissa swallowed. What *were* they arguing about? That he'd expressed a few doubts, or that he wasn't paying enough attention to her? He was right, she was upset—furious, to be exact. She felt like picking a fight, felt like confronting him—she just wasn't sure it was for reasons she could discuss with him. The fact was, the anger had felt good, it had felt safe.

"About the boys' attendance record," she explained, it sounding foolish now, even to her.

He blinked, trying to remember what he'd said that had gotten her so angry. "All I meant was, it is a little early to tell about attendance, that's all."

"Well, the implication being that attendance will fall off as the semester goes on," she insisted, now wishing she could just drop the whole thing.

"I didn't say that."

"You implied it."

"No, Marissa, I didn't," he said deliberately.

She glared at him, the fact that he'd used her first name only making her angrier. "Well, *Sheriff,* I think you did. As a matter of fact, I think you'd like it if Josh or one of the other boys screwed up. I think you'd like to see them violate their probation so you and Ron Cox would have an excuse to lock them up again. That's what you wanted in the first place, wasn't it?"

Dylan sat staring at her for a moment, feeling a little like a character in a Kafka novel—dropped into the middle of a situation and not entirely sure how he'd gotten there.

"Look," he said in the same calm, rational voice he used to talk to unstable suspects. "We seem to have gotten off on the wrong foot here. Let me clear the air on a few things. I might not have agreed with the sentence the judge handed down, but look—that happens all the time in my line of work. He's made his ruling, the sentence has been agreed on—it's all water under the bridge as far as I'm concerned. I'm just here to do my job, nothing more." He paused, leaning forward and noticing how the sunlight from the small window behind her shone brilliantly through her hair. "Despite what you might think, Marissa, I'm not the enemy. I want to see Josh make it, too."

Marissa felt the emotion well up in her throat. She didn't want to see the soft look in his eyes, didn't want to think of him as concerned or caring—especially not about Josh. In a way, his quiet, candid words made her feel even worse. Now she not only felt stupid, she also felt contrite. She'd made a fool of herself, arguing with him, trying to make something out of nothing. Despite the circumstances of the past, there was nothing personal between them, yet she'd let her emotions talk herself into a corner, and now there was no graceful way out.

"Let's just drop it, shall we?" she suggested stiffly, embarrassed and angry—with herself this time. "I admit, I might be a little sensitive. It's not just a professional thing for me—it's personal, too."

"I understand, no problem," he said, thinking it was a whole lot more personal for him, too, than he cared to admit.

It took only a few minutes more for him to finish with the last folder. He found the documents he wanted and stacked them with the others.

"I think these are all I need," he said, glancing over Josh's registration form a last time. "If you could just point me in the direction of the copy machine, I'll just..." His voice faded as something on the form caught his attention.

Marissa waited for a moment, nervously fingering the paper clip in her hand and feeling the hair at the base of her neck start to tickle. "What is it?"

"What?" Dylan glanced up, then gave his head a little shake. "Oh, uh—nothing really. I guess I'd just assumed Josh was born here in Jackson."

The paper clip slipped from her hand and landed silently on the blotter below.

"Oh? Did you?" she said noncommittally, feeling the muscle just above her lip begin to twitch. She'd handed Dylan Josh's file without considering what information was in it. He was a cop, used to looking below the surface, used to questioning things. Would he figure out Josh was really her son? Would he make the connection between Josh's birth date and the time they'd been lovers?

"Yeah, it says here he was born in Maryland."

She nodded, turning to the open file drawer and busying herself by rearranging a few files. "That's right, he was."

"Huh," Dylan mused, watching her pull out several file folders from the drawer, then slip them back into place again. "Isn't that where you got that scholarship for our last year of high school? Some private school in Maryland?"

She turned to him, remembering the story her parents had circulated to explain away her reason for leaving home. "Yes, it is. The Hardwick School in Maryland."

He gave her a deliberate look. "That's kind of a coincidence, isn't it?"

She shrugged, feeling a cold line of sweat form along her upper lip despite the air-conditioned room. "Is it?"

"You don't think so?"

"Not really," she said, giving him another careless shrug and thankful her voice wasn't trembling as badly as her legs were. "You were aware Josh was adopted, weren't you?"

"Sure, I thought that was pretty much common knowledge."

"I think it is," she said, pushing the file drawer closed. "Caleb and Penny certainly never kept it a secret. Did you also know I have an aunt who lives in Maryland?"

"Didn't you live with her while you were there, or something?"

"That's right, in Bowie," she explained, taking a deep breath. "Anyway, Aunt Bea knew that Caleb and Penny were interested in adopting. It was through her that they heard about Josh."

Dylan slid the folders down onto her desk. "She kind of put things together?"

"Something like that," Marissa murmured, trying to read his expression, trying to determine just what it was he was thinking, but it was impossible. His dark eyes and rugged features revealed nothing.

"So your Aunt Bea knew Josh's birth parents, then?"

Marissa's heart pounded so loudly she was actually afraid he might hear. She'd already made a fool of herself once by letting her emotions run away with her, she couldn't risk doing it again. But his questions frightened her. Did he suspect something? Had the dates of the registration form started him thinking, had him putting two and two together, made him suspicious?

"I don't know that she knew them, exactly," she said nonchalantly. "I don't know if I was ever clear on all the details. It wasn't really any of my business. Why?"

Dylan shrugged casually. "No reason, I just wondered now with both Penny and Caleb gone, if Josh would ever want to find out about his past."

"What?" Marissa chocked, surprised.

"You know—find his birth parents."

"Whatever for?" she demanded, nerves making her respond with more emotion than she'd intended. "Why would he want to do that? He has all the information about his past that he needs. *We're* a family now—he and I. He doesn't need anybody else in his life."

Dylan glanced up at her slowly, the vehemence in her voice surprising him just a little. "I just thought . . . forget it."

Marissa sucked in a deep breath. What was happening to her? She was doing exactly what she'd told herself not to do—letting her emotions get the best of her. She had to stop, had to start thinking about what she was doing, or everything was going to fall apart. Dylan was smart, and as a cop he was used to dealing with people who were often less than honest. The last thing she needed was to appear like a person with something to hide.

Letting out a long sigh, she gathered her composure and forced a smile across her face. "No, look, I'm sorry. It's been kind of crazy around here the last couple of weeks, I've been under a lot of pressure. I guess it's got me over-reacting a bit."

"Well, I wasn't suggesting anything," he added quickly. "Or *implying* anything."

Marissa smiled. "I know. I'm just a little sensitive where Josh is concerned. I want it to work out for us, and there's so much I want to do for him—things I think I can help with." She stopped and shook her head. "Looking into the past just isn't something I'd want to encourage right now. There's been enough upheaval in his life in the last couple of years, and who knows what he'd find if he started asking questions about his birth parents." She stopped for a moment, forcing herself to take a breath and not come on too strong. "Maybe someday, just not now. Besides, things happen for a reason. I don't think stirring up the past will solve anything."

Dylan saw something flash bright in those blue eyes of hers—some feeling, some emotion he couldn't quite pin down. It was more than sadness, something closer to regret.

But what she said was right, of course. Stirring up memories served no useful purpose. How many times in the last two weeks had he told himself that same thing?

"Yeah, I guess you're right," he said after a moment, picking up the folders from the desk and handing them back to her. "I guess we all have things in our past that are better left forgotten."

Marissa took the folders from him and turned her chair toward the credenza. She prayed that was what he had done—forgotten all about what had happened between them. If only she could do the same thing—just put it aside and move on. But that would never happen when every time she looked into her son's face she was reminded of what she'd had, and what she'd lost.

Her son. From the moment she'd discovered she was carrying a child in her womb, she'd thought of Josh as *her* child. Josh was the one thing Dylan had given to her that could never be taken away, the one part of him she could keep with her forever. And even though she'd had to give Josh up temporarily, in her heart, she'd never stopped thinking of him as her son.

But perceptions had a way of changing, and hers had changed a lot since she'd come back. Seeing Dylan again made her realize that everything about him—his humor, his voice, his expressions and demeanor—served as a reminder that Josh was part of him, too... like it or not.

She rose quickly to her feet, disturbed by the troubled thoughts in her head, and reached for the documents he'd pulled from the files. "I'll get these copied for you."

Dylan stood then, too, handing her the registration forms and watching as she moved around the desk. Something had caused the soft line of her mouth to tense and tighten. She wasn't the calm and efficient principal any longer. She was a woman—soft and vulnerable.

As she moved to pass, he reached out, slipping a hand around her upper arm and stopping her. "You look upset again."

For a moment, Marissa, surprised by the sudden move, could do nothing but stare up into his dark eyes. He was so close, so close, she could see the tiny flecks of color in his dark eyes. It was as though suddenly all the air in the small office had been sucked away, leaving her gasping and breathless.

Memories became electric, assailing her with images and sending her heart to her throat. She remembered his lips on hers—searching, seeking, and his hands restless and desperate. She heard his voice in her ears whispering hungry, fervent words— *I love you. I love you. I love you.*

But of course, he hadn't loved her. It hadn't been her name he had whispered, her lips he'd wanted to kiss, or her love he'd sought. He hadn't wanted her, he'd wanted Mallory. Marissa had merely been a substitute, a stand-in whose heart had gotten in the way.

"No," she said, shaking her head. "No, I'm not, I'm not upset."

"But I can see it," he insisted, his voice barely above a whisper. "In your eyes."

"Dylan, please," she whispered, pulling against his hold.

Dylan. Not "Sheriff" this time, but Dylan. The sound of his name on her lips sent a jolt of emotion running through him. He knew then he never should have touched her, because he wasn't entirely sure he would be able to let her go.

His hand around her arm flexed slightly, allowing him to feel her firm, smooth flesh through the fabric of her clothes. The sad, vulnerable look in her eyes had something flaming inside. He wanted to see them spark again, flare with fire and anger and passion.

The scent of her perfume swirled around him like a fragrant, heady cloud, filling his senses with its delicate scent. But its fragile aroma reacted like a powerful narcotic in his brain, infiltrating his thoughts and making him remember the fantasy.

He told himself he didn't want to pull her into his arms, and yet he ached to do so. He didn't want to ravage her mouth and muss up her hair. He didn't want to kiss her. His gaze drifted to her lips, his hand on her arm pulled her a fraction of an inch closer, and he heard the roar of his own heart thundering in his ears.

"Marissa," he murmured, watching her lips with his eyes, but tasting them in his mouth. He pulled her closer, feeling the softness of her breast against the back of his hand. "Marissa."

Marissa watched him draw closer and closer, thinking somewhere in her consciousness that he looked as though he were going to kiss her. But she couldn't allow that, she just couldn't seem to make herself turn away.

"Hey, boss, how about a refill?"

For a moment, all Marissa could do was turn and stare at the young woman who stood in the doorway with a coffeepot in her hand. But Karen's voice had been as effective as a glass of ice water in the face, breaking the mood and bringing reality back with a jolt.

"Karen," Marissa stammered in a hoarse voice. "I thought . . . I didn't know you were back."

"I'm sorry," Karen Hamilton said with an embarrassed smile, her full cheeks filling with a deep, florid red. "I didn't know you had someone with you."

Marissa realized Dylan still held on to her arm, still stood close. She and Karen were in the process of getting to know each other, and she didn't even want to think what kind of picture she and Dylan made standing so close.

"The sheriff was here checking up on Josh," she explained quickly, feeling the color in her own cheeks start to rise. She carefully pulled against Dylan's hold, relieved when he offered no resistance and let her slip her arm free. She took a few shaky steps forward, holding the documents out in front of her. "Now that you're back, do you think you could make some copies of these?"

"Sure, I'll do it right now," Karen said eagerly, grabbing the documents with her free hand and holding up the coffeepot she held in the other. "Could I bring either of you some coffee?"

"No," Marissa said quickly, shaking her head. "Actually, the sheriff and I were just on our way out to the construction site." She turned to Dylan, glancing up into his dark eyes for just a split second, and gestured to the door, "Shall we?"

Chapter 5

"How come you let him in here to harass us?"

Marissa pulled her gaze from Dylan, whose muscular frame was almost completely hidden behind Randy O'Riley's broad, hulking one. The two stood beside a large stack of lumber on the far side of the construction site talking. She turned and looked up at Skip Carver, who towered behind her. The ruddy, youthful face beneath the shock of flaming red hair was twisted and distorted with anger.

"Is that why you think he's here?"

"Well, isn't it?" he demanded, holding a long screwdriver by the shaft and tossing it angrily to the ground. The tool made several slow spins as it fell, but failed to stick into the soft earth and rolled clumsily along the grass. Skip scowled and muttered, "He's always poking around, trying to stir up trouble." He lifted his gaze and glared across the common to where Dylan and Randy stood. Dylan had asked to speak with each of the boys individually, and Skip was waiting his turn. "Marshal Dillon needs to get a life instead of getting his jollies from harassing us." He turned back to Marissa. "Shouldn't you be protecting us from him?"

Marissa folded her arms across her chest and leaned back against the low concrete-block wall that separated the maintenance yard from the rest of the campus. She'd heard Skip refer to Dylan as "Marshal Dillon" before, hoping to get a rise out of her, but she hadn't given him the satisfaction. She'd learned early in her teaching career that when a kid was as angry as Skip, reprimands did little good. A more subtle approach was usually more effective.

"You know the terms of your probation," she pointed out. "He has a right to be here to check up on you."

"Torment is more like it," Skip scoffed. He looked up at her, as though he were about to say something more, then shook his head. "Aw, forget it. You're probably in on this with him."

"In on what?"

"This . . . this plan Marshal Dillon has to keep his hooks in us."

Marissa regarded the teen carefully. "Sounds like you think the sheriff really has it in for you?"

"Well, doesn't he?" Skip demanded, bending down and picking up the screwdriver and tossing it again. It failed to stick again. "First, there's his following us all over the place—just looking for something to pull us in for. Then those phony arson charges, and now this." He gestured to the work site. "This is slave labor, you know that, don't you—slave labor!"

Marissa laughed. She'd seen Skip's aptitude tests. He was a smart kid—maybe too smart—and he was headed for trouble unless someone got to him soon. "Phony charges? Come on, Skip, you're making this sound like a bad teen movie—the nasty old sheriff threatening to outlaw dancing at the prom. You expect me to buy that?"

"Don't laugh, Miss Wakefield, it's true." He knelt down and snatched the screwdriver from the grass.

"You forget, Skip, I was in the courtroom. I heard them read the charges, and I sure don't remember hearing you saying anything about being innocent."

He looked up at her and shrugged. "I said what my lawyer told me to say."

She gave him a skeptical look. "I wouldn't have thought anyone could get you to say anything you didn't want to."

"It got me out of jail, didn't it?"

Marissa raised a brow. "So what you're telling me is that you didn't have anything to do with torching the toolshed, is that it?"

He gave her a smirk, his pale green eyes narrowing. "Hey, nobody saw me lighting any matches, did they?"

"That's not exactly the same thing, though, is it?"

He looked down at the screwdriver in his hand, and then back to her. "Maybe it was Josh who struck the match."

Marissa's glaze flicked to Josh, who was bent on all fours, working with Rick Mathers to smooth the wet cement they'd just poured for the shed's foundation. She didn't believe that. Josh had told her all about that night, how he'd been there with the others, and he'd done his share of vandalizing—breaking windows and spray-painting walls. But he hadn't been responsible for setting the fire—neither had Randy. The fire had been all Skip's idea.

She looked back at Skip, who'd risen from his haunches. His smug smile revealed more than he knew—his cockiness, his confidence, but also his vulnerability. She recognized a power play when she saw it. She also understood a veiled threat—and she wasn't going to sit still for it, either.

Marissa walked over to where he stood, reaching up and snatching the screwdriver out of his hand. Without missing a beat, she tossed it down hard into the ground, its long shaft solidly piercing the soft earth, leaving the handle wobbling with the force.

"And maybe it would be in everyone's best interests if all three of you just concentrated on fulfilling your obligation to the juvenile courts and getting on with your lives."

Skip stared down at the screwdriver, then back to her, taking a step closer. He was tall and big—even for fifteen—and he knew how to use his size to intimidate. "That doesn't bother you? I mean, that your precious nephew might be a firebug?"

"What I know about Josh doesn't bother me a bit, Skip." Her heart pounded loudly in her chest, but she held her ground. "Does it bother you?"

"The only thing bothering me is Sheriff James and this stupid job I'm stuck with," he insisted.

Marissa bent down and pulled the screwdriver out of the ground. "Then you'll take some consolation in knowing your friends are stuck with the same job." Straightening up, she gave him a smile. "You all received the same probation."

"Yeah, right, the same probation," he muttered. "And I really believe you and Marshal Dillon are going to ride Josh as hard as you will Randy and me."

"Well," she said, slapping the handle of the screwdriver into the palm of his hand. "I guess you're just going to have to stick around to find out, aren't you."

"Okay, Carver," Dylan called from across the work site. "You're up."

Dylan let his gaze follow Marissa as she made her way across the maintenance yard toward Rick Mathers. He liked the way she moved—the motion of her arms, the set of her shoulders, the sway of her hips. There was a confidence to her movements, an assurance that enhanced that subtle air of sensuality. He thought of that moment in her office, that moment when she'd stood so close, when he could all but feel her body against his.

"So you and Mathers getting along okay?" he asked, watching as she and the industrial arts teacher disappeared into a trailer that served as a maintenance office, forcing his mind back to business. He turned to Josh, who sat on a huge bag of concrete mix absently tossing pebbles onto a weathered-looking football lying in the dirt in front of him.

"Okay, I guess," he said, shrugging a shoulder.

"For a teacher," Dylan added dryly.

Josh looked a little surprised. "Something like that."

"Not working you too hard?"

Josh shook his head. "Not too bad."

"How's school going?"

Josh snorted, tossing a pebble and watching it spring off the football and land somewhere in the dust. "It's school."

Dylan smiled to himself. He remembered all too well long, boring classes that seemed to go on forever and dull, lifeless teachers whose monotonous monotones sent even the brightest minds wandering. Was it any wonder kids got into trouble? What was it about the school system that took so much of the pleasure out of learning? How many more young minds would go to waste before somebody woke up and changed things?

"Skip seems to think you guys are being pushed a little too hard, that you got too much work."

Josh's mouth twisted into a crooked smile as he bent down and scooped up another handful of pebbles. "Skip thinks any work is too much."

Dylan studied him carefully. From his conversations with the other two boys, he'd picked up on some tension. "You and Skip been spending much time together outside school?"

Josh stopped and looked up, his face stiff and defensive. "Look, I haven't done anything wrong. If there's something going on, it's not me."

Dylan gave him a dubious look. "Is something going on?"

"I don't know," he insisted, his voice cracking just a little. "That's what you said."

Dylan shook his head. "I just asked if you and Skip see much of each other outside school—simple question."

Josh took a deep breath and shook his head. "No."

"You two still friends?"

"Kind of."

"Randy tells me Skip seems to think you're getting special treatment around here—because your aunt's the principal. You think that?"

"No," Josh insisted angrily. "It's not like that. Skip's just full of sh—"

"I get the idea," Dylan said quickly, cutting him off. "Tell me about home. Everything going okay with you and your aunt?"

"Oh, sure," Josh said, his voice softening.

"The two of you getting along okay?"

"Yeah, Aunt Mar's great."

Dylan thought of Marissa, of her soft eyes and smooth, flawless skin, and forced her image from his mind with a shake of his head. "So it doesn't make it awkward for you—her being principal?"

"Maybe a little."

"Like with Skip?"

Josh looked up at him. "I can handle Skip."

Dylan nodded thoughtfully and took a few steps into the yard. He surveyed the concrete pad that had been poured earlier. "Looks pretty good."

Josh glanced across the yard in the same direction. "Yeah, wasn't as tough as I thought it would be. Actually, it..."

Dylan looked back around when Josh's voice trailed off. "You were saying?"

Josh glanced down, flipping a few more pebbles in the direction of the football. "Nothing—just that, well... it wasn't all that bad to pour the stuff and smooth it out. It was kind of . . . fun.''

Fun. Dylan turned that over in his mind. It was almost a strange concept—fun. In his line of work, he'd almost begun to believe the only fun kids believed in anymore was causing trouble.

He watched as Josh reached down and grabbed up another handful of pebbles and began tossing them again. Josh Wakefield and his friends had been a giant pain in the neck and had kept the switchboard at his office lit up like a Christmas tree on a pretty regular basis. He'd come to think of the kid as a spoiled brat, a wise guy, a punk with an attitude.

But watching him now as he sat alone, away from his friends, away from the attitude and the wisecracks, he didn't look much like a punk. He just looked young—very young. Like a kid who could help pour a pad of concrete and discover it could be . . . fun.

"You ever toss that thing?" he asked, gesturing with his chin in the direction of the football.

"Sometimes."

Dylan bent down, snatching up the ball and dusting it off. He placed his hands carefully into place around it. "I used to be pretty good with one of these."

"Oh, yeah?" Josh said, his interest picking up. "My dad used to play."

"Yeah." Dylan nodded, lifting the football over his shoulder and making a few imaginary passes. "I remember—of course, that was a little before my time." He lowered the ball, feeling muscles in his shoulder he hadn't felt in a long, long time. "You ever think of going out for the team?"

Josh gave him a deliberate look, motioning to the school building behind him. "Sutter is a continuation school, remember. No football team."

Dylan grimaced, nodding. "I forgot."

Just then, Marissa stepped out of the maintenance trailer with Rick Mathers in tow. Dylan squinted his eyes, watching as they stood together, talking and laughing, and felt his stomach muscles tighten. Suddenly Mathers reached over, settling his hand at Marissa's waist, pointing to something at the work site. Rick Mathers stood only a scant few inches taller than Marissa, so when she cocked her head to look in the direction he pointed, it brought them nearly face-to-face.

"I used to go to school with him," Dylan said suddenly, feeling tension in his stomach turning to a gnawing. When Josh looked up, Dylan nodded in the direction of the industrial arts teacher. "Mathers, I mean." He watched as the teacher turned his head, making it look almost as though he were whispering something in Marissa's ear. "Your aunt did, too."

"Oh, yeah?" Josh mumbled absently, uninterested.

"Yeah." Dylan mumbled. Whatever Mathers had said in her ear made her laugh, and she reached out and touched him on the arm. "He ratted on me once to the football coach."

"Yeah?" Josh turned to Dylan, his interest picking up.

"Yeah. I broke training once—stayed out late one night drinking a few beers."

"Oh, yeah?" Josh said again. Suddenly Dylan James seemed a lot less like a sheriff and a whole lot more like a regular guy.

"Yeah," Dylan mumbled, his lips thinning into a narrow line as he watched the two of them head toward the trailer again. "The little creep turned me in."

Josh's face broke into a wide grin. "You know, he wears a pocket protector."

Dylan glanced down at Josh. "You're kidding."

"Swear to God," Josh averred, chuckling.

Dylan glanced back and watched as they disappeared inside the trailer. "What a nerd."

"You got that right."

"I figured," Dylan muttered. "The little worm."

"A bug," Josh corrected him. "A real goofus bug."

Dylan's head snapped up, and he turned back to Josh. He suddenly realized the kid had dropped his guard, had forgotten about attitude and acting tough. "What did you say?"

"What?" Josh asked, his defenses going back up. "I didn't say anything."

"You called him a goofus bug?"

"Oh, that," he said, his face relaxed. He grimaced a little, and for just an instant his expression turned wistful. "It's just something my dad used to say."

Dylan nodded. "Your dad?"

"Yeah, it was kind of a joke we had about this goofy-looking dry fly," Josh explained, tossing the whole handful of pebbles he held to the ground. "You know, for fly-fishing?"

"Yeah, I do know," Dylan said, reaching into the breast pocket of his shirt. He pulled out a ratty little wad of feathers and string, holding it up. "But for trout, I generally prefer an Adams."

"Sure I can't bring you back a soda?"

Marissa shook her head. "I'm sure, Rick, thanks."

Rick Mathers dug deep into the pocket of his jeans, bringing out several coins. "I think I'll just run over to the machine in the teacher's lounge. I'll be right back. You won't change your mind? They've got iced tea in there, too."

"No, thanks," Marissa insisted, turning away from the window. She looked into his eager face and cringed inside. He was a truly lovely person—polite and attentive. But the fact was, he got on her nerves, and she was edgy enough at the moment. She just wanted to be left alone. "But look, Rick, why don't you just take off? It's not necessary for you to stick around. You're through for the day. I have to wait around for Josh, anyway.''

Rick grinned, the sunlight from the window catching the thick lens of his glasses and glaring back bright. "That's okay, I don't mind. Besides, I have some questions for James. After all, I'm responsible for those three boys for a good part of the day. We've got a schedule to keep, and I'm curious how often he plans to make these random checks.''

Marissa nodded, then turned back to the window. She let out a long, exasperated sigh, trying to calm her jittery nerves. It was nearly five o'clock, and frankly, she was tired of waiting. Rick had sent the other boys home nearly a half hour ago, and she still had work to do back in her office. She knew she should just go back and try to get some of it done, but she was too antsy to concentrate. What was taking so long?

She peered through the tinted trailer window of the maintenance office and glared across the yard to where Dylan and Josh sat talking. What could they be discussing? Dylan hadn't kept the other two boys this long. What did he want with Josh? *What were they talking about?*

"I'm afraid I'm going to have to leave now."

Marissa jumped just a little, turning to Harold Wise, the school's custodian. "That's okay."

"I'd offer to stay and lock up, but the district won't authorize overtime any longer."

"Don't worry about it, Harold, I'll take care of it." She glanced back out the window, and then to him again. "I shouldn't be much longer."

She watched as he picked up his black plastic lunch pail and headed for the trailer door. "You just have to push the button in," he explained, pointing to the large round button on the lever handle of the door. "And pull the door tight."

"Thanks," Marissa mumbled, giving him a little wave. Hot air rushed into the small trailer when he opened the door to leave. It was the heat that had driven her inside the small, air-conditioned office in the first place. The afternoon had turned sweltering.

But apparently Dylan and Josh were impervious to the heat. They'd been huddled in conversation across the yard for the last hour.

She sank down onto a worn brown vinyl chair, frustrated and edgy. The chair groaned, squeaking loudly when she swiveled around to the small metal desk behind her. She leaned forward, resting her elbows on the desk and cradling her chin with her hands. She ignored the clutter of work orders and stale cigarette butts that were littered about. Her mind was focused on Dylan and the conversation he was having with their son.

Their son. Again the thought had every muscle in her body tensing up.

She glanced up at the clock on the wall. An hour. They'd been talking for an hour. Was it just talking? Skip had accused Dylan of harassing them—was he harassing Josh now? Was he questioning him, accusing him of something? Sixty minutes hardly constituted questioning—it qualified more as interrogation.

And what was that business with the football? she thought, making a face. She remembered having glanced across the lawn just as he waved that stupid football around. What was all that about?

Surely he didn't think Josh had done something wrong. She and Josh had been together almost every minute since he'd been released from jail, and she knew for a fact he'd been good. But if he wasn't questioning Josh, what was taking so long?

She slammed her hands down hard onto the desk, sending paper and cigarette butts flying. She was tired of waiting, tired of sitting there doing nothing. She was going to find out for herself what Dylan was doing with her son.

She marched to the trailer door, angrily yanking it open.

"Hi," Josh chirped, a wide grin on his face. His expression quickly changed, however, when the blast of cold air from inside the trailer reached his overheated skin. "Boy, does that air-conditioning feel good." He stepped inside and leaned down to give Marissa a sweaty kiss on the cheek. "Do you know how hot it is out there?"

"Uh, no—I mean, uh, yeah, I do," Marissa stammered, sputtering to recover from the surprise. She watched as he stepped past her and made a dash to the small water cooler in the corner. As far as she could tell he looked okay, not exactly like someone who'd spent the last hour being interrogated.

He pulled a paper cup from the dispenser, filling it to the brim. He turned, holding the cup out. "Water, Sheriff?"

Marissa reared around to find Dylan on the step outside. The collar of his uniform was unbuttoned and loose, and the sleeves were rolled causally to the elbow.

He turned his dark gaze to her, giving her a cursory look. "May I?"

"C-come in," she stuttered, stepping to one side to allow him room to pass.

She closed the trailer door behind him, closing out the hot cloud of air that had come in with them. She watched as they stood by the cooler, downing one paper cup of ice water after another and feeling herself become flushed and uncomfortably warm for entirely different reasons.

"So...you two all through now?" she asked after a moment. She'd tried to make the question sound casual, but even to her own ears it had sounded stiff and awkward. "With your...talk, I mean?"

Dylan exchanged a look with Josh. "All through," he said, turning back to her.

"Everything...okay?" she asked when it became obvious neither one was going to elaborate.

"Fine," Dylan said, nodding.

"Fine," Josh said, nodding.

Marissa could have screamed. Weren't they going to tell her anything? She searched Josh's face in an effort to see what it was he might be feeling. Had Dylan upset him, frightened him? But Josh simply smiled back at her, lifting the water to his lips and gulping down another cup.

She turned to Dylan. "You have everything you need for your report for Judge Kent?"

"I think so," he said, crushing the paper cup and tossing it across the length of the trailer toward the green metal wastebasket beside the desk. It landed squarely inside. "For now."

Marissa's gaze bounced between them, from one to the other. They just stood there, staring at her, and the silence was driving her crazy. Her curiosity was exploding, she wanted to scream and launch into her own interrogation, put them both beneath the white light and demand to know what they'd talked about, why it had taken so long—who and what and why. She searched her brain for a subtle approach, some sort of clever lead-in to get them talking, but she couldn't come up with much.

"Rick let Skip and Randy leave about a half hour ago," she said, taking great pains to keep her voice causal. "We'd just assumed you were through with them. I hope that was all right."

Dylan glanced down at his wristwatch, surprised to find it was after five. Kim was going to wonder what the hell had happened to him.

"Sure," he said, looking up and watching her knot her fingers together. She looked like she was about ready to leap out of her skin. What was making her so jumpy? "We were all through."

"Oh," she said, nodding more than she needed. "I just wondered, well, since it seemed that you and Josh . . . since it was a bit longer. I thought maybe there was something more you might have wanted to see them about."

Dylan shook his head. "No, I think that was everything."

"Great," she murmured, stepping back a few paces toward the cluttered desk. "That's . . . great."

The small trailer suddenly seemed cramped and airless, despite the noisy air conditioner that blew down on her from the vent in the roof. She almost wished Dylan wasn't standing between her and the water cooler—she could have used a cool drink herself.

"Karen called down before she left, said she'd made those copies you'd wanted." She walked back toward the door. "She was going to leave them on my desk. We can stop now, if you'd like, on your way out."

"Sure, thanks," Dylan mumbled, getting the distinct impression she wanted him out of there. Why was she so anxious to get rid of him? He turned to Josh, giving him a nod. "Take it easy, kid. I'll be in touch."

"Yeah," Josh mumbled, nodding back.

Marissa was just about to reach for the door when it suddenly pushed open.

"Oh, good, you're finished," Rick Mathers said, stepping inside the trailer, holding an opened soft drink can in his hand. He kicked the trailer door closed with his foot, shutting out the glare of the sun.

"We were just on our way to my office," Marissa explained, wishing there was some diplomatic way she could get him to move away from the door. "The sheriff needs to pick up some papers for his report to the judge."

Rick nodded, then turned to Dylan. "So, Sheriff, what did you think?"

Dylan's dark eyes narrowed. Was this why she'd been so jumpy, because she'd known Mathers was coming back? Was this why she'd been so anxious to get rid of him? "I thought everything looked good."

Rick smiled, lifting the can to his lips and taking a drink. "So you think this will be typical of the checks you plan to make—taking the boys aside and talking to them?"

Dylan's gaze flickered to Marissa, then back to Mathers. He remembered having watched the two of them together, how they had looked—heads together, talking and laughing. Just what was it Mathers had said to her when he'd leaned so close and made her laugh? What little secrets did they share, what private jokes were there between them?

"Maybe," he said, being deliberately vague. He wasn't entirely sure he liked being questioned by this little pipsqueak, especially since it seemed Marissa was perfectly comfortable with allowing him to do it. "I really haven't decided yet."

Rick Mathers nodded again, obviously unaware of the undercurrents in Dylan's voice. He finished the can of soda and tossed it in the direction of the metal trash bin. It clanged noisily against the rim, then fell to the floor and rolled under the desk. "Have you decided how often you plan to schedule these random checks—once a week, every other week, once a month?"

Dylan took several steps forward, glowering down at the teacher and remembered Mathers's smug expression when the coach chewed him out for breaking training. "If they're scheduled, they wouldn't exactly be random, now, would they?"

"I guess not," Rick conceded with an embarrassed laugh. He walked to the desk, picking up a pack of cigarettes and slipping them into his pocket. "But it's a little hard for us to keep to a schedule if you'll be popping in at any given time and putting a halt to everything."

"I guess that's just something we'll have to work out when the time comes," Dylan said, giving him a cold smile. "Unless, of course, you have a problem with that?"

"Me? No, of course not," Rick said with a nervous laugh. He turned to Marissa, pointing out the window. "I see a few tools in the yard that I need to put away. I'll talk to you later?"

"Sure," Marissa said, reaching over and opening the door of the trailer for him. When he was gone, Marissa slammed the door shut and turned to Dylan. "Look, I'm sorry about Rick. He gets a little carried away sometimes."

Dylan shrugged carelessly and shook his head. "Don't worry about it," he said, turning a sly eye then to Josh. "Goofus bug."

Josh nodded. "Goofus bug."

Chapter 6

"What's a...goofus bug?"

Josh glanced up from his plate of linguini smothered in red sauce and smiled. Swallowing his mouthful, he laughed low in his throat. "Mathers is a goofus bug."

"That's *Mr.* Mathers, if you don't mind," Marissa corrected him, giving him a stern look. But her eyes sparkled with humor, and they both knew she wasn't serious. "And that doesn't answer my question."

Josh regarded her for a moment, his grin growing wider. "You really don't know what a goofus bug is?"

"No, I really don't know what a goofus bug is," Marissa repeated, making a face and mimicking his voice. "But apparently Sheriff James does."

"Yeah, he does," Josh said, scooping up another forkful of pasta and twisting it into a mouth-size ball. "'Cause he fly-fishes."

"Fly-fishes?" Marissa lowered her fork to the plate.

"Yeah, you know." Josh reached out a hand and made a few casting motions with his free hand. "Fly-fishing."

"You mean, like your dad used to do?"

"Yeah, like that," Josh said, casting into the air a few more times. "Remember he used to take me?"

"I guess," Marissa mumbled, taking another bite of pasta, chewing it, then swallowing. God, she'd always hated fishing. "You mean Dylan—Sheriff James fly-fishes?"

Josh nodded, his mouth full of pasta.

She curled more linguini around her fork and took another bite, thinking as she chewed. Fly-fishing. She tried to picture him in her head—standing on the bank of a lake or wading through a stream in hip boots. It wasn't that she couldn't see him doing that exactly—with the abundance of streams and lakes in the Mother Lode, it was certainly a popular-enough sport. But still it surprised her. It surprised her to think that he actually had a real life, with hobbies and interests and concerns. He was, she begrudgingly realized, more than just the football quarterback, or a sheriff with a gun.

"So what does that have to do with a goofus whatever-it-is-you-call-it?" she asked after a minute.

"Goofus bug," Josh clarified, wiping his mouth with his napkin. "It's a dry fly. You know like a parachute, a blue-winged olive, a gray ghost. Dad used to use a goofus bug once in a while." He smiled, thinking back. "It's this dopey-looking thing—even for a fly." He looked across the table to her. "Didn't you ever hear my dad call anyone a goofus bug—like when he was driving and somebody cut him off?"

"I guess I didn't," Marissa replied, thinking of her brother and the kind, gentle man he had been. Goofus bug. She wouldn't say she could exactly remember hearing Caleb refer to anyone in that way, but it certainly sounded like something he would have said—especially around Josh. Caleb never would have wanted his son to hear him curse or swear, and goofus bug sounded just like the kind of silly thing he would substitute for what he really wanted to say.

Josh shrugged. "Anyway, it got to be kind of a joke with us—anyone who was kind of nerd or a jerk, a pain in the butt— Oh...sorry." He grimaced, giving her an apologetic smile. "I mean, anyone who was a pain in the neck was a—"

"Goofus bug," Marissa finished for him.

Josh reached for his glass of milk, his dark eyes shining. "Jerk," he mused. "A pain in the neck. Huh..." He grinned wider. "Remind you of anyone?"

"Now, stop that," Marissa scolded, trying her best to keep a straight face. "Rick's okay."

Josh peered at her over the rim of the glass, pausing before taking a drink. "Okay for what?"

Marissa gave him a look, but couldn't quite suppress a smile. "Well, okay, I admit, maybe Rick is a little..."

"Nerdy?"

"*Persnickety,*" she corrected him pointedly. "But he's a good teacher and knows a lot about industrial arts, manual arts, and he's great with computers. Actually, I'm lucky to have him on my staff."

"Wow, lucky," Josh joked, rolling his eyes. He reached for the platter in the center of the table, sliding it toward him.

She watched as he refilled his plate with another heaping mound of pasta and dug in. She'd read somewhere that teenage boys were the perfect eating machine, and, watching as he dove into his second helping, she was inclined to believe it was true.

She glanced down at her own half-finished plate. She'd eaten only a fraction of what Josh had consumed, and she felt overstuffed and uncomfortable. Pushing her plate to one side, she leaned back in her chair.

"Well," she said, pulling the napkin from her lap and dabbing at the corners of her mouth. "I'm not asking you to like him—just put in your time, do your work and co-operate.''

Josh lowered his fork to the plate, his smile fading. "I've been trying to, honest. I'm not doing anything wrong."

"Oh, sweetie, I know, I know," Marissa said earnestly, sitting back up and reaching across the small table. She covered his hand with hers, cursing under her breath. What was she doing? She knew he was sensitive about everything that had happened, and the last thing she wanted was to make him think she planned to bring up the past every time something came up. "I'm *really* impressed with the efforts you've made. You buckled down, accepted your punishment. You haven't whined or made waves. You've shown a lot of maturity and a lot of responsibility. I'm not only impressed, I'm very proud."

Josh's cheeks flushed with emotion, and he quickly looked away. "Yeah?"

"Yeah," she said, squeezing his hand. And then, because she knew she'd embarrassed him, she quickly changed the subject. "So...did you and Sheriff James have a nice talk today?"

"Yeah," Josh said, scooping up another forkful of food. "It was okay."

"Did he ask a lot of questions?" she prompted, making an effort to keep her tone light.

"Some," he said with his mouth full.

"I'd just wondered," she said casually, leaning back again in the chair. "Because he seemed to keep you out there so long. I was getting a little worried. Skip told me the sheriff has harassed you guys before. I thought maybe...you know, maybe he was giving you a hard time or something."

"No," Josh said, shaking his head and swallowing. "Skip's just paranoid. He thinks everyone's out to get him."

Marissa frowned. So much for being subtle. It looked as though the only way she was going to find out exactly what he and Dylan had talked about for so long this afternoon was to come right out and ask.

She drew in a deep breath. "So what did you two talk about for so long?"

"Fly-fishing," Josh said, chewing.

"Fly-fishing?"

"Yeah."

"All that time?"

"Yeah," Josh said, shrugging. "Well, mostly. He asked me some stuff about school, and Skip." He smiled again. "And *Mr.* Mathers. But mostly we just talked fly-fishing."

"And that's how this goofus insect thing came up?"

"Goofus bug."

The dinner in her stomach rolled queasily around. "That's it?"

"Pretty much," Josh said. With a small corner of garlic bread, he shoveled the last bite of pasta onto his fork and downed it in one gulp. "He said he'd take me sometime, if I wanted."

Marissa came forward in her chair. "Take you fishing?"

"Uh-huh."

"You and Dyl...uh, you and the sheriff fishing? Together?"

Josh glanced up, giving her a curious smile. "Yeah, together."

"Why would he want to take you fly-fishing?"

"I don't know," Josh said, settling back and tossing his napkin down onto his plate. "We just got talking about it. I told him about that place Dad and me used to go up near Long Barn. He told me about some of the places he goes around here." Josh flicked his wrist, practicing a few more air shots. "Just asked if I'd want to tag along sometime, that's all."

"What did you say?"

"I said maybe." He glanced at her again, his dark brows knitted together. "Was there something wrong with that?"

Marissa shook her head. "No, no. Of course not. I guess I'm just a little surprised, that's all." She stood up and began to clear the dishes away. "I never thought of Dylan James fishing."

"Not just fishing," Josh pointed out, air casting a few more times, and wiggling his eyebrows. "*Fly*-fishing. There's a difference."

Marissa laughed as she carried the dishes to the sink. "Well, its just so much smelly fish if you ask me."

"Girls," Josh muttered with a smile as he carried the pasta platter into the kitchen.

"Women," she corrected him.

They continued to talk as they worked together in the kitchen, clearing the table and stacking the dirty dishes in the dishwasher. Josh told her about the new girl in his algebra class, and Marissa asked his opinion on the new menu in the school cafeteria. It was a casual conversation—idle chitchat, really, but the kind of comfortable, relaxed talk she enjoyed the most, the kind she'd missed all those years she'd spent without him.

After a while, Josh headed for his room to start on his homework, and Marissa finished up in the kitchen.

It wasn't until she heard the low rhythms coming from Josh's CD player that her mind turned to Dylan again.

She told herself his offer to take Josh fly-fishing had just been a casual gesture. She could almost imagine how the thing had come up—they'd been talking, one thing had led to another, and Dylan had just brought it up. It was simply a spur-of-the-moment thing that neither of them had taken very seriously. But she couldn't help feeling a little uneasy about it. The thought of Dylan and Josh developing any kind of a relationship made her uncomfortable. As far as she was concerned, the less time the two of them spent together, the better.

But she had to be careful. If she'd learned one thing from that fiasco in her office this afternoon, it was that she couldn't afford to panic, couldn't afford to let her fears and her paranoia make either of them suspicious. She and Josh were just starting their life together, and as long as Josh was on probation, Dylan James was going to be a part of it. It was up to her to find a way to cope, to set the tone for the others to follow.

She snapped the lid down tight on the plastic bowl that held the meager leftovers of their dinner and pulled the refrigerator door open. It was only then that she noticed the empty milk carton.

Picking up the empty container, she tossed it into the trash. Keeping a house stocked with enough food for a hungry teenage boy was proving quite a challenge. Having lived alone for so many years, she was forever having to throw away food that had gone unused and forgotten. But now with Josh, it seemed she couldn't keep enough food in the house.

Snatching up her purse, she walked to the stairwell and called up.

"Hey, Josh."

Immediately the music died, and she heard the sound of his door opening.

"What's up?" he called down the stairs.

"We're out of milk. I'm going to run down to the market and get some. Be back in a minute."

Dylan looked down at the folder on the seat beside him. He might as well go ahead and admit it. This was just an excuse—plain and simple. An out-and-out excuse he'd come up with—and not even a very good one at that. After all, getting Marissa's signature on the report he'd compiled for Judge Kent was really nothing more than a formality, nothing that couldn't have waited until morning. Yet here he was, parked in front of her condo as though he were delivering a vital organ on which a human life depended.

He reached up, switching the key off and bringing the Jeep's motor to an abrupt halt. He sat there for a moment, listening to the engine creak and groan and trying to find some justification as to why he was doing what he was about to do.

It really made no sense. After all, he'd been perfectly content these last couple of weeks doing what he could to avoid her, concentrating on work and trying to forget she was even back in town. If it hadn't been for this damn report for the judge, maybe he would have forgotten about her completely.

Dylan made a face. Even he didn't buy that. It had been sixteen years since he'd held the woman, and he hadn't done a very good job of forgetting.

He peered out of the window, looking across the lawn toward her door. The sun had all but disappeared behind the mountains, just the meekest of rays drifting through the twilight sky. So why was he there? What had him racking his brain, coming up with this flimsy excuse just so he could see her again?

He thought of that moment in her office—that moment when he'd pulled her close, when she'd looked up at him with emotion so evident in her eyes. When she'd looked so much like the girl he'd loved, the girl he'd wanted all those years ago.

But that wasn't the reason. He'd come because he'd had to, because he couldn't stay away. He'd left the small maintenance trailer and walked back with her to her office. He'd dutifully picked up the copies of the documents he'd requested, then he'd shaken her hand, walked to his Jeep and driven away. But something hadn't felt right,

something nagged at him as though it had been left un-
done, or unsaid.

He glanced down at the folder again, staring at it as
though he expected it to spring to life, as though it would
suddenly come alive and advise him on what he should do.
But instead it did nothing—just lay there staring up at him,
mute and pathetic—just like the excuse he was using it for.

It was stupid—this whole thing was just one big stupid
mistake. He had to get out of there, get out before anyone
saw him, before he made a bigger fool of himself than he
had already.

He reached for the key in the ignition, but before he
could twist it on, before he could crank the engine back to
life and speed away, the light above her door suddenly
switched on, flooding the small porch with light.

Dylan froze. She was down the steps and halfway across
the lawn before she spotted his Jeep—but then, it would
have been a little hard to miss sitting there at the curb
parked right behind her car. She came to an abrupt stop,
peering through the darkness.

Dylan swore under his breath, reached for the folder
from the seat beside him and opened his car door. It was a
flimsy excuse, but it was the only one he had.

"Looks like I caught you at a bad time," he said, stepping out of the car and giving her a small wave from across
the hood of his Jeep.

"I was . . . I was just on my way to the market," she
stammered, walking to where he was parked. Her defenses
were immediately up. She stopped on the curb, resting her
hands on the warm hood, gazing across at his tall, dark
form. "Did you need to see me about something?"

He held up the folder. "Just a signature on this report for
Kent, but it can wait." He reached for the door handle,
feeling almost relieved. She looked entirely too soft, and
too vulnerable, in the pale glow of the porch light. The

tight, constricting bun was gone, and her hair fell long and free. "I'll catch you some other time."

"Are you sure?" she asked, stopping him. "If it's important . . ."

"No, that's all right," he insisted, pulling the door open. "Go do your grocery shopping, we can talk later."

"It was just milk," she said, stepping away from the patrol car.

He stopped, poised in the open door, and glanced back at her. He tried not to notice how the light formed a golden halo behind her. "Just milk?"

Marissa laughed, realizing that might have sounded a little strange. "Yeah, milk. We're out. I think Josh goes through a couple of gallons a day. I was just going to the corner market for some."

Dylan didn't even miss a beat. "Hop in, I'll drive you."

"So, what do you think?"

Marissa lowered the folder to her lap. The report was straightforward and accurate, and she could find nothing to complain about.

"I think it sounds fine," she said, opening her purse and slipping her pen from its holder in her checkbook. She rested the folder on her lap, signing the cover letter in the space he'd left for her. She closed the folder and handed it to him. "Do you think I could get a copy of this for my files?"

"Sure," he said, taking the file from her and depositing it on the seat between them. He pulled into a free spot in the small parking lot, turning the motor off. "I'll have Kim send one over."

"Thanks," Marissa said, gathering up her purse and pushing the door open. "I won't be more than a minute."

"No hurry," he said, opening his door, too. "I'll go with you."

Marissa headed down a narrow aisle of the small market, feeling self-conscious and uncomfortable. Each step she took she was aware of Dylan following closely behind. The small store was nearly deserted, and no one paid any attention to them at all, but in her mind she felt as though every eye in the place was watching.

It had given her quite a start to look up and find him parked at the curb in front of her house. For a moment, all she'd been able to do was stand there and stare. A million different things had run through her head, a million reasons as to why he'd come—another random check on Josh, a question about the visit at school, another troubled student. But just for an instant, just for one brief fraction of a millisecond, she'd thought that maybe he'd come to see her.

She reached the dairy case, her eyes scanning for the low-fat milk. Reaching for the largest container she could find, she picked it up.

"Here, let me help you with that," Dylan offered, relieving her of the heavy container.

For a brief moment, their hands brushed, and Marissa felt the reaction of that brief contact reverberate through her entire system.

"Thanks," she mumbled.

"Wow," he said, surveying the size of the carton. "I didn't even know they made them in this size."

"You'd be surprised what you learn when you have a teenager living with you," she said, heading back down the aisle toward the checkout line. "And you'd be surprised how much more time you spend in a grocery store than you used to."

"Growing boy," Dylan commented dryly, following her to the end of the line.

"Growing and hungry," she said.

They waited silently in line. Marissa concentrated her attention on studying the busy pattern on the blouse of the woman in line in front of her, and Dylan scanned the headlines of the tabloid newspapers that lined the racks on either side of the counter.

The line grew longer as other shoppers moved in place behind them, and Dylan stepped close to make room. His arm brushed hers, and the sudden contact caused her to jump. She tried to step back, but the conditions were too crowded, and she only succeeded in banging her knee into his.

"Sorry," she mumbled, feeling clumsy and embarrassed.

"No problem," he said, shifting the heavy carton of milk from one hand to the other.

Marissa turned and watched with growing impatience the slow, steady pace of the checkout clerk. It seemed to be taking forever. When she'd finally finished ringing up one customer and started on the next, the tape on her cash register suddenly ran out, and she had to call the manager to come help her install another spool of paper.

Dylan shifted the milk again, causing their arms to brush again. Marissa closed her eyes. She felt like screaming. She just wanted out of there, wanted to get moving again, but it seemed that forces were conspiring against her to prevent that from happening. It made her nervous having him so close—nervous and uneasy. It made her think of that moment in her office when he had touched her arm, when he had said her name.

"Marissa?"

Marissa's eyes snapped open, and she looked around, confused and flustered. But it wasn't Dylan who had said her name. It was the woman who stood at the end of the line behind them.

"Marissa Wakefield, it *is* you?"

Marissa looked into the woman's smiling face, recognition coming to her in a rush. "Jill? Jill Lawrence?"

"You remember," the woman screeched, leaving her basket at her spot at the end of the line and rushing up to give Marissa an enthusiastic hug. "You know, my sister told me you'd moved back to Jackson, but I could hardly believe it."

"Jill Lawrence," Marissa murmured again, remembering the face of her childhood friend. "You haven't changed a bit."

"No? You don't think so?" Jill laughed, stepping back and pointing to her extended tummy.

Marissa laughed, her cheeks darkening as she realized how that sounded to her very pregnant old friend. "Well, maybe a little."

"Oh, Marissa," Jill said again, giving her another hug. "You look great. You're the one who hasn't changed. My God, how long has it been? Fifteen years? Sixteen?"

"Long enough that it's probably better not to count," Marissa laughed. The line moved forward, and they all took a step closer to the counter. "Jill, do you know Dylan James?" She looked up into his dark eyes. "Dylan, this is Jill Lawrence."

"I don't think there's anyone in Jackson who doesn't know Sheriff James," Jill said, extending her hand to him. "We've never met officially, Sheriff, but I know all about you." She leaned forward, lowering her voice. "I'm Kimberly's sister. She talks about you all the time."

Dylan made a face, giving her a crooked smile as he took her hand. "Well, I hope you don't believe everything she tells you."

"Oh, it's all good," Jill assured him. "And it's Scaletti now. Jill Scaletti."

"You and Dom got married," Marissa said, remembering Dom Scaletti and his kind brown eyes. He used to joke and tease with her and Mallory whenever they stepped into his father's deli for salami sandwiches and potato salad. "That's wonderful."

"Sixteen years this fall," Jill announced proudly. She tapped her tummy again. "This one's number five. How about you?"

Marissa's gaze flicked momentarily to Dylan. "About three hundred," she said with a laugh. "I'm the principal at Sutter High."

"Kimberly mentioned that. My oldest son's a student there." She stopped, grimacing a little. "He ran into some problems with grades at Jackson High. But he's doing better now at Sutter, so I'm delighted you're there. You always were great with kids." She turned to Dylan. "When my brother Kevin was little, he used to be such a pain in the neck—a real handful, you know?" She put her arm around Marissa, giving her a squeeze. "But Marissa...she knew just what to do, really knew how to handle him. I swear she had him wrapped right around her little finger."

"Is that right?" Dylan murmured, looking down at Marissa. He remembered Kim telling him the same story, and wondered just how many other men there were in her past still wrapped around that little finger of hers.

"How is Kevin?" Marissa asked quickly, turning away from Dylan's gaze. "What's he doing now?"

"Actually, he just got married a few months ago," Jill said, reaching back and pulling her stuffed grocery cart closer. "He and his wife are expecting, too—their first, though. They live in Sacramento. He's a doctor now, can you believe it?"

"Wow," Marissa said with a laugh, trying to picture the disheveled little boy she used to know in a white coat and stethoscope. "Boy, do I feel old."

"Yeah, well, don't feel bad," she laughed, glancing up at Dylan. "I still call him my baby brother." Her smile faded. "I heard about your brother and his wife. I'm really sorry. That must have been terrible."

"Yeah, it was, especially for Josh," Marissa said, patting Jill's hand. She was sometimes skeptical of people's concerns, thinking that they used it as an excuse to gossip about Josh's trouble, but it was easy to see that Jill's concerns were heartfelt.

"Kim also said he's living with you now."

"Yes, he is."

"Well, teenagers can be a real challenge," she said, giving her a sympathetic pat on the arm. "Believe me, I know. I've got two of them."

Jill went on to tell Marissa about her children, and the half-finished nursery she was redecorating, and the changes at the deli Dom now ran after his parents retired several years ago. Marissa listened with interest, caught up in Jill's amusing wit and easy, relaxed manner. As she looked into Jill's lively face, she couldn't suppress a small pang of regret. She remembered what it was she'd always liked about Jill, and why they'd become such good friends. There wasn't a pretentious bone in the woman's body, she was what she appeared to be—an open, honest and sincere individual.

Marissa almost regretted that she hadn't kept in touch with Jill and her other friends over the years, but she'd told herself it had all been for the best. Her child was going to be raised in Jackson, and she didn't dare do anything that might make anyone suspect the truth about his birth. Still, she remembered how lonely she had been. She'd known no one in Maryland, and as good as her Aunt Bea had been to her, it hadn't been the same. She'd missed Mallory that first year, until she'd finished high school and they'd gone to the University of Maryland together, and of course she'd missed the rest of her family terribly. But despite all the awful things he had said to her, she'd missed Dylan most of all.

She kept her attention on Jill, but there wasn't a moment that passed that she wasn't aware of him standing at her side. She could literally feel his presence, just as if he were touching her—but of course, he wasn't. He simply stood close, listening to Jill, making a comment here and there, and nodding his head from time to time.

Marissa couldn't help wondering if Jill found it odd to find the two of them together. She had never told anyone about her love for Dylan—not even her best friend. Only Mallory knew about that, and only Mallory had known how she'd traded identities, how she'd let Dylan believe he was seeing Mallory instead of her. But there had been talk once Dylan had discovered the truth, there had been teasing, and joking, and gossip about the "trick" she'd played on him.

Did Jill remember all those old rumors? Would seeing her and Dylan together cause her to draw the wrong conclusions, make the wrong assumptions? Would the gossip start and the old rumors begin to fly again?

Marissa watched as Jill chattered on. If she found it unusual to find Dylan with her, if she was the least bit curious, it didn't seem to show.

The truth could be a terrible thing, she reminded herself as she laughed at Jill's account of her four-year-old's latest antics. It could be a heavy burden, and it could sometimes make her see things that simply weren't there.

She'd been so absorbed in her thoughts, and with listening to Jill, that she hadn't even been aware that the line had moved. It wasn't until Dylan had reached around her and hoisted the milk carton onto the counter that she realized they'd made it to the clerk.

"Well," Jill said in a conspiratorial voice, glancing back at the people standing in line behind them, "I'd better get back to my spot in line before there's a minor riot here." She turned and gave Marissa a quick hug. "This has been so great. Could we get together sometime? For dinner, maybe? I know Dom would love to see you."

"I'd really like that, too," she said, feeling Dylan's hand at her elbow. She gave Jill a wave. "And I want to meet all your kids."

She let him lead her out the door and into the parking lot. He held the door for her as she climbed into the passenger side of his Jeep, and she watched as he walked around to the other side.

"Oh, wait," she said suddenly as he climbed into the seat beside her. She reached for the handle of her door. "I forgot to pay for the milk."

He stopped her with a hand on her arm. "It's okay. I took care of it."

"What?" she gasped. "You paid for my milk?"

"Well, I couldn't very well let you walk out of there without paying, could I?"

"Well, no," she replied, confused. "But—"

It had grown quite dark, and the only light inside the Jeep came from the small sign in the market's window. Her pale hair reflected the faint rays, and her eyes sparkled large and clear. She looked beautiful in the dim light, her lips full and inviting, and he felt a twist of emotion in his chest—an almost painful spasm tightening around his heart. For a crazy moment he wanted to reach across the seat and pull her to him, wanted to press his mouth against hers and kiss her long and deep.

His hold on her arm tightened, and he leaned close. "And how would it look if the sheriff had to arrest the principal?"

Chapter 7

Marissa felt her world skitter to a stop. She watched in a kind of daze as Dylan leaned across the seat, pulling on her arm and bringing her close. She felt the strain of the seat belt pressing hard against her chest, felt the throb of her heart pulse thick in her throat and the pant of his breath against her cheek. He was going to kiss her. There was nothing sudden or unexpected in his moves, nothing questionable or unclear. He'd made his intentions clear, given her plenty of time to consider. He was going to kiss her, and she wasn't doing anything to stop him.

He didn't caress her lips, didn't brush or lightly graze against them. He pushed his mouth to hers, determined and decided, pressing her lips apart, and allowing his tongue to plunge deep. It wasn't the kiss she'd expected, and she wasn't reacting as she thought she would. It was far from a first kiss, far from a staid, inquiring introduction. It was the kiss of a lover, the kiss of a man hungry for a woman, and who would tolerate nothing getting in his way.

Dylan felt the air in his lungs grow hot and humid. It had been years since she'd been his, years since she'd whispered his name and yearned for his touch. He had pushed her away, had told himself he hated her and would never forgive what she had done. He had gone on—to other women and other relationships. He'd done his best to put her out of his heart and out of his mind.

But with her lips against his, with her taste shooting through his system like a high-speed chase, he realized a part of him had never let go, a part of him had never stopped thinking of her as belonging to him.

Marissa parted her lips, welcoming the invasion of his tongue and feeling her breath stop and her heart thunder in her ears. It wasn't the fact that he was kissing her she found surprising. It was discovering just how much she wanted him to. There had been other men in her life since he'd been her lover—other men who had kissed her, and who had wanted her. But this man was different, and his kiss was different, too.

This was Dylan—her Dylan—the father of her child, the man she had loved. Years had passed, emotions had come and gone, but this was what she wanted, this was where she was supposed to be.

The kiss deepened. Somehow her hand had found the front of his shirt, and she clutched at the smooth khaki uniform. His hand had found her cheek, sliding to the back of her neck and burying itself deep in her hair.

Marissa wasn't sure if it had been him who had intensified things, or her, and she was swiftly approaching that point where it no longer mattered. All she knew was that there was a magic in his touch—a magic she had been without for far too long, a magic she didn't think she could live without another moment.

He pulled his mouth away, staring into her smoky blue eyes and hearing the soft groan that escaped her parted lips reverberate through his entire system. His breath came in labored, rasping gasps, and the hand in her hair flexed and caressed. It had been sixteen years since they'd been together, but he remembered with uncanny clarity the sounds she had made when they had made love, when he'd buried himself deep inside her and sent them both spinning out of control. He longed to hear those sounds again, longed to return with her to that special place they had found together. He wanted to recapture magic, wanted to find the happiness he had shared with her. It had been so long since he'd been happy—so very long.

Marissa saw the desire etched on his face, felt the wild beat of his heart beneath the palm of her hand. This couldn't be happening—it shouldn't be. It was crazy, dangerous, and it made no sense. She couldn't let him hurt her again, couldn't risk letting herself start to feel again. There was too much history between them, too much water under the bridge, too much that had gone wrong.

And yet none of that seemed to matter—the past, the present. Nothing seemed to matter in the face of the passion that arced between them. It was powerful and potent, born of too many years spent alone, and too many nights without the man she wanted.

Dylan stared into her eyes, watching as they cleared and focused, as the world took shape in them again. He had wanted to kiss her—had wanted to since that moment in her office. It was what had him camping out in front of her house, what had him drumming up lame excuses, and seeking opportunities. He'd wanted to kiss her, and everything in him that was a man told him she'd wanted to kiss him, too.

"Don't forget to call."

They both jumped violently as Jill wrapped on the window and waved as she walked to her car.

Dylan pulled away, sliding back into the driver's seat and starting the engine as Marissa gave Jill a meek smile and a small wave.

They drove the few blocks back to her condo in silence. Marissa was too absorbed in her own thoughts, too preoccupied by the inner turmoil of her trembling emotions, to have time to be awkward or uncomfortable.

Dylan made a U-turn in the street, pulling to a stop at the curb in front of her house. He stepped out on to the pavement, and walked quickly around the Jeep, but Marissa had already gotten out by the time he reached her door.

The summer night was warm and clear, and the hint of a breeze that blew down from the foothills lazily stirred the limbs of the huge scrub oaks that lined the quiet street. The light on her porch glowed pale and bleak in the darkness, and from the bedroom above, she could hear the faint sounds of Josh's stereo.

"I need to pay you for the milk," she said, juggling the milk carton to one side and fumbling with her purse.

"No," he said, putting a hand out to stop her.

She froze at his touch and looked up at him. The porch light cast his face into shadow, but she didn't need to see his gaze to feel it on her. "Oh, but I—"

"Maybe we should talk about what happened," he said, the hand on her arm sliding to her elbow.

"I...I don't know what to say." She took a deep breath. "This all seems a little . . . crazy."

"Crazy good?" he asked, slipping his other hand around her. "Or crazy crazy?"

She smiled a little, shaking her head. "That's what's so crazy. I don't know what happened back there."

"That's interesting, I thought what happened was pretty clear. Maybe I was mistaken."

Marissa dropped her gaze, and the smile faded. He was right, of course. And it would be ridiculous to try to deny it. After all, they were hardly kids anymore. She shook her head. "No."

The concession pleased him, and a slow smile broke across his lips. "Any suggestions as to where we should go from here?"

"I don't know," she admitted honestly. "But maybe we need to give it a rest. I mean . . . I need time to think."

"Fair enough," he said. It wasn't exactly what he'd wanted. He would have preferred something more along the lines of her dragging him by the arm into her bed, but it would do. He could be patient, if she wanted—for a while. He pulled her close, crushing her purse and the carton of milk between them. "And while you're at it, think about this, too."

His mouth settled on hers with the same assurance, the same determination, that it had before, and Marissa found herself wanting nothing more than to yield to its silent demands. And when he let her go, she stood there on the curb in a crazy kind of stupor, watching as he walked back around the Jeep and climbed inside. It wasn't until he'd started the engine and sped off down the street that she finally turned and started back toward her door.

She glanced down at the milk in her arms, feeling a little dazed and shell-shocked. What the hell had happened to her? She'd left the house for a simple carton of milk. She hadn't even been gone a half hour, and yet it felt as though her whole world had changed.

She walked slowly to the porch, fishing her house keys out from the bottom of her purse. She glanced up at the light in the bedroom window above. Josh's room. Once again Dylan James had stepped into her life and changed everything. Only she wasn't some love-struck teenager any longer, and she wasn't about to make the same mistakes twice. After all, she didn't just have herself to look out for—she had Josh to think of now, too.

She unlocked the door and stepped inside, tossing her purse and her keys down on the table in the entry. She needed time to think, time to try to figure out just what it was she was doing. She couldn't afford any mistakes this time—not this time. There was too much at stake. She wasn't worried about a broken heart, she was worried about Josh—her son.

Their son.

"He wants me where?" Dylan asked again, pouring the last of the coffee into his mug. The morning staff meeting had just broken up, and except for Kim and himself, the small break room was empty.

"In his chambers," Kim said again, perusing through the large pink box in the center of the table. Finding a cream-filled éclair, she lifted it out of the carton and plopped it down on the napkin in front of her. "Around twelve-thirty."

Dylan brought the cup to his lips, gingerly taking a sip. The coffee was hot but tasted particularly bad. He swallowed, making a face, and examined the contents of the cup more closely.

"Jeez, what are they trying to do with this stuff? Poison someone?" he muttered, tossing the coffee into the sink and down the drain. "Did Judge Kent say what it was about?"

"Nope," Kim said, shaking her head. Taking a bite of the donut, she licked her fingers. "Just that he expected you to be there."

Dylan reached for the tea bags in the cupboard above the sink, slipping one out of the paper package and dropping it into his cup. There was only one thing Kent would want to see him about—it had to be the progress report he'd sent over to the courthouse five days ago. But the summary had been straightforward and thorough, what could there be about it that would cause Kent to summon him to the courthouse? If he had questions, couldn't they handle them over the phone?

Dylan shook his head, filling his cup with tap water and placing it and the tea bag into the microwave. He liked Randolf Kent, but couldn't help being just a little annoyed. He did have a job to do. After all, he was the county sheriff and there were appointments to keep and duties to perform. Dropping everything on a moment's notice wasn't always easy to do—even at the request of a superior court judge.

"Heard you were out shopping the other night."

Dylan set the timer on the microwave and turned back to Kim. "What do you mean?"

"My sister—Jill. She said she met you the other night at the market."

Dylan clenched his jaw tight. "Yeah."

"She . . . also said you weren't alone," she said, popping a piece of éclair into her mouth and chewing.

The microwave beeped behind him, and Dylan turned around and retrieved his mug from inside. The tea was steeped, and steamed in the cup strong and potent. He'd wondered how long it was going to take before Kim brought it up. He'd known it would be just a matter of time, and frankly, he was surprised it had taken as long as it had. It had been nearly a week since that night at the market, and it had been six *long* days since he'd seen Marissa, as well.

He pulled the tea bag from the cup, dropping it into the trash can and turned back to Kim. "No, I wasn't."

Kimberly looked at him, waiting. "Well?"

Dylan looked at her and shrugged. "Well, what?"

Kimberly made a face. "You know exactly what. Jill said you were with Marissa Wakefield."

"Yeah."

"So . . ." Kimberly started, urging him on.

"So?"

"So what's going on?"

Dylan's frown deepened slightly. He'd been asking himself that same question for the last six days. "What makes you think there's anything going on?"

"Oh, come on," Kimberly insisted. "She was with you, wasn't she?"

"Yeah."

"You came together."

"Yeah."

"Jill said you gave her a . . . you know . . . a *ride.*"

Dylan laughed. "I give Emma Crandall a ride to the post office from time to time also. I suppose you think there's something going on there, too?"

"Emma Crandall is eighty-seven years old," Kim pointed out dryly. "And the two of you didn't date back in high school." She started to take another bite of the éclair, then stopped. "At least I don't think you did, did you?"

Dylan laughed again, and gave his eyebrows a wicked wiggle. "Don't underestimate those little gray-haired ladies."

"Very funny, very funny," Kim said, rolling her eyes. She finished the last of the éclair and walked over to the sink, pushing him aside and washing her hands. "So I guess you and Emma make out in parking lots all the time, too, then, is that right?"

"Make out?" he asked stiffly. "I'm not sure I'd know how to *make out* anymore."

"Oh, is that right, Grandpa?" Kimberly said sympathetically, tweaking her fingers and flipping a few drops of cool water in his direction. She reached for a paper towel and dried her hands. "According to Jill, it looked like you knew exactly what you were doing."

Dylan's smile slowly faded. He was rather hoping Jill hadn't seen them—not that he was interested in keeping secrets. He'd wanted to kiss Marissa very much, and it didn't bother him who knew, or who saw them. It was just that he didn't feel like talking about it. "Shouldn't you be getting back to work? I mean, if you don't have enough to do, I could always find something more for you—''

"Okay, okay. I can take a hint," Kimberly conceded, cutting him off. She crumpled the paper towel and tossed it into the trash, heading for the door. After a few steps, she stopped and turned around. "Did I ever tell you I hate it when you start sounding like a boss?"

He laughed, but as he watched her head out the door and down the corridor toward the main desk, the smile slowly faded from his lips. It had been a long week—long, and tiresome, and hectic. There had been more budget headaches and useless wrangling with the board, and a freak rash of summer colds had left them short-staffed and scrambling. He'd stayed late at the station every night, and had taken several of the night patrols himself.

He glanced up at the clock. It was almost noon. What he really needed to do was work through lunch and try to make a dent in the paperwork that was piling up on his desk—not go rushing off to the courthouse for a command performance in front of the judge. But that was what he'd do—like it or not. And he didn't like it much.

He finished his tea and rinsed out his cup in the sink, then headed back for his office. He rounded his cluttered desk, ignoring the stack of unfinished paperwork, and settled into his chair. He thought about Kim, and the questions she'd asked him.

If Kim was asking about Marissa, there was a good chance others in his department were curious, as well. It was safe to say he wasn't crazy about the idea of his private life being the subject of office gossip, and he didn't want to encourage or condone rumors and innuendos. Their work was too serious, the service they provided the community too important, for him to tolerate that. But he was realistic, and knew that it didn't matter how dedicated or how hardworking an employee was, loose tongues and idle chitchat seemed to be an inevitable part of the work experience.

So he didn't doubt that the grapevine was alive and well in his department, and that he was probably the subject of it from time to time. But the truth of the matter was, he really hadn't been thinking about who might be watching, or what kind of gossip might follow, when he'd leaned across the seat of his Jeep and kissed Marissa. All he'd had on his mind was the woman, and how much he'd wanted her right then.

Then—and now. He swiveled his chair around, staring out the window and picturing her in his mind. She'd asked him for time, and maybe he'd needed some, as well. But it had been six long days, and not one had passed that he hadn't wanted to call, hadn't wanted to hear her voice, to hold her again. But he hadn't, he'd tried to be patient.

It wasn't as though he'd thought this all out, as though he had a plan or had charted a course to follow. He hadn't driven over to her house that night with the intention of kissing her. It just happened. He hadn't known what his feelings for Marissa Wakefield were—maybe he still didn't—but he understood something now he hadn't when he'd pulled up in front of her house almost a week ago. He wanted her, and he had a pretty good idea she wanted him, too.

He remembered how it had felt to hold her again, to kiss her, to feel her soft mouth against his. He had no idea what her reaction would be, but she hadn't pulled away from him, hadn't lashed out in fury and indignation. Instead, she had sighed sweetly, her lips growing soft and compliant, and she'd leaned into his kiss—intense and hungry.

He closed his eyes to the sudden surge of desire that clutched at him. There had been women in his life—a string of them since he and Stephanie had split up. But he was far from being a ladies' man, hardly the kind of guy who went around making moves on the women he knew. But he'd made a move on Marissa Wakefield—a big one—because Marissa was different, and she had a way of making him different, too. She made him want to reach out and do things he didn't normally do—like thinking up excuses to see her, and impulsively kissing her in a public parking lot.

Impulsive. That's what the kiss had been—impulsive. Impulsive, and foolish, and dangerous, and...unbelievable, and he hadn't been able to stop thinking about it since.

He glanced at his wristwatch, sighing heavily. If he didn't leave soon, he would be late for his meeting with Judge Kent—and he'd discovered it was never a good idea to keep a judge waiting.

He rounded his desk, heading out the door and down the corridor. Maybe it was just as well that Judge Kent was waiting for him. Otherwise he'd probably do something stupid—like get in his Jeep and drive to Sutter High School and storm into her office unannounced and unexpected. That would not only be stupid, it could prove disastrous. She wasn't the kind of woman you could push, and he understood the need for patience. After all, they weren't a couple of kids anymore, and couldn't go jumping into something without considering the circumstances. He'd tested the waters, and she hadn't told him to get lost, so the ball was in her court. He just had to wait for the serve.

"You have to understand, this is just a rough outline," Marissa pointed out anxiously, leaning forward in her chair. "There is much more that would need to be worked out—points that could be added, or modified." She clasped and unclasped her hands. It was ridiculous to be nervous, but she couldn't seem to help it. "Hopefully there is enough there to give you the basic idea." She hesitated. "Basically."

Randolf Kent lowered the folder and leaned back in his high-backed leather chair. His bushy white brows were scrunched together tight, making him look much like a gaunt, sinister version of Santa. "I have to tell you, Miss Wakefield, I studied your idea very carefully. I found it very...interesting."

Marissa felt her heart sink. She could all but feel the "but" coming—as in *"I loved your idea, but..."* She forced herself to lean back in the chair, preparing herself and keeping her composure.

Judge Kent had been a friend of her father's for years, but that wasn't why she'd come to him with her idea. She'd submitted her idea to him because he'd seemed open and receptive to her plans for Josh. She wasn't looking for special attention or favoritism, just fair consideration. Of course, she'd doubted Dylan would believe that. She remembered how he'd accused her and her family of using their influence and connections in the community to get what they wanted.

Dylan. Reluctantly her thoughts moved back six nights to when he'd kissed her, and she felt color warm her cheeks. She'd asked for time to think—and God knows she'd been thinking. She was wondering now *what* she'd been thinking. Not only had she let him kiss her, but *she'd* kissed *him* back. Didn't she realize she was playing with fire—again? This wasn't just any man, just some man she found herself attracted to. This was Dylan—*Dylan*.

He'd made his intentions very clear. They were two responsible adults, unattached and uncommitted. There was an attraction between them—for her to deny it would be stupid. Maybe the idea of an affair wasn't unreasonable under normal circumstances, but there was nothing normal about their situation. She could probably handle an affair with another man, but not with Dylan. She had loved him once, and his love had changed her life forever. And now, with Josh in her life, there was just too much at stake.

Judge Kent picked up the folder containing her proposal and perused it once again, and Marissa forced her mind back to business.

"Yes, very interesting," Kent murmured again, removing his glasses and peering at her from over the top of the folder. "So much so that I passed it along to a few friends to get their feedback. I hope you don't mind."

Marissa's eyes widened, and she sat up. "Uh, no. No, of course not."

"Good," he said, smiling and setting the folder down again. "I think you might know them—Tom Dyer, the county's chief probation officer, and Maureen Porter, who's on the county's board of supervisors? And I have to say, they were both impressed with the idea, I might add. As a matter of fact, I've asked them to join us this afternoon. They should be along any time now." He slipped his glasses back on and picked up the folder again. "I think we've got something to discuss here."

Marissa stared at him, smiling and feeling just a little light-headed. She was thrilled. This whole plan had come to her because of the situation with Josh. While the arrangement that had been made with Judge Kent and the juvenile courts—making it mandatory for Josh and the others to attend school and do the actual work on construction—had been rather unique, it was proving to be a productive one. Early reports from their teachers indicated that their progress in class had been good, and construction on the shed was actually moving ahead of schedule. It was becoming apparent that not only were all three of the boys putting in their time in the classroom, but they were also working hard at the site and learning a lot about construction.

Marissa figured if the arrangement worked for Josh, Skip and Randy, why couldn't it work for other young people in the same situation—kids who had gotten into trouble with the law and who needed help and a second chance more than they needed a jail sentence? She'd felt if a coordinated effort could be made between the juvenile courts and the school district, a program could be devel-

oped that would direct youthful offenders away from juvenile hall and back into school—providing them with not
only an education and practical skills so they could com-
pete in the workplace, but also with hope.

She'd worked with a lot of troubled kids in her ten years
in the education system, and she firmly believed all kids
deserved a chance at a better life—no matter what kind of
mistakes had been made. A program that worked to give
these troubled kids self-respect and encouraged them to
become useful members of society would be good for everyone. In addition it would help keep a lot of kids off the
street and out of trouble.

Marissa had written up an outline for a program, knowing it sounded hopelessly idealistic—but when it came to
kids, she believed in being idealistic. She'd submitted the
proposal to Judge Kent in the faint hope that some small
effort would be made to start the ball rolling. But this…this
was more than she'd ever hoped.

"That sounds wonderful," she said, her excitement
starting to build.

"Well, of course, I think we should be careful about
starting out too ambitious. It would be wise to take it slow.
Perhaps start out with a test program." He searched
through a stack of files on his desk, pulling one out. "This
first report on your nephew by Sheriff James is very encouraging, *very* encouraging." He slipped the folder down
on top of the written report. "This just might serve as our
pilot program."

They were interrupted as Maureen Porter rapped at the
door. Judge Kent had just finished introducing Marissa to
Amador County's only female supervisor when Tom Dyer
arrived. Marissa shook his hand, excited and happy. She
was thrilled to see their enthusiasm for her idea, and eagerly looked forward to discussing it in detail with them.
After a few moments of idle talk, the judge invited them all
to take a seat around his desk.

"I also thought it would be good to bring the sheriff in on this. His department could be instrumental in targeting those juveniles who would benefit the most from a program like this. I called over to his office this morning and asked him to join us as well."

Marissa felt her entire system react. "Sheriff James will be here?"

"Yes," Kent said, checking the time on the watch at his wrist. "He should be coming any time—" A loud rap on the door interrupted him, and he reached up and pulled his glasses from his nose. "That should be him now."

Chapter 8

The last thing Dylan had expected when he arrived at Judge Kent's chambers was a roomful of people—no, actually, the last thing he'd expected was to find *Marissa* there with a roomful of people. And then suddenly they were a committee—including *him*—formed to explore ideas for a juvenile offenders alternative work-study program Marissa had proposed. He'd been assigned by the committee to work with Marissa to come up with a formal proposal to submit to the board of supervisors.

"You look a little confused."

Dylan followed Marissa out through the side door of the small courthouse and into the hot afternoon sun. "Do I?"

She stopped, shifting the satchel she carried from one arm to the other. "Yeah, you do. You going to be okay with this?"

He smiled down at her. "You mean us working together?"

Marissa felt her cheeks warm, and it had nothing to do with the brilliant sunlight. "Actually, I was referring to the program we're suppose to be developing."

"Ah, yes, the program," Dylan said, his smile fading. He held the copy of her proposal Judge Kent had given him, leafing through the pages. There hadn't been time to study it yet, but he'd given it a brief skim. "You think this could really work?"

"Sounds like you think it won't."

He shook his head. "It's not that. It's just..." He shrugged, giving his head a shake. "I've seen programs that look good on paper, but when you get down to dealing with real people with real problems... I don't know. I just think it might be a little optimistic."

She bristled just a little, remembering how they'd gone head to head over the situation with Josh. "What's wrong with being optimistic?"

"Nothing," he said, flipping the pages closed. He really didn't want to talk about reports and programs. He wanted to talk about time, and if he'd given her enough. "But I've worked with a lot of these kids, these 'juvenile offenders' you call them in your proposal."

"And?" she added testily when he hesitated.

"And some of them are just bad news."

"I'm not saying it's an option for every kid in trouble, and I certainly don't claim it's a cure for juvenile crime or anything like that, but I think there are some kids who could really benefit from a program like this."

"Maybe," Dylan said, considering this. "But not every kid can be saved."

"Of course not, but does that mean we're not supposed to try and save any?"

He looked down into her bright blue eyes, seeing the fire and the passion in them. He took a step forward. "Do we have to talk about this now?"

"What's wrong with now?" she asked. "Judge Kent has scheduled another meeting in a month. I'd like something concrete to show them then—that's not much time."

"That's four long weeks away," he said, running a hand along her arm and cupping her elbow. "Besides, there's something else I think we should be talking about."

Marissa felt every muscle in her body go rigid. She knew what he meant and dreaded it. But if they were going to work together, it was probably a good idea to set the ground rules right away. "Look, Dylan, if this is about the other night."

"Six nights," he corrected her. The hand on her elbow tightened. He'd warned himself not to push, but there was something in her eyes that caused a hard knot to form in his stomach. "You said you wanted time."

"Yes, I know," she murmured, dropping her gaze, wanting to look anywhere but his eyes. "And maybe you're right. Maybe it would be a good idea if we cleared the air."

The hand on her elbow fell away. "Cleared the air?"

She glanced back up at him, hearing the change in his voice. "I'm afraid I might have given you the wrong impression."

The knot in his stomach tightened, then doubled in size. "When was that? When I was kissing you, or when you were kissing me?"

She felt the color in her cheeks deepen. "I admit that things did get rather heavy—I think maybe we both got a little carried away."

Dylan's clenched his fists tight, seeing the writing on the wall. What an idiot he'd been, an idiot and an egotistical fool. He'd been walking around for the last six days as though he were in some kind of a trance—hardly able to function, hardly able to think. When she'd said she wanted time, he'd just assumed it was to get used to the idea of the two of them together—again. It never occurred to him she would use the time to change her mind.

"And now with the committee, and this project and everything, and us...working together," she continued when it became obvious he wasn't going to respond. "I'm not sure it would be a good idea for us to be...you know, involved."

Involved was such a bland, expressionless way to describe what he'd been feeling, what he'd pictured in his mind happening between them. It wasn't as though he'd thought very far into the future, about where a relationship might take them, but the chemistry between them had been so explosive, so volatile, he'd felt compelled to follow it.

But it was obvious now that he'd read her wrong, obvious that some remnant from the past, some spark of feeling from those summer nights so many years ago, had roared to life and was making him see things that simply were not there. A cold, dead feeling spread through him, but he steeled himself against it. After all, it wasn't the first time.

He would do what he always did—squelch the disappointment, suppress his real feeling beneath a facade of good-natured humor. He would kid and tease—even make light of the very thing that hurt him the most. He knew just what to say, just what to do, and no one need ever know just how hard it really had been.

"Look, Marissa," he said with a small laugh and a dismissing wave of the hand. "It's no big deal. If you're not interested, you're not interested."

"It's just that I—"

"Hey," he said, cutting her off. "No explanations necessary. Can't blame a guy for trying though, right?" He turned, making a sweeping gesture with his hand, and walked with her to her car. "So how would you like to handle this with the program?" he asked, pulling the car door open for her. "Should we arrange a time to talk about it now, or would you rather give me a call?"

Marissa felt off-balance and a little confused. He'd taken her by surprise being so good-natured about everything. She'd just told him she didn't believe they could be lovers, and he was already making jokes and moving on to business. He'd practically seduced her in the front seat of his patrol Jeep, yet now he stood there calmly talking about scheduling appointments and charting timetables as though it had meant nothing at all. Had offering to become her lover really meant that little?

Of course, she knew she should be grateful. He'd made it very easy for her. There had been no messy scene or unpleasant words, no awkwardness or embarrassment. But as unpleasant as all those things would have been, at least she would have felt it mattered to him. As it was, he had acted as if she'd just turned him down for a lunch date—not an affair. How many times did you have to enter and exit relationships with women for it to become that easy?

"Why don't you take some time," she said, slipping down on the seat behind the wheel and starting the car. She just wanted to get away and not think about working with him—or even seeing him again. "Study the proposal a little more, and give me a call next week. We'll set something up then."

Dylan watched as she pulled out of the parking lot, wondering when he was ever going to learn. He should have learned his lesson sixteen years ago—he and Marissa Wakefield just didn't mix. He'd been foolish to think there could be something between them now. It was time he accepted there just wasn't anything there.

He glanced down at the proposal in his hand, feeling a dull pounding in the back of his head. What the hell had he gotten himself into?

"You sound disappointed."

"Don't be silly," Marissa snapped, shifting the telephone from one ear to the other. Her long Saturday morning telephone conversations with Mallory were becoming a regular thing—something they both looked forward to. "If anything, I'm relieved."

"Hello," Mallory called out deliberately, tapping the phone receiver noisily with her finger. "Is that *my* sister talking? The one I share everything with? The one who can't hide anything from me?"

Marissa sighed, and rubbed at the tension building in the area between her eyes. Why couldn't that "twin radar" of theirs have come with an on-off switch? "Okay, okay, maybe I was just a little disappointed—not that I wanted to get involved or start something with him in the first place, but..." Her words drifted off as she remembered how he'd carelessly waved off her concern.

Mallory waited, picturing Marissa's scowl. "But maybe you should have found out."

"What?" Marissa gasped, her eyes opening wide.

"Marissa, what would it have hurt?"

"Are you crazy?" Marissa demanded. "Mallory, I would think you of all people would understand what a mistake that would be. My God, we're talking Dylan James here. Have you forgotten what he did to me? About the past, about Josh?"

"I haven't forgotten about anything," Mallory reminded her quietly, feeling her sister's anger but knowing it wasn't really directed toward her. "But that was a long time ago, for heaven's sake. You're both different people now, and maybe it's time you started to come to terms with some of those feelings you still have for him."

"I don't have *any* feeling for Dylan James," Marissa insisted, but even as she spoke she knew Mallory would know differently. She stopped and drew in another deep breath, her headache growing worse. "Not *those* kinds of feelings, anyway."

"You mean you aren't in love with him anymore?"

"How could I be in love with him? You said yourself we're different people now. I don't even know who the man is anymore."

"Well, maybe you would know if you hadn't slammed the door in his face."

Marissa closed her eyes. It had been three days since their conversation in the parking lot, and she was sick of thinking about it. "Look, I don't want to talk about this anymore." She opened her eyes and checked the clock on the wall. Josh had volunteered to ride his bike to the post office to mail several letters for her, and she'd promised him a driving lesson in return. Knowing how excited he was about learning to drive, she assumed the trip wouldn't take very long at all. She expected him to come bounding through the back door at any moment now, and didn't want to be talking about Dylan when he did. "Let me grill you for a while now."

"I haven't exactly been grilling you," Mallory pointed out dryly.

Marissa smiled. "You call it what you want, I'll call it what I want. Now tell me what's going on with you? All I'm able to pick up are these disgustingly happy vibes. I suppose that's because of Graywolf. How is he, by the way?"

She listened as Mallory told her about her husband and their activities on the reservation. Marissa let her mind drift back, remembering the reservation and the places Mallory described. When she'd lived in Arizona, she had spent many weekends on the "Big Res" tutoring at reservation schools, and working with the children. She was grateful now for the chance to escape into her sister's happiness for a while, to remember the beauty of the reservation and forget all about Dylan, and the way it had felt when he'd kissed her.

"So except for this cold or flu, or whatever it is that's got me feeling so yucky, things are going great," Mallory concluded with a deep breath. "Although I'll admit, they'd be going even better if I could hear about the article I'd submitted to *Arizona Magazine*."

"The one on the reservation rehab center? But you just submitted it a couple of weeks ago." Marissa not only felt her sister's frustration, she could hear it in her voice. "Give them a chance."

"I know, I know," Mallory groused. "It's just that this waiting kills me."

"What about Graywolf? He doesn't pick up any vibes?" Marissa asked, referring to her brother-in-law's "special" talent—occasional flashes of precognition.

"If he does, he's not sharing them with me," Mallory complained.

Marissa laughed. "As if that man could keep anything from you. I hope you're still planning to come next month for a visit?"

"We'll be there," Mallory assured her. "Besides, Graywolf promised Josh they would take the Jeep off-road and let him try to drive."

Marissa heard the back door. She turned around just as Josh came running into the kitchen, his face flushed with color and his breath coming in heavy heaves. "Speaking of driving, guess who just showed up for his lesson."

"Makes me almost glad I live in another state," Mallory joked. "Give him a hug for me."

"Well?" Josh asked anxiously when Marissa had hung up the phone.

Marissa looked into his young face and felt a tight constriction around her heart. He looked young, and excited, and she loved him so much. Reaching for her purse, she slipped the strap over her shoulder. "Well, let's do it."

"Uh-oh," Josh said, his hold on the steering wheel tightening and his deep voice cracking. "Now what do I do?"

Marissa stopped rubbing the sore spot on her forehead and glanced behind them. "Damn," she muttered, surprised to see the flashing red lights from a squad car behind them. "We're getting pulled over."

"What did I do?" Josh asked again, panic causing his voice to raise higher.

"Nothing that I know of," she said, glancing around.

"So what do I do now?"

"Stay calm," she instructed, doing her best to bank down her own anxiety. "Slow down and pull over." She pointed to a shady spot near the curb. "There. Pull over there and stop. Let's find out what's going on."

Josh edged the car to a stop, but his face was awash with sweat from nerves. "What did I do?" he asked again, turning to her. "I didn't do anything wrong."

"I don't think you did anything, either," Marissa admitted honestly, watching as the squad car pulled to a stop behind them. "It's probably nothing at all."

Josh gave her an uneasy look. "You've never been pulled over by a cop before, have you?"

"Not exactly," she said, giving him a shrewd look. "But I don't exactly think we have to make a run for it just yet." She twisted around in the seat, but from the passenger's side of the car her vision was obscured, and all she could make out was the uniformed torso of an officer approaching the driver's side of her car. Her mind spun in a million different directions, ready to launch into a defense and offer a reasonable explanation. But when the officer bent down and peered into the car, she forgot everything.

"Dylan!" she gasped with a mixture of anger and relief. "What are you doing? You scared us half to death."

"I suppose it would be pointless for me to ask to see an operator's license," he said dryly, arching a brow from behind his dark glasses and shifting his gaze from Josh to Marissa.

"Especially since you know he hasn't got one. This is only a first lesson. Nobody ever has a license for their first lesson," she pointed out snippily. The dark sunglasses made it impossible to tell where he was looking, and she glared up at him uneasily. "And why are you driving a squad car?"

"Mine's in the shop," he said, turning to Josh and giving him a pat on the shoulder. "First lesson, huh?"

"I'm getting my learner's permit next week," Josh said excitedly. He was visibly relieved, and he loosened the death grip he had on the wheel.

"Depending on your progress report from class," Marissa corrected him.

"I guess the time you and Skip were pulled in for joyriding in your mother's car last year didn't count," Dylan remarked sarcastically.

Josh cringed a little, looking appropriately embarrassed. "Skip did all the driving that night. I was just along for the ride."

Dylan chuckled low. He'd discovered that without the "attitude," Josh Wakefield had a pretty good sense of humor—clever and pretty sophisticated for a kid his age. That wasn't something Dylan was used to seeing in the kids who were brought into the station. "You look pretty comfortable behind the wheel. How's it going?"

"Great!" Josh replied, his hands flexing on the steering wheel. "I think I'm a natural."

Dylan let his gaze slide across to Marissa and felt something tighten in his chest, but he did his best to cover. "You don't look too convinced."

Marissa jumped, realizing he was talking to her. Her hand went to the tender spot on her forehead again. Josh had hit the brake a little too hard when they'd first started out, and she'd had a painful encounter with the rearview mirror. "We've had our moments."

"Judging from that knot on your forehead, I'd say some were better than others," he said, his voice growing serious. "Uh, just so you'll know. Josh really should have his permit before he gets behind the wheel. It's a violation to drive without it—even for lessons—which for most people would normally be no big deal. But for Josh, technically it's also a violation of his probation."

Marissa's face fell. "I hadn't thought of that."

Dylan shrugged. "Like I said, it's no big deal. Just something you should be aware of."

"Oh," Marissa mumbled, her frown deepening. Josh had been after her for weeks for driving lessons, and frankly, she'd been glad it was something she could do for him. It never occurred to her they would be breaking the law. "Is that why you pulled us over?"

Dylan faltered just a little. He'd been asking himself the same question. It would have been a whole lot easier just to let them pass. After all, the woman had made it very clear she had no interest in him beyond the scope of their business together. It wasn't as if he needed to invent excuses to see her any longer.

But the fact was he'd been concerned when he'd seen them drive by. Josh was on probation, and driving without a license might be a technicality, but it was just the kind of technicality that could prove explosive when mixed with an overzealous patrol office. And Dylan had realized as he watched the teen maneuvering the car slowly down the street that he didn't want that to happen, didn't want something to interfere with the progress Josh had made.

Josh Wakefield might have been a giant pain in the butt for him and the department for the last two years, but the kid honestly seemed to be changing. Dylan was beginning to think Josh just might be one of the lucky kids who really could straighten out, who really might make it.

And for some reason, Dylan was also discovering that whether Josh Wakefield made it or not mattered very much to him.

"Just being careful," he explained, noticing how the shape of Marissa's blue-green eyes was almost the same as Josh's dark brown ones. "It could maybe be a problem if you were pulled over by someone else—a California Highway Patrol or a unit from another jurisdiction—someone who wasn't up on the situation. I just wouldn't like to see things get sticky, or anything like that."

"I see," Marissa said to the reflection of herself in his dark glasses, wondering whether or not he was even looking at her. She felt uneasy, but not because of the glasses. Without being aware of it, Dylan's actions were very close to being paternal—a father protecting his son. "Thank you."

"Actually, it just occurred to me," he added thoughtfully, turning to Josh. "Something you might do in the meantime—I mean, until you *officially* get your permit, that is. You know the old creek road, down by the fairgrounds?"

"Sure," Josh said, nodding. "We used to go out there all the time to..." He stopped abruptly, grinning sheepishly. "Well...I know the place."

"Yeah." Dylan laughed, aware that the secluded area was a popular spot for late-night drag races and keg parties. "I thought you might. Anyway..." He tilted his head, glancing back to Marissa. "It's pretty deserted out there, nobody around, nothing much to run into. No nosy cops." He stopped and gave her a little smile. "Not a bad place to practice."

"Well," Marissa mumbled. Was he smiling at her or Josh? "Maybe we'll give it a try."

"Good." He took a step back, straightening just a little, then stopped. "Oh, I almost forgot." He reached into the top pocket of his shirt, flipping back the buttoned flap and pulling out a small clump. "What do you think of this?"

Josh's eyes narrowed, scrutinizing the ratty mass of color. "What is that? A black gnat?"

Dylan's eyes widened with surprise behind the sunglasses. "Damn, you're good."

"Hey, I wasn't three-time junior fly champion at the county fair for nothing, you know," Josh said, reaching out the car window and taking the fly from Dylan, then examining it closely. "Under-ten division."

Marissa watched as Josh and Dylan studied the fly, discussing the weight, the size and the materials used. Again she was struck by not only the remarkable physical resemblance between father and son, but by the similarities in their personalities, as well. They had the same dry, self-deprecating wit, and both used that good-natured humor to ease themselves out of awkward situations.

She thought of Dylan and the conversation they'd had in the parking lot of the courthouse earlier in the week. His nonchalance and casual remarks had certainly eased what could—or should—have been an awkward situation between them. Had that been his way of coping with an unpleasant moment, or was it that his feelings about her were really that casual?

She shook her head. It was moot now, anyway. The ground rules had all been laid out. From now on it would be strictly business between them—no more, no less. And she knew better than anyone else, that was all it ever could be.

"I'm heading up toward Fiddle Town next week," Dylan said to Josh, slipping the fly back into his pocket. "To that spot I told you about. Thought I'd test it out, see if I have any luck." He hesitated a moment, then shrugged. "Interested in coming along?"

Josh turned to Marissa, his eyes wide with excitement. "Can I?"

* * *

Dylan reached into his tackle box, past the neatly assorted trays of flies and lures, to the set of small silver clippers he kept in the bottom of the box. Finding them, he straightened up, tying off his line with a neat doubt knot and snipping it free of the spool.

The sun beat down on his back, scorching his bare skin, a marked contrast to the frigid chill of the stream, whose waters flowed with the runoff of last winter's snowpack. But Dylan ignored the sun's searing heat, just like he ignored the water's icy bite. The morning had been too good, too productive, to worry about sunburn or soaking feet. Especially since he was well on his way to catching his limit.

With the toe of his wet boot, he kicked the lid on the tackle box closed, and reached for his fishing vest that lay beside him on the rock. He slipped in on over his bare chest, inspecting the pockets again, double-checking that he had what he needed—flies, line, needle-nose pliers. He and Josh had decided they weren't going home until they'd each caught their limit, but the way the fish were biting, they would easily make it back in plenty of time for dinner.

It had been well before dawn when he'd pulled up in front of Marissa Wakefield's condominium. But Josh had been ready and waiting, standing on the porch with rod and reel in hand.

Dylan had been a little surprised to see the kid standing there alone. He'd expected to see Marissa waiting there with him—or maybe it was just that he'd hoped she'd be there.

He pulled the black gnat from the breast pocket of his fishing vest, attaching it to the end of his yellow monofilament leader. But a frown etched deeply into the rugged lines of his mouth as he thought about those moments in front of her house. He didn't like thinking about what it had felt like to look up to see her run out the front door toward him as he'd loaded Josh's gear into the back of his truck. At first he'd been too caught up in the sight of her, too distracted by the short robe wrapped around her and the long hair falling free and loose down her back to feel much of anything at all—but then later . . .

Dylan shook his head, trying to push his thoughts aside. He felt beads of sweat form along his upper lip, knowing they had nothing to do with the sun blazing down from overhead. He'd been trying to purge the image of her from his mind all morning.

His gaze glinted to the blanket spread on the shore, and to the bleached wicker picnic basket that sat on top of it. In his head he saw her running down the sidewalk with that basket in her arms, carrying the lunch she'd packed for them—fried chicken, potato salad, cold sodas and a beer. But it wasn't the food he was thinking about, it was the satiny material of her robe, and how it caught the light of the street lamp and shimmered pink with every move that she made.

He swiped angrily at the perspiration on his lip, swearing beneath his breath.

"You okay?"

Chapter 9

Dylan looked up, surprised to see Josh standing in the ankle-high water just beside him. "Yeah, I'm fine, why?"

"Just wondering." Josh shrugged, tilting the baseball cap he had on backward away from his forehead and setting his tackle box down onto the rock next to Dylan's. "You just had a funny look on your face, that's all."

Dylan shook his head. "No, I'm fine." He gestured with his chin to the creel basket Josh had slung over his shoulder. "Any more?"

Josh flipped up the lid and smiled. "Just three more little beauties."

Dylan peered into the basket and muttered under his breath. Looking up at Josh, he shook his head. "They don't look so little to me."

Josh's grin widened. "I was being modest."

Josh lifted each of the sizable rainbow trout from the basket, one after the other, and added them to the line of others he'd strung earlier and had anchored in the cold rushing water of the stream. He peered deliberately at the shorter line of trout on Dylan's line anchored nearby.

"Gosh," he mused, making a play of comparing the two lines of fish. "I'd say I might be one or two up on you. What would you say, Sheriff?"

Dylan's eyes narrowed. "I'd say it's not nice to mess with the sheriff." He glanced up at the lure dangling from Josh's pole. "What are you using now?"

"Same thing, the gray ghost," Josh said, pulling the fly close and inspecting it. He looked up at Dylan and smiled. "What did you think? A goofus bug?"

Dylan laughed. "So how is our friend Mathers, anyway?"

"That's *Mr.* Mathers," Josh corrected prissily. "According to Aunt Mar I should be respectful of my elders."

Dylan's smile stiffened. "Sounds like your Aunt Marissa and ... *Mr.* Mathers are pretty good friends."

Josh shrugged. "I guess."

Dylan nodded, busying himself with something on his reel. A picture of Marissa and Mathers flashed into his mind and the muscles in his jaw clenched tight. "Spend a lot of time together, do they?"

"Sometimes," Josh said, looking down and making an adjustment on his line. "You know—at school."

Dylan nodded again, but his hold on his reel relaxed just a little. "How's it going, anyway—at school, I mean, and with the toolshed?"

"Okay—for school, that is," Josh said, tightening a knot around his lure. "And the shed..." He stopped and looked up at Dylan. "You know, actually, it's been kind of...neat. I mean, Mathers is kind of a jerk—you know. But the other stuff..." He nodded his head. "It's actually been okay."

"You and Randy getting along okay?"

"Sure," Josh said simply.

"How about Skip?"

Josh's smile faded, and he shrugged.

"You two don't talk much, I take it."

Josh shook his head. "Not much."

Dylan studied him for a minute. "He giving you trouble?"

Josh looked away. "I can handle Skip."

Dylan didn't doubt that he could, but he also didn't doubt that the strain between the two had gotten worse. He suspected if Skip were to know Josh had gone fishing with the sheriff, it wouldn't help matters.

"Well," Josh said, sighing, "my line's getting dry, and I hate it when my line gets dry." He waded a few steps through the water, then turned back to Dylan. "Something tells me I'm going to catch my limit before you."

"Get out of here, kid," Dylan said in his best tough-cop voice, tossing a water-soaked piece of bark at him. "You're buggin' me."

Dylan watched as Josh waded through the rushing water—baseball cap turned backward, T-shirt dangling from the back pocket of his shorts.

With his hair away from his face, Dylan couldn't help thinking how much he reminded him of Kenny, his brother Michael's son. They were both about the same age, had the same dark eyes, the same solid build. Dylan had brought Kenny fishing with him before, but Kenny didn't have the interest in it like Josh had, didn't have Josh's coordination and natural abilities.

It was easy to see that Caleb Wakefield had loved fly-fishing, because he'd certainly passed his passion for the sport on to his adopted son. Josh was not only a knowledgeable fly-fisherman with a relaxed style and impeccable form, he also had an uncanny knack for catching fish. He'd mentioned to Dylan more than once during the morning how his dad had told him how he should "listen" for the fish, and how important it was to rely on his instincts as much as his skill and equipment.

Listening as Josh talked about his dad had Dylan under-standing just how Caleb's death had affected the kid, and just what a void it had left in his life. Dylan thought of Marissa, and her fervent concern for her nephew. Maybe she'd been right, maybe jail time wasn't the kind of disci-pline he'd needed. Maybe what the kid needed was some-one to step in and fill the void left by his father. Maybe what he really needed was a father figure.

Dylan thought of Marissa's proposal and the program they were supposed to develop from it. He'd had a chance to read over it thoroughly in the week since he'd pulled them over during their driving lesson. The plan was as op-timistic and idealistic as he'd suspected, but he had to ad-mit that for the right kid, at the right time, it might help.

He glanced up, watching Josh's fluid motions as he cast the long line back and forth into the churning water. A year ago all he wanted was to see Josh Wakefield locked up be-hind bars, now...

Just then Josh pulled another twisting trout from the icy-cold water, and Dylan chuckled silently to himself. Maybe he hadn't made up his mind whether Josh was a juvenile delinquent or just a troubled kid, but there was one thing he knew for certain. The kid was one hell of a fisherman.

"I just what?" Marissa glanced down at the sink full of rainbow trout, trying very hard not to look at the staring eyes.

"Just cut off the heads," Dylan explained again, pick-ing up one of the fish and laying it down on the cutting board. He reached for a meat cleaver from the knife rack. "Like this."

"No!" Marissa gasped, stopping him with a hand on his arm. She'd nervously drank a glass of wine while waiting for them to return, and the thought of watching him lop off a fish's head had it resting uneasily in her stomach. "Please, don't."

Dylan shifted his gaze, looked at her and smiled. "Something tells me you don't like trout."

"I love trout," she insisted, reaching for the chilled bottle of chardonnay and pouring him a glass. "With a light *amandine* sauce and a glass of white wine."

He smiled as he washed his hands in the sink. "So I take it you've never cleaned one before."

She gave him a . . . look and offered him the glass. "You make it sound as though it was some kind of crime, Sheriff."

He leaned close and took the glass from her. "This is fishing country. It practically is."

"It's cattle country, too," she pointed out, crossing her arms in front of her. "Yet I still manage to resist the urge to run out and rope a steer every time I want a steak."

He laughed. "Spoken like a true outdoorsman—or should I say outdoorswoman?"

"I like the outdoors. I camp, I hike," she insisted, picking up her glass from the counter. "Just because I can't cut off a fish's head with any degree of enthusiasm doesn't mean I've got anything against nature."

He laughed again. "I can't believe you grew up around here and never learned to clean a fish. Didn't your dad or your brother ever take you fishing?"

"Sure they did. But I was the *smart* one, remember?" she reminded him. "The one bird-watching back in camp. Mallory was the one who did all that fun stuff—like cutting fish heads off."

"Oh, I don't know," Dylan murmured, the smile slowly fading from his lips. "I seem to remember you liking *fun* stuff, too. He clinked his wineglass to hers. "Remember the fun stuff we did together?"

Marissa felt a jolt of emotion bolt through her system like an electrical current running through a power line. She looked up into his dark eyes, her throat feeling strangled and tight. She felt warm and breathless, as though suddenly all the air had been sucked out of the room. She couldn't seem to move, to think. For one glorious, crystallized moment there was nothing else—only feeling and sensation, and the haunted, hungry look of desire in his eyes.

"Dylan," she whispered, unaware until she heard her voice that she'd even spoken at all.

"Finished cleaning the fish yet?"

The fragile spell shattered into a million tiny fragments, and Marissa felt herself catapulted back into reality with a harsh, cold rush. She looked quickly away, not wanting Dylan to see just how flustered she was. She turned just as Josh came through the back door, his fishing pole banging against the door frame as he passed.

"Are you kidding?" she said, her voice sounding breathy and coarse to her ears. "And take all the fun away from you? No way."

"Get over here, kid," Dylan said, putting the wineglass to his lips and draining it in one gulp. The wine moved through his system, feeling weak and impotent in the wake of the emotion it followed. "You've got some work to do."

Marissa stepped back, sipping at her glass of wine and forcing herself to calm down. She tried not to think about the picture the two of them made—father and son standing there at the sink, cleaning the fish and laughing. She'd never forget how Josh had looked when he'd come running up the walk toward her, proudly displaying the reeking string of fish, and looking happier and more relaxed than he had in a very long time.

She took another sip of wine, watching Dylan cut and clean the fish, watching him joke with Josh, watching him so relaxed and at home in her kitchen. He was so comfortable with Josh. Was there something about the blood they shared, something in their biological connection that made it so natural and easy for them? Would Josh relate as well to any other man who took the time with him, with whom he had a common interest, who offered him the same kind of attention?

Marissa finished her glass of wine, and poured herself yet another. She felt jumpy and nervous. Frankly, she'd felt uneasy all day, and her little encounter with Dylan just now hadn't helped. And even her weekly phone call with Mallory hadn't made her feel any better.

Marissa watched Josh as he listened to something Dylan was saying, watched the look in his eyes, the smile on his face. She knew Josh missed his father—missed Caleb. But she was only beginning to realize just how much he missed the kind of camaraderie and bonding he got from a strong male role model.

She lifted her glass to her lips for another sip of wine, but ended up taking a gulp. She wasn't much of a drinker, but watching Dylan laugh and joke with Josh was enough to drive her to drink. It just didn't seem fair. She loved Josh and would do anything she could for him. But no matter how much she loved him, no matter what she said or what she did, a father was the one thing she couldn't be for him.

She took another swallow of wine—too much this time and it caught in her throat. For a moment her airway was blocked, and she coughed loudly.

"You okay?" Josh asked.

She glanced up, nodding, embarrassed to find both Josh and Dylan staring across the kitchen at her, the same look of concern on their faces. "F-fine," she croaked, taking a breath and covering her mouth with her hand. "Went down the wrong pipe." She coughed again. "I'm okay."

"You sure?" Dylan asked, taking a step toward her.

Marissa nodded her head and grabbed a kitchen towel to muffle another cough, waving him off. He hesitated for a minute, giving her an uncertain look, then turned back to the fish when she gave him another dismissing wave.

She rushed into the small bathroom near the stairwell, clearing her throat loudly. She quickly splashed water on her face, reached for a towel, then stared at herself in the mirror.

"Stupid," she muttered to the image staring back at her. Her eyes were red and watering, and mascara trailed down her left cheek. What was she doing, drinking glass after glass of wine? She certainly didn't need something to dull her senses when she was around Dylan James. She needed something to sharpen them.

She took a few deep breaths, cleared her throat again, and did a quick patch-up job on her makeup. By the time she walked back into the kitchen, Dylan and Josh had the kitchen looking spotless—and smelling a lot fresher. They stood proudly examining the row of cleaned fish laid out before them.

"Pretty impressive," she said as she walked up behind them. "At least we won't go hungry."

"Not for a while, anyway," Dylan commented, turning around and looking at her closely. "You okay now?"

"I'm fine," she said with a careless wave of her hand. "Fine. Just swallowed wrong, that's all."

"I invited the sheriff to stay for dinner," Josh said, pointing to the large kettle simmering on the stove. He picked up a wooden spoon and tasted the chili bubbling in the pot. "There's plenty, and nobody makes better chili than Auntie Mar."

Marissa's smile faltered, but she struggled not to let it show. She wanted Josh to feel comfortable enough to invite his friends for dinner, but why did it have to be Dylan? It would take more than a few sips of wine to get her through an entire meal.

"Sure," she said brightly, avoiding looking directly into Dylan's dark gaze. "Like Josh said, there's plenty."

"Looks good," Dylan mused, peering into the kettle. "But you mean you're not having trout?"

Marissa laughed, glancing down at the fish on the counter. "Oh, something tells me we'll be eating plenty of that in weeks to come. So," she said, clearing her throat and pasting a placid smile across her face. "You'll stay, then?"

"Uh . . . thanks, but I'm not exactly dressed for dinner," he said, pulling at the T-shirt he'd tossed on over his sunburned chest. "And I really should check in at the station. Besides, I think there are laws against dinner guests who smell like a pile of dead fish."

"I think it's okay," Josh joked back, giving his own shirt a tug and making a face. "As long as at least one of the hosts smell the same way?"

Dylan laughed, walking to the small table in the breakfast nook and gathering up his gear. He wasn't sure he could last a whole evening—sitting across a dinner table from Marissa, smiling and making small talk as though everything was just fine and dandy. He wanted her so bad it made his insides hurt. "Thanks, kid, but maybe some other time."

"You sure? We—"

"Josh," Marissa said pointedly, cutting him off. She certainly wasn't crazy about the idea of having Dylan James share a meal with them, but she couldn't help feeling just a little insulted knowing he didn't want to. Did he have another woman waiting? A date? "The sheriff said he can't stay. Just drop it."

Marissa ignored Josh's confused look, turning instead to Dylan and following him to the front door.

"Well, kid, I enjoyed it," Dylan said to Josh, offering him a hand. "And how you managed to catch every big one in the stream, I'll never know. You're a hell of a flyfisherman."

"Thanks," Josh said, the color in his cheeks deepening. "And thanks for taking me. I enjoyed it, too."

Dylan turned to Marissa. "I looked over your proposal. Think you'll have some time next week to get together and talk about it?"

"Sure," Marissa said, opening the front door. She'd wondered when he would get around to reading it. "Give me a call."

She closed the door behind him and started back for the kitchen. She glanced up at Josh as she passed him. "Chili?"

"Yeah," Josh murmured, following in line behind her. "Chili, you bet."

"Will you stop worrying?" Jill said, giving Marissa's arm a pat. "It's just two nights. What can happen in two nights?"

Marissa gave her a deliberate look. "I really wish you hadn't asked that."

Jill laughed, putting one hand to the small of her back and patting her round tummy with the other.

"Besides, with me having to stop every twenty minutes to go to the bathroom, we'll be spending most of our time on the road this weekend."

Marissa laughed. She had to admit she was happy that Josh and Jill's oldest son, Nico, were becoming friends. When he'd called earlier in the week and invited Josh to spend the Fourth of July weekend with their family at their beach house in Santa Cruz, she'd happily agreed—even though it meant spending the three-day holiday weekend without him. Nico was a good kid and certainly a better influence on Josh than Skip Carver. She was anxious to do what she could to encourage their friendship.

Still, watching as Josh tossed his sleeping bag and packed sports bag in the back of the Scalettis' oversize minivan wasn't easy. Maybe it was just going to be for a few days, but she was going to miss him.

She turned to Jill. "You know, this is really sweet of you to include Josh. I really appreciate it."

"Listen, I should be the one thanking you," Jill insisted. "Normally Nico likes to use these little family trips to do what he can to make his brother's and sisters' lives miserable. Josh will keep him occupied and out of everyone's hair. Hallelujah.''

''No, I mean it,'' Marissa said seriously. ''Josh has had some . . . problems in the past. Not many parents would be as understanding about that as you and Dom have been.''

Jill's face grew serious, too. ''Look, Marissa. Josh has had some tough breaks, and he's made a few mistakes. But what kid hasn't?''

''I know, but I still appreciate it. I really do.''

Jill took both Marissa's hands in hers. ''Hey, maybe all the kid really needed was someone to believe in him, and now he's got that—he's got you.'' Reaching out over her protruding belly, she gave Marissa a hug. ''He's crazy about you, by the way. Anyone can see that.''

Marissa watched with stinging eyes as Dom Scaletti herded all the kids into the minivan, and helped his pregnant wife up into the passenger's seat. Josh came running up, his dark eyes shining.

''Have you got your spending money?'' Marissa asked quickly, busying herself with trivial matters so that she wouldn't burst into tears. ''And your extra pair of swimming trunks and your beach towel?''

''I've got it, I've got it,'' he assured her, wrapping his arms around her for a big hug. ''Thanks, Auntie Mar,'' he whispered against her ear. ''I love you.''

''I love you, too, baby,'' Marissa whispered back.

She stood on the curb and waved until the minivan turned the corner and disappeared. It was only Friday, and the long weekend stretched out before her empty and endless. What she really felt like doing was running back into the condo and crying her eyes out. But instead she squared her shoulders and headed for the car. With school out, her office would be quiet and she could get some real work done.

She pulled out of the driveway, heading down the quiet street toward school. It wasn't even ten yet, and already the sun was hot. The Fourth of July promised to be a typical one in the Mother Lode—sweltering.

She glanced down at the thick folder on the seat beside her, thinking about the proposal inside. It had been nearly a week since Dylan and Josh went fishing together, nearly a week since he'd told her he'd call to discuss the program they were supposed to be working on together.

He'd called all right, she thought darkly. One brief telephone conversation. He'd been abrupt and noncommittal with her, ambiguous in his comments and ideas for the program, and vague about when they could schedule a time to get together. It had been a frustrating and completely unproductive conversation as far as she was concerned— hardly worth the effort. Why had he even bothered? But while the call had upset her, finding out from Josh that Dylan had stopped by the construction site one afternoon last week and hadn't even bothered coming by to see her had really made her mad.

Her grip on the steering wheel tightened. Well, that was just fine with her, she thought as she pulled into her parking space in the school lot. She didn't need his help, and certainly didn't want it. She would put a program together, and she would present it to the committee on her own—let him make what explanations he wanted to Judge Kent.

"Hi, Karen," she said, feeling the cold blast of the air-conditioning against her face. "I told you it wasn't necessary for you to come in today."

"I know what you told me," Karen said, lifting a heavy stack of files from her desk and onto the file cabinets behind her. "And I also know just how good I'm going to feel when I walk in here Monday morning and be caught up on my filing and have a clean desk." She turned around, dusting her hands off. "Besides, the boys are with Larry for the day, and the thought of rattling around alone in that empty house isn't exactly appealing, if you know what I mean."

"I know exactly what you mean," Marissa said with a sad smile. She'd seen how painful the recent breakup of Karen's marriage had been for her and understood her desire to want to keep busy. "Josh left this morning for the weekend." She jostled the folder in her arms. "So guess what I'll be doing for the next three days."

"I thought Sheriff James was supposed to be helping you with that?" Karen said, putting her hands on her hips.

Marissa laughed. "Yeah, well, if I waited around for him, I don't think it would ever get done."

Karen shook her head, turning back for the file cabinet. "Men," she muttered, pulling out a drawer. "Can't live with them, can't shoot 'em—although God knows they give us reason."

Marissa laughed again as she passed Karen's desk and headed into her office. She tossed the folder holding all her ideas and thoughts for the juvenile program onto her desk and sat down. She stared at the thick file, trying hard to ignore the anger gnawing at her stomach. It had taken her hours of research to compile all the information inside that folder, and Dylan couldn't seem to find the time to even meet with her. Just who did he think he was, anyway?

With a heavy sigh, she reached for the folder, opening it wide. She'd just begun sorting out its contents across her desk when her phone buzzed.

"Yeah, Karen," she said, depressing the intercom button. "What is it?"

"I think someone's ears were burning," Karen said drolly over the line. "Dylan James is on line one."

Chapter 10

Dylan stared at the door, wondering exactly how he'd gotten himself into such a mess. He didn't want to be here, didn't want to be anywhere near Marissa. In fact, he'd spent a good part of the last week doing what he could to avoid her. But time had run out.

The fact was, when he'd left her condo last Saturday after spending the day fishing with Josh, he simply didn't know if he had the strength or the energy that another encounter with her would require. He knew he was good at keeping up a front, knew he could joke and kid and make a good show of pretending that everything was just fine. But even he had his limits, and like it or not, he had feelings for the woman. Maybe they were real, or maybe they were just remnants from the past; it really didn't matter. They were there, and he wasn't made of stone. He couldn't just ignore what he felt—even though at this particular moment, he wished very much that he could.

He shifted the large, flat pizza box and wicker-wrapped bottle of Chianti from one hand to the other, balancing them carefully. He wasn't sure why he'd brought a pizza and wine with him—as a peace offering, maybe, or maybe just as a shield. Her icy tone over the phone this morning had been anything but inviting. She'd agreed to this meeting, but not willingly. He'd had to explain to her that Judge Kent had cornered him at the courthouse and asked for an update on their progress. She hadn't been happy with him, with the judge, or with the situation, and she hadn't minded letting him know.

And of course, it didn't help that they'd had to shift the meeting from her office to her house. The drug bust that had thrown his entire department into chaos had made it necessary for him to stay late at the station. He'd offered to meet at her house instead of her office in an effort not to inconvenience her any more than he already had—even though the quiet atmosphere of her house was the last place he really wanted to be.

Except that now he was running late for this "late" meeting, too, and that wasn't going to make this any easier. At least Josh would be there. Maybe Marissa wouldn't light into him too badly with the kid around.

He reached for the doorbell and depressed the small round button. Through the heavy wooden door, he heard the soft chimes and felt a knot of apprehension start to form in his stomach. He heard the distant sound of her footsteps, and took a deep breath.

"I know I'm late," he said quickly, making an effort and giving her a bright smile. He held up the pizza box and the bottle of wine. "But I came bearing gifts."

Marissa slowly crossed her arms over her chest. He looked entirely too handsome in jeans and a polo shirt, and it only added to her annoyance with him. "I'm tempted to slam this door right in your face."

"I know, I know," he said sympathetically. "And I wouldn't blame you. But you know it takes time to make the streets safe for all you good citizens." He gave her a pathetic look. "And it's such a thankless job."

Marissa rolled her eyes, feeling her anger ebb even though she tried very hard to hang on to it. "You were supposed to be here an hour ago."

"I'm here now, and I'm ready to work," he said simply. He sensed a softening in her voice, and decided to go with it, pushing past her. "And the pizza's getting cold. Let's eat."

Marissa watched as he walked through the house as if he owned it, depositing the pizza box onto the kitchen counter and opening the cupboard and bringing out two wine-glasses.

"Make yourself at home," she muttered as she followed him into the kitchen.

"Thanks, I will," he said good-naturedly, giving her another smile and ignoring the sarcasm in her voice. Setting two wineglasses on the counter beside the pizza box, he reached for the bottle of Chianti and uncorked it. He poured them each a glass, picking them both up and offering one to her. "Bottoms up."

Marissa stared down at the glass he offered, debating on whether to take it from him or toss it in his face. She elected for the former, bringing the glass to her lips, but, watching the smile on his face turn into a full grin, she decided to keep her options open.

Dylan took a gulp of wine, then reached across the counter and flipped open the top of the pizza box. "Call Josh. Let's eat."

"Josh isn't here."

Dylan's hand hesitated as he reached for a slice of pizza. "He's not?"

"No," Marissa said, walking over to the kitchen cabinets and pulling out two plates and two forks. "He went to Santa Cruz for the weekend with the Scalettis."

"Oh, yeah? The whole weekend?" he asked, picking up his glass of wine and taking another gulp. So much for relying on the kid to keep him out of trouble.

"Yes," she said, walking back across the kitchen and offering him a plate.

"You aren't supposed to put pizza on a plate, and you sure don't eat it with a fork," he told her.

"You don't?"

"No, you don't."

She sighed, and gave him a tolerant look. "So, exactly how are you supposed to eat it, then?"

"With your hands," he said reasonably, taking another drink of wine. "While you lean over the box."

"No."

"No?"

"No," she said again.

"You . . . put pizza on a plate?" he asked warily.

"*I* do," she said pointedly, shoving a plate into his flat belly. "And tonight you do, too."

"Yes," Dylan said dubiously, wincing as he took the plate from her. "You're right, I do."

"Actually, getting back to Josh," she said as she reached into the box and picked out a slice. She lifted it onto her plate, plucking a bit of pepperoni off the top with her fingertips and popping it into her mouth as she walked to the table and sat down. "I have to admit, as much as I'm going to miss Josh this weekend, I was pleased he wanted to go. I'd like to see him make more friends like Nico Scaletti."

Dylan plopped a big wedge of pizza onto his plate, picked up his wineglass and joined her at the table. "As opposed to Skip Carver?"

She lifted her wineglass toward her lips and peered at him from over the top. "I didn't say that."

"You didn't have to," he said, determinedly lifting the pizza up with his hands and taking a bite. He offered her the fork as he chewed. "I'll use a plate," he said, swallowing in a gulp. "But I'll be damned if I'll use this."

"I don't doubt that you will," she muttered, trying very hard not to smile. "Be damned, that is."

She didn't want to like him, didn't want to find anything about him amusing or charming. But there was something there just the same, a certain quality, a certain way he had of endearing himself that really got to her, despite the fact that she had every right to be angry. He'd put off meeting with her for almost two weeks now, and then when he finally had agreed to a meeting, he'd shown up late. She should be furious.

So why was she sitting there smiling across the small table at him?

"Frankly, Sheriff, at this point I don't care how you get it in your mouth," she told him, forcing the smile off her face. "Just eat it. We've got work to do, and you're going to need all the strength you can get."

Marissa walked to the sliding glass doors that led to the small patio just off the living room. She pushed the door open, feeling the cool night air against her face.

"I think it's finally cool enough to turn off the air conditioner," she said, turning back to Dylan, who sat hunched over the coffee table. "I'm going to run upstairs and open the bedroom windows."

Dylan nodded, scribbling a few additional things on the legal-size tablet in front of him, then tossed the pen down. He straightened up, closing his eyes and stretching back into the soft cushions of the sofa. His neck was stiff, and his leg muscles felt tight and cramped. It was late, after midnight, and they'd been working almost nonstop for the last few hours.

He opened his eyes and leaned forward to reach for his coffee cup, then decided against it. He must have drunk a couple dozen cups in the last two hours, but it just wasn't helping. The fatigue of an eighteen-plus-hour day was simply too much for even caffeine. Exhaustion had gotten a toehold and wasn't going to let go.

He sank back into the cushions and looked around the cluttered living room. Papers and reports were scattered everywhere—stacked on the hearth and strewn over the plush carpet. The screen of Marissa's laptop computer glowed amid the chaos, the lengthy blueprint for the alternative juvenile sentencing program safely stored in its hard drive—and backup disks had been made for each of them.

His eyes felt scratchy, and he rubbed at them. He was exhausted, but it was a good kind of weariness. Marissa was a taskmaster and had all but demanded blood from him. But they'd gotten a lot done, and he had to admit she'd pretty much made him a believer. The program they'd outlined was not only sound and sensible, but it just might work.

"Join me?"

He opened his eyes to find Marissa standing over him holding a fresh bottle of wine and two glasses.

"I don't know," he said cautiously, sitting up. She'd surprised him with the offer. "Are we going to be doing much more tonight?"

She shrugged, pouring the wine into one of the glasses and placing it into his outstretched hand. "I don't know how much more I'm good for. Do you realize it's after midnight?"

He rubbed at a kink in his neck. "It feels like it."

"Maybe we should think about unwinding a little," she said, pouring herself a glass of wine. Cradling the glass in her hand, she sat the bottle down on the cluttered coffee table and walked back to the sliding glass door, looking out into the night.

"It's nice out now," she said, letting the breeze filter through her hair. "I like it when I can open all the windows and let the breeze in."

The sight of her in front of the open door, her tall, slender body silhouetted against the moonlight, was almost more than he could take. Pouring over reports and compiling information had been exhausting work, but it had also kept his mind occupied, kept him from thinking about being here, having her so close. But now...

He put the glass to his lips and emptied it, welcoming the wine's numbing warmth as it spread through his system. Reaching for the bottle, he filled his glass again. It wasn't that he had it in mind to get drunk, he just wanted to dull his senses a little, just take the edge off the images in his mind and the desire stirring in his body.

"I'd be careful about leaving windows open at night if I were you," he warned, rising to his feet. He reached down and grabbed the bottle of wine and slowly crossed the living room toward her. "In most residential robberies the perpetrator enters through an open door or window."

She turned around and gave him a dirty look. "Do you think you could stop being the sheriff just for a little while?"

He took another drink of wine, and gave her an innocent look. "Just stating a fact."

"Cops," she muttered, rolling her eyes and slowly shaking her head. She slid the screen open and stepped out onto the dark patio. "You really have a way of taking the joy out of things, don't you?"

"What?" he persisted, following her out and feeling the beginning signs of the alcohol that coursed through his bloodstream. "What did I say?"

Marissa walked to the two cushion-covered redwood patio loungers and sat down on one. "Stop seeing criminals around every corner and pull up a chair," she said, patting the seat of the lounger next to hers. She felt a delicious combination of exhaustion and exhilaration. Their evening had been productive, and she was pleased and excited with what they'd come up with. Dylan, for all his tardiness and excuses, proved to be both a tireless and a surprisingly enthusiastic worker. His hard work and input had taken the sting out of the fact that he'd kept her waiting so long. "We put in a good night's work. Drink your wine, and just enjoy this cool night for a while."

"Good idea," he mumbled, looking down at the bottle and the glass in his hand. He emptied his glass again and refilled it, lowering his tired body onto the chair next to hers. Maybe this wasn't exactly masochistic, but it was getting awfully close. After all, what more delicious a torture could there be than to be sitting alone in the darkness with her, and not be able to touch her?

The late night was quiet, with only the low song of crickets disturbing the silence. The adjacent condominiums were dark, Marissa's neighbors having gone to bed long before this, and they sat in darkness—quietly relaxing and winding down.

"We got a lot done tonight," she murmured, staring up at the moon and sipping at her wine.

"Yeah," he mumbled with a nod, noticing it took a little more time to negotiate the route of his glass to his mouth. "Good work, a lot of good work."

"I was concerned we wouldn't have anything ready by the time the committee met again, but now…" She stopped just long enough to take another sip from her glass. "Now I think we'll really have something concrete to show them."

"Yeah," he murmured, closing his eyes and feeling the chair begin to gently sway beneath him.

They drifted back into silence, and Marissa gradually finished her glass of wine. She reached for the bottle on the table beside her. "Would you like more?"

"Oh, oh," Dylan said with a silly giggle that was out of character for him. "I'm afraid I've already had some more." He handed her the empty bottle. "All of it, actually."

"Oh, my," Marissa murmured, hearing the slur to his words. She sat up, regarding him carefully in the darkness. "Sheriff James, I do believe you're tipsy."

He heard himself give that silly giggle again. "I believe the technical term, Miss Wakefield, is 'under the influence.'"

"I believe the technical term, Sheriff James, is potted," she corrected him, standing up and thinking for a minute, trying to decide exactly what to do. "Come on, let's get you inside. You need some coffee."

"Oh, no, not coffee," he moaned, allowing her to pull him to his feet and lead him back into the house. "I can't drink any more coffee."

"Yes, you can," she said in a firm voice. "And you will—lots of it." She pushed him down on the sofa, taking the empty wine bottle and glass from him. With that goofy, kidlike grin on his face, and his hair falling carelessly over his forehead, he looked years younger—like the young high school quarterback she'd fallen in love with. "Now, stay put, and try not to get into trouble. I'll be right back."

"Marissa," he murmured, grabbing her hand before she could walk away. "You're so beautiful."

"Oh, my heavens," Marissa said with a sigh, looking down into his dazed expression and seeing Josh's face in his.

"I think about you *all* the time, all the time," he said, tugging on her arms, pulling her closer. "Do you ever think about me?"

"Dylan," Marissa protested, trying to pull her hand free. It was obvious he didn't know what he was saying, but it embarrassed her, anyway.

"Do you ever think about how it used to be with us?" he murmured. He kept pulling on her arms until she had bent close, bringing her face level with his. "When we were together, when we made love?"

"Dylan, now stop this," she said sternly, but her heart had leapt to her throat.

"Because I do—all the time," he whispered. "All the time."

"Dylan," she said again, trying to ignore the rush of heat sweeping through her. "Just stop."

"Beautiful," he murmured, his hand reaching up and caressing her cheek. "So beautiful."

"L-let go," she stammered.

"But I don't want to let go. I want to look at you," he said dizzily. "So beautiful. So beautiful. You were always the beautiful one—more beautiful than your sister."

Marissa felt her whole system react to the rush of memories. In one simple sentence, he'd managed to strike at the very heart of what had been wrong between them—what would always be wrong between them. She wasn't the woman he'd wanted, she wasn't the right twin. For him she would forever be the second string, the one who would never be good enough.

She snatched her hand away. "I'll get the coffee."

She ran into the kitchen, her hands trembling and her heart beating frantically in her chest. He was drunk and was talking out of his head. Besides, it was all water under the bridge, old news. She had a new life now, a life she'd always wanted with her son, and she couldn't let herself start looking back.

In a sort of numb haze, she went about the job of brewing the coffee. When it was finished, she grabbed a coffee mug and the carafe, and headed back for the living room. The state he was in, it would no doubt take the entire pot to sober him up.

"Okay," she said brightly, forcing back the feelings of discomfort. All that was important right now was getting him out of there. "Coffee's ready. Sit up and let me pour you a nice, hot—"

She stopped abruptly, the hot coffee nearly spilling from the carafe.

"Oh, no," she groaned when she saw Dylan sprawled out across the sofa sound asleep. "No, no, no, no." She rushed around the sofa, setting the coffee and the mug on the cluttered table. "Dylan, wake up," she said, bending down and giving his shoulder a little shake. "Wake up. Time for coffee."

But there was no response from him.

"Hey, Sheriff, now come on," she insisted in a louder voice this time, giving his shoulder another jostle. "Time to go get the bad guys. Come on, Dylan. Wake up."

But there was still no response—not a grunt, a groan or a snore.

"Dylan," she said again, growing a little desperate. She lowered herself onto the cushion beside him, squeezing down between him and the edge. "Come on, now. You have to wake up, you have to get out of here."

She stared down at him, lifting one of his hands from his chest. When she let it go, it dropped lifelessly back onto his chest.

"Dylan?" she repeated, concern creeping into her voice. On impulse, she pressed her ear to his chest, hearing the slow, steady cadence of his heart.

"Well, at least you're not dead," she muttered, sitting back up. What was she going to do?

In one last desperate effort, she put her hands on his shoulders and gave him one more good shake. But it was hopeless. He was out cold.

She stared down at him and couldn't help noticing how vulnerable and defenseless he looked—and so very handsome. She reached up, pushing his hair back from his eyes, thinking how soft it felt against her fingers.

"Marissa," he murmured sleepily.

Marissa yanked her hand away, startled and embarrassed. But it was obvious that he was still deeply asleep.

He looked so much like Josh lying there, with his face motionless and relaxed—so much like the son he didn't know he had. The irony wasn't lost on her. Father and son were getting to know each other, anyway. They were forming a loose sort of friendship despite the circumstances that had brought them together.

"Marissa."

He mumbled her name again, but she didn't jump this time. Was he thinking of her? Was there something in his dizzy dreams, something in his subconsciousness that had him thinking of her? And was it really her, or just someone who looked like her?

It would be so much easier if she could just hate him, but she didn't. Despite everything, he'd been a good friend since she'd moved back to Jackson. He'd been good to Josh. He'd given her son his time and his attention. He'd been the kind of father figure he desperately needed, and for that she was grateful. But how would he react if he were to know the truth? What would his dreams be filled with then?

Rising slowly to her feet, she walked quietly through the house. She climbed the stairwell, then flipped the switch at the head of the stairs, flooding the narrow hallway with light. She pulled a blanket and pillow from the linen closet, shoved them under her arm and headed back to the living room.

"Okay, Sheriff, looks like you're staying," she said as she slipped the pillow under his head and covered him with the blanket. She paused for a moment, looking down at him. "I always wondered what it would be like to spend the night with you again," she said, bending close and giving him a quick, impulsive kiss on the forehead. "Somehow this isn't what I'd expected."

She walked through her quiet house, turning off lights and securing doors and locking windows. She remembered what he said about perpetrators and thieves, and quickly gave everything a double check.

Why wasn't she more upset? she wondered as she made her way quietly up the steps. Maybe she was just tired, or maybe it was the wine she'd drunk, or maybe it was just that she was losing her mind completely—but for some reason it felt kind of good knowing he was there, he was close by, and that she'd kissed him good-night.

There it was again. Marissa skittered to a stop, pausing with one foot on the step, the other on the landing, and listened intently. But the only sound she could hear now was that of her own breath rushing in and out of her lungs.

A shiver of fear slithered down her spine. At first she'd thought it was Dylan moving around in her dark living room, confused and disoriented, bumping into things, but the sound she'd just heard had not come from the living room.

She crept the rest of the way down the stairs, her bare feet soundless on the carpeted steps. It was only a little after three, and she'd slept for only a couple of hours, but she was anything but sleepy. Apprehension had her feeling wide-awake and scared to death.

"Dylan?" she called out in a stage whisper, tiptoeing toward the living room. "Dylan?"

She stopped for a moment, listening for a response. But she could hear nothing, just her heart and her quivering breath. She thought about how she'd tried to wake him up earlier, and how impossible it had been. What if she needed him and he was still out cold?

She shivered again. Despite the summer night, she felt cold and numb, and her short nightshirt offered little protection. She wrapped her arms around herself, rubbing at the gooseflesh on her skin. She hadn't thought about a robe or slippers, but modesty hadn't exactly been foremost in her mind. She was more interested in waking Dylan and finding out what—or who—was making that sound outside.

"Dylan?" she breathed urgently, taking a few steps closer to the sofa. "Dylan, wake up, wake—"

"Shh," Dylan whispered, stepping silently behind her and placing a hand over her mouth. He turned her in his arms, forcing her to look up at him, and felt every muscle in her body tighten. "He's moving around the house."

Marissa's eyes were bright with terror, and she wanted very much to scream. But she fought against it, banking down her panic and forcing herself to think. She stared up at Dylan, hearing his voice in her ears and trying as best she could to make the words register sense in her brain.

"W-what's happening?" she whispered. "What's going on?"

Dylan turned his head, nodding to the patio doors. Marissa followed his gaze, looking up just as a dark silhouette appeared through the thin drapes.

"Oh, God," she gasped as she watched the shadow move across the patio.

Dylan pulled her tight, bringing a finger to his lips. "Is it locked?"

She looked up at him, her eyes growing wide in the darkness, and nodded. She turned back, watching as the shadow moved across her patio, hearing the sound of the door being tested.

"He's...he's trying to get in," she whispered almost soundlessly, clutching at Dylan's shirt.

Dylan nodded. "He's tried all the doors."

"Sh-shouldn't we call the police?" Her hold on his shirt tightened. "Shouldn't we be doing something?"

Dylan quieted her again, watching as the shadowy figure moved and backed away. Dylan slowly released his hold on Marissa and walked soundlessly across the living room. Through a crack in the drapery, he peered outside.

"What's he doing now?" Marissa asked, having followed him on tiptoe.

Dylan watched for a moment longer, then turned back to Marissa. "He's gone."

Marissa straightened up and looked at him. "Are you sure?"

Dylan reached up and pulled the curtain back a little to show her the patio was empty. "I'm sure."

"He was trying to get in," she murmured, a cold chill making her shiver.

Dylan felt her trembling. "But he's gone now, don't worry about it."

"Where's your gun?"

He couldn't help smiling. "Marissa, I don't need a gun."

She looked up at him. He was being so casual about everything...almost cavalier and unconcerned. "Shouldn't you be calling a patrol car or something?

"Trying to catch him, find out who it is?"

"I already know who it is."

Marissa's eyes grew wide again. "What? You know?" She shivered again, but this time it had nothing to do with the cold air or the threat of an intruder. It was his unemotional, ominous tone that bothered her. "Then why aren't you going after him? Why aren't you doing something?"

Dylan glanced out the window, then pulled the drapes closed again. He turned slowly to Marissa, resting his hands lightly on her upper arms. "I can't go after him."

Marissa pushed away, shaking her head. "You're talking crazy. Someone was trying to break into my house. I don't understand. If you know who it was, why aren't you going after him?"

"Because if I go after him, I'd have to arrest him."

Marissa stopped for a moment. "What is it you're not telling me?"

It was dark, with only the dim light from the street lamps outside filtering through the curtains, yet he knew she was confused. "It was Skip."

Chapter 11

Marissa's eyes widened, and a cold flush spread through her veins. "Skip Carver? He was trying to break in?"

Dylan nodded, reaching behind the end of the drapery and testing the locked slider. "It would appear that way."

"But why?" Marissa asked, raising her hands up helplessly. "Dylan, why would he want to break into my house? Josh is a friend of his. Why would he do that to a friend?"

"I'm not sure," Dylan said, taking a step closer in an effort to calm her down. "Maybe he's angry with Josh, or... or maybe to get back at you for something."

"Me," she repeated, shocked. "Why would he want to get back at me? I've never done anything to Skip."

"I know," Dylan conceded. "But Skip Carver—" He hesitated for a moment. "You know as well as I do the kid is bad news."

Marissa's eyes narrowed, and she took a step back. "There's something you're not telling me. Something's happened, hasn't it. Skip's done something."

"Look," Dylan said cautiously, drawing in a deep breath. "I don't know anything for sure. It's just that . . . well, I've suspected for a while that Skip has been having a hard time." He reached a hand out and brushed a long lock of her hair back into place. "That he might be developing some problems."

"What do you mean? Like what? What kind of problems?" she demanded, gripped by a worse fear than when the prowler was outside. "I check his progress in class almost every day. His grades aren't the greatest, but they're passing. And he's not giving his teachers a problem, or any of the other students."

Dylan's hands settled on her upper arms. The gold necklace around her neck caught a flicker of light, the cluster of stars sparkling shiny and alive. "I don't mean that kind of problem."

"You mean you think he . . . that he's . . ." Her words drifted off, and she closed her eyes tight. Her mind rushed to remember those times in the last several weeks when Josh hadn't been with her, when he might have been with Skip, he might have been . . . She squeezed her eyes tighter. Things had been so wonderful the last few weeks. She and Josh were becoming so close. He couldn't be getting into trouble again, he just couldn't.

"I think maybe Skip is doing some things he shouldn't," he said evasively, knowing the truth would only make her worry. "And that he's headed for trouble—big trouble."

Marissa's brows arched together. "You're not talking about graffiti or vandalizing, are you."

Dylan didn't have to see the worry and uncertainty in her eyes, he could hear it in her voice, and he weighed his options. The truth was harsh, but maybe knowing the truth would be better than dealing with the worry. "No, I'm not. I think Skip's been taking drugs, and I think he's committing residential robberies to get money to buy them."

Marissa opened her eyes, sucking in a breath. She'd been involved with education long enough to know that alcohol and drug use were an unfortunate fact of life for some kids. And while she wasn't naive enough to think that it wasn't a problem at Sutter, or that none of her students were involved in those kinds of activities, it didn't make hearing Dylan's suspicions any easier.

"How do you know?"

"I've been a little suspicious for a while," Dylan admitted. "And I've been hearing things from the streets. I've asked Josh about—"

Marissa's gasped, and clutched at his arms. "You don't think that Josh—"

"No," he said adamantly, cutting her off. His grip on her tightened. "I honestly don't. I think Josh is really tying to straighten himself out and has stayed out of trouble. Randy, too, for that matter." He took a deep breath, his voice dropping a degree. "But I think Skip's put them in a bad position. I think they might know something about what's going on, maybe know what he's into. They're with him every day at school and at the construction site. And if you talk to them, it's pretty clear that there's tension between them." He stopped, noticing how her white nightshirt looked almost iridescent in the darkness. "The problem is, if I haul Skip in . . ." He hesitated, shrugging. "I do that under the terms of the court's ruling, the D.A.'s going to want me to pull all three of them in."

Marissa looked up into his face, which was dark and streaked with shadow. She was faced with the irony again—the irony that was becoming her daily companion and her daily burden. Dylan was protecting Josh—protecting him the way a father would protect his son. Was it just a fluke, a coincidence? Was it just Dylan doing his job, looking out for a kid in trouble the same way he was looking out for Randy? Could it possibly be that simple, or was there something more? Dylan had no way of knowing that Josh was his son. Was it just her guilt that saw the link between them, or was there an awareness there?

"That's why you did it, isn't it," she said in a whisper. The darkness and the emotion had the whole night feeling surreal and illusory—as if it were happening just outside the realm of the real world, in another time, another place. "That's why you didn't go after Skip—to protect Josh and Randy."

Dylan's jaw clenched tight. There was something in her voice, something in the words she had said that had him uneasy. He'd heard the emotion, heard the gratitude, and it made him uncomfortable.

Where Marissa Wakefield was concerned, he struggled with his own emotions—both the assortment of emotions from the past, as well as a whole battery of new ones. From the moment she'd walked into his office on that hot summer morning all those weeks ago, he'd been fighting against the feelings that had lain dormant in him for sixteen years—feelings like anger, disappointment, pain and...love. He'd done his best to cope with them, to try and understand what he was feeling and why. But it hadn't been easy when she stirred in him a myriad of new emotions—emotions that had nothing to do with the past and everything to do with the fact that she was a very desirable woman.

The last thing he wanted was for her to start feeling grateful to him. That would simply be asking too much on his already frazzled emotions. Gratitude only made it more difficult, muddied waters that were already dark and murky—and he was barely able to keep his head above water as it was. He couldn't handle her looking soft and vulnerable right now—not now, not with the two of them alone in the dark, empty house.

"Look," Dylan said dropping his hold on her and taking a step back. "Before you start pinning any medals on me, you should know that if Skip had actually succeeded in busting in here tonight, I'd have had him down at the station so fast his head would still be spinning." He was pleased that his voice sounded harsh and cold, and he turned around and walked through the dark living room to the sofa. "The fact is, there was no break-in, no robbery. I would only have had a trespassing charge at best." He reached down and grabbed the blanket Marissa had tossed over him several hours before and made an attempt to fold it. "Skip Carver isn't going anywhere. I can wait. I'm not going to blow a real case against him for a trespass. As far as Josh goes, if he keeps his nose clean, he's got nothing to worry about."

Hearing his caustic tone and gruff words, Marissa watched his dark silhouette fumble with the blanket, and she felt a burst of awareness free itself from some hidden place in her heart. It was dark in the room, but she felt like she was seeing things clearer than she ever had in her life. She thought back to the countless times he had joked, how he had scoffed and jeered, in order to cover what it was he really felt.

He talked so tough, acted so jaded, it almost had her believing he didn't care. But she'd seen something just now—something he was trying very hard to cover up with harsh talk and tough words, something that had all the pieces falling into place.

He was afraid of her—had been afraid of her all along. Afraid of being alone with her, afraid of touching her, afraid of getting too close. But what did he have to fear from her? It didn't make sense, it didn't add up, unless . . .

"You know, you're very good at that," she said, unable to keep the smile from stretching across her face. She crossed her arms over her chest and started across the room, her bare feet soundless on the carpet.

Frustrated, he stopped grappling with the blanket and tossed it down onto the cushions in a wadded mess. "What?" Dylan asked sarcastically. "Folding blankets?"

"Hardly," she snorted, peering down at the blanket lying in a heap on the sofa, then shook her head. She looked back up at him. Even in the darkness she could see his smirk, and the way he worked his jawbone—clenching and unclenching—and it only made her smile wider. She suspected the Sheriff of Amador County wasn't accustomed to squirming, because he looked awkward and uncomfortable doing it now. "No, I was referring to the *tough cop* routine. You've really got it down."

"You think it's a *routine,* do you?" he asked caustically. But with the windows shining behind her, he could see her willowy figure through the nightshirt, and his mouth suddenly went as dry as sand.

"Sure do. Isn't it?"

He shifted uneasily. She was moving again, and the closer she got, the more uncomfortable he became. "I guess I wasn't aware of that."

"Sure you were," she insisted. He was uncomfortable, she realized, almost edgy. "You do it all the time." *She* was making him nervous, and she found that not only empowering—but exhilarating. "As a matter of fact, you're doing it right now."

"Am I?" he mocked, making a play of indulging her. "I must say, that's very interesting."

He'd forgotten about Skip and his nocturnal visit, forgotten about sheriffing and devotion to duty. He was too busy trying desperately not to think of the darkness, and the silence, and the quiet, empty house. And he really didn't want to think of the woman before him who was naked beneath the nightshirt.

"I find it interesting, too," Marissa was saying as she watched him fidget and take a step back. She wasn't aggressive by nature, and she certainly had never been overly confident when it came to men. Maybe if she had been, she never would have felt the need to impersonate her sister in order to get a date with him in the first place. But she felt aggressive now—aggressive, powerful, and not only sure of herself, but sure of what she wanted. She had the sheriff on the run, and she was in full pursuit.

"Well, I'm glad you find this so entertaining," Dylan taunted, but his fists clenched tight at his sides. He felt jumpy and agitated, a little like an animal trapped in a cage. Things were moving too fast; she was giving him no time to recoup or recover. He wanted to get as far away from her as he could. But he couldn't move, could no longer make his body obey his commands.

"Oh, I do find it entertaining," she continued, dropping her arms to her sides as she slowly made her way towards him. "And I suppose it comes in handy, too—you know, in those awkward moments."

"Awkward moments?" he snorted carelessly. "What are you talking about?"

"Oh, you know, those sticky situations that deal with emotions and having to feel something," she said, pausing only briefly. "Like now."

"Now? You're talking crazy," he said glibly. "Is this a sticky situation?"

"Oh, sure it is," she said, moving close. Watching him stumble back a step had her laughing just a little. "And I think it's about to get a whole lot stickier."

Dylan took another step back. "Look, Marissa, I don't know if this is such a good idea."

"What?" she asked, reaching out and sliding her hand up his shirt. "This?"

Dylan swallowed hard. He could stop himself from touching her, but he was helpless to stop her from touching him. "Yes."

"You don't think so?"

"No, I don't," he said honestly. "Maybe it would be better if I left."

"But, Sheriff, wouldn't that be running away?" she asked, backing him up against the sofa. "And you know, tough guys never run away."

She had worked him like a big-game hunter works her prey. He was trapped, cornered—snared in a trap he hadn't even known was set. He watched as she reached out her other hand, flattening it against his chest.

"Marissa, what are you doing?"

"What do you mean?"

"Why are you doing this?"

"You mean this?" she asked, sliding her hands slowly up his chest. "Or this?" She pressed her body close.

Dylan closed his eyes, his chest rising and falling with heavy breaths. "I...I don't think you realize what you're doing."

"Yes, I do," she said, moving her hands along the solid wall of his chest. "I might be a little rusty, but I'm going to seduce you."

"Look, Marissa, okay," he conceded, feeling more desperate, more helpless, than he had in his life. "You made your point. You can stop now. This isn't funny anymore."

"You're right," she murmured, moving her body against his. "It isn't."

"Marissa, please." He groaned, feeling the soft pressure of her breasts against him. "Maybe...maybe we should wait—"

"Dylan, I don't want to talk," she said, cutting him off. "And I don't want to wait." She moved her body again, feeling him hard and hungry against her. She looked up into his dark eyes, bringing her lips within a whisper of his. "It's been sixteen years. Don't you think we've waited long enough already?"

Dylan capitulated, powerless to do anything. He'd hoped for caution, had searched for reason, but both had heartlessly deserted him. If there were arguments to be made, he'd forgotten them. If there were hazards to be alerted to, he'd risk them. Maybe it wasn't so important that they hadn't charted a path, hadn't mapped a route, or steered a straight course. None of that seemed important with her mouth on his. At the moment there was nothing else—just the woman before him—and a need clawing at him like no other he'd known.

He'd held out as long as he was able, had given her every chance that he could. But he was, after all, just a man—a man whose greatest sin was wanting this woman more desperately than he wanted his next breath. The movements of her beautiful body along his fueled the desires he'd been trying for weeks to suppress—stoking the embers, bringing them to flame, causing an inferno. With a groan that came from the very depths of his soul, he moved his arms around her, and gave himself over to her capable hands.

Marissa settled her lips squarely on his, coaxing them apart, and tasting him deeply. She heard his groan, felt it reverberate through her, and savored the flavor of it in her mouth. She sunk her hands into his hair, pulling him close, holding him fast. She'd never been so determined, never felt so sure, or acted so boldly. She knew exactly what she wanted, and had no qualms, no reservations, no doubt about going after it.

She understood his need to struggle, knew he'd tried to resist and hold back. But she'd known the war he'd waged hadn't been against her—it had been against himself. She had let him grapple with his conscience, let him fight with his pride; she had let him argue and scrap because she'd already declared herself the victor. She wanted Dylan James, and she wasn't going to take no for an answer.

"Marissa," he moaned almost painfully against her lips. He looked down into her eyes, the world reeling in a blur of color and mass around him. "Tell me you're sure. *Tell me,* because . . . because I don't think I can stop."

Marissa felt a bubble of silent laughter rise to the surface. Sure? He wanted to know if she was sure? She couldn't remember having been so sure of anything in her life. This was Dylan—the man she'd fallen in love with a lifetime ago, the man who had filled her dreams, who had changed her life, whose child she had carried in her womb. She'd spent years trying to hate him, trying to forget and move on with her life, but she'd failed miserably in her attempts. He was her man, and she was his woman. She wanted him—for the moment, for tonight, or for however long he wanted.

"Dylan," she whispered, slowly pulling at his polo shirt, slipping it free from the waist of his jeans. "I don't want you to stop."

He'd capitulated, now he surrendered. His arms came around her, crushing and unyielding, and his mouth ravaged against hers. He was flesh and bone, not ice and stone—but even if he had been, she would have been able to melt him. She wanted him, and that was all his weary brain could comprehend.

For one brief, fleeting moment Marissa could only stand there. His almost violent submission had left her stunned, unable to think. The air left her lungs, making her feel shaky and faint, and the floor beneath her suddenly seemed less steady, less firm.

She felt his mouth on hers, felt the force of his arms, and the heat from his body. A shiver traveled up her spine, causing her to tremble in anticipation. It was only then that life began to slowly seep back into her dazed senses, and purpose returned to guide her. She felt every nerve come alive, and with it came the hunger, the need and the desperation.

She wrapped her arms around him tightly, meeting his kiss and giving herself over to its special magic. She felt wild and reckless, invincible and invulnerable. She'd always been the practical one—the one who had played it safe, who had played by the rules. But this time there were no rules. She'd wanted him from the moment she'd laid eyes

on him, and she'd wanted him every day that had passed
since then. With him she had not only broken the rules,
she'd obliterated them completely. When it came to Dylan, there would be no playing it safe.

Dylan's hands moved over her, restless and hungry. She
felt lush and supple through the thin cotton of the nightshirt, and it made the ache in him almost unbearable. His
heart pounded like thunder in his ears, and the blood in his
veins turned to fire. He found the end of the nightshirt and
slipped his hands beneath.

The skin along her leg felt like liquid silk—alive and
bursting with heat. He felt her body tremble beneath his
touch, his hand traveling the length of her—thigh, hip,
belly, waist. When his hand skimmed the delicate nipple of
her breast, her entire body reacted. She gasped against his
mouth, and a deep growl sounded from somewhere deep in
her throat. Dylan felt it rumble through him, echoing
through the canyons of his soul like a phantom plea—urgent and heartfelt.

He lifted his mouth from hers, staring down into her
fervent blue eyes. To him she was perfect—like a fantasy
come to life. Her skin looked flawless, and glowed like fine
porcelain in the faint light of the room. Her long hair
spilled over her shoulder, and framed her face in an aura of
white gold.

Had he ever noticed how truly perfect her face was before—how blue her eyes, how delicate her chin, how fault-
less her skin? Had he ever held another woman without
thinking of her, had he honestly thought he could want
anyone else when it was her his soul cried out for? He had
come full circle—into the arms of the woman he'd loved
and lost, the woman he wanted never to lose again.

"So beautiful," he whispered almost soundlessly, as the
blue in her eyes darkened into a rainbow of green.

"Tell me, Dylan," she murmured thickly. Her mind was
made up, for her there would be no going back. But she had

to hear the words. "Say that it's me. Tell me I'm the one you want."

"Oh, God," he groaned against her lips. "Marissa. Beautiful Marissa. Don't you know? Can't you tell?" He placed one gentle, feather-light kiss along her lips. "It's you. It's always been you."

And she was—the one he'd always wanted, the one he would want forever. All that mattered now was that she was in his arms, and he didn't intend to ever let her go.

Slowly, his hand settled over her breast. The round fullness weighed gentle against his palm, and he felt her whole body react to his touch.

Marissa's lids shuttered closed, his touch causing a surge of longing in her that was almost more than she could bear. Her blood had turned to a molten substance, flowing hot and unchecked through her veins. Needs were catapulted to a critical degree, and desires were sent raging out of control.

She felt the nightshirt fall as he lifted it away, felt the rush of cool air against her body, against her skin. She stood naked before him, but there was no time for modesty or shame, no time to think about misgivings and uncertainties. He was kissing her, and his hands were on her again—moving and stroking, making the need in her so great it bordered on agony. She'd started out the aggressor, but it was she who was submitting now—submitting to a fate she'd waited her whole life to encounter, and a passion that threatened all else.

She pulled at his shirt, pushing the fabric aside and letting her hands move over his chest. He felt hard, and strong. There were no soft edges to his body, nothing delicate or frail. He was all man—his lean, hard frame issuing strength and determination, and a vulnerability that came from wanting a woman.

Dylan's hands moved over her body, caressing and massaging. Desire pounded at him, and his ability to hold it at bay diminished with every stroke of his hand. She was beautiful beyond belief, her tall, slender body forming soft, womanly curves. His hands settled on her breasts, brushing over the sensitive centers, making them hard and taut.

With a groan, he tore his mouth from her lips, his body shuddering in its struggle for control. He couldn't seem to get enough—couldn't touch enough, taste enough, feel enough. She filled his senses, took up the middle and both ends of his consciousness. He could think of nothing but touching her, pleasing her, loving her.

His lips made a wet trail down her jaw, kissing and tasting the supple skin first at her neck, then at her shoulder, and then gloriously at the gentle swell of her breasts. He pulled a delicate nipple into his mouth, paying homage to it with his lips and tongue, then searched for the other, paying tribute to it in the same, sensuous manner.

He could feel her body trembling, could hear her soft moans, and the restless motions of her arms and legs. His body surged with new strength. He was filled with the knowledge, and the certainty that he could give her what she wanted, that he could please her as no other man could.

And please her he would. Because for the first time in sixteen long years, he was where he knew he should be. Like a knight fulfilling a prophecy of old, he knew his purpose, understood his charge, and was ready to yield to it completely. His destiny was upon him. He was Marissa Wakefield's lover—and that was all that he wanted to be.

Marissa gasped for breath. Her heart pounded so loudly and so fiercely she thought it sought a path out of her chest. She had gone into this with her eyes wide open—there had been no promises, no guarantee of what there would be for her next, but she would have no regrets. If it all came crashing down tomorrow, let the pieces fall where they may. This was what she wanted—this man, this moment.

Dylan clutched at her, raising her up and pulling her close. Her hands were tugging at his jeans. The feel of her against him sent him flying to a whole new level of need, pulling what thin line of reason he had left, and snapping it.

He lifted her up, stepping around the sofa and taking what scant steps were needed to lower them onto the softness of the cushions. He pulled her beneath him, hearing the sound of her jagged breath in his ear and feeling his hold on the real world start to slip. His body cried out for solace, his mind begged for mercy, and his soul reached out to be with the one that it loved.

His hard body trembled as he rose up above her. He searched her face for any sign of question or doubt. But he could see nothing in her beautiful face except longing and hope. The ache in him had become an anguish, and his body had reached the outside edge of its tolerance. In one strong, sure, glorious stroke, he pushed into her, bringing their two lives together, and making them one.

Marissa felt the breath catch in her throat, felt her heart pause in her chest and her spirit soar to the stars. The feel of him within her, the movements of their bodies together, sent her safe, cautious world careering out of control. There was no balance left to the universe, no semblance of order or stability. Like her staggered senses, the cosmos had fallen into chaos, and there was no going back. She was traveling toward a place she'd visited only in her dreams, a place she'd longed for all her life, where desire met fulfillment, where touch became serenity and peace meant the man in her arms.

And then she was there—to that spot on the hill, that castle in the sky. Her body convulsed as the rapture showered over her like a million tiny stars—glowing, glittering, full of light. She was sent hurling into space, floating through a void that left the real world behind. She was at one with another—at one with the man she loved.

Chapter 12

Dylan felt her body move beneath him, felt the eruption of mind and body, heart and soul, and it shattered what little command he had left. Feeling her explode into bliss was like feeling poetry in motion—like holding a moment suspended in time, and everything within him reacted. Destiny was calling, and with all that he was, all that he had, he relinquished control.

"Marissa," he cried out, breaking through into the abyss, and finding pleasure purer and far sweeter than he'd ever known.

It was a long time before he drifted back to earth, before the world took shape and the night settled back around them. But he couldn't bring himself to let her go. He held her close, her head was beside his on the cushion, and their bodies were still joined in their intimate embrace.

It had never been like that for him—not even sixteen years ago when he'd been flush with youth and love. His body still trembled from the onslaught of emotion. He'd been intent on satisfying her, had become so focused on bringing her pleasure, on fulfilling her needs, he'd been taken by surprise. But even as he lay there beside her, his hard body spent and physically depleted, the taste of her still on his lips, his heart was far from sated. It would take more than one act of love, more than one night of magic, to satisfy the need in him—more than a lifetime.

"You okay?" he whispered, his lips brushing a small kiss along her neck.

She turned her head on the cushion to face him. She'd heard his light, casual tone, but in the darkness his eyes were filled with emotion, and her heart swelled in her chest. "I'm fine."

"You sure? I got a little carried away. I wasn't exactly...smooth just now," he said sheepishly, his eyes narrowing. He gestured to their current condition among the dislodged cushions, with her nightshirt strewn on the floor and what clothes he still wore gaping half on, half off. "This looks more like a crime scene than a seduction."

She had to smile, finding his humor oddly touching. She felt the tension in his body, heard the uncertainty in his voice. He was far from being as relaxed and as comfortable as he tried to sound. Tonight had been unexpected, and they both needed time to accept and understand. In the past, his light remarks and teasing tone would have seemed awkward and out of place to her. But she understood the man better now. She understood how he used the humor and the teasing, in just the way he did the "tough guy" act—as a cover, as a way of coping. It was his way of saying something when he couldn't find the words to say what he felt.

But the humor couldn't hide what was in his eyes. She looked into their dark depths, seeing the emotion and feeling it. Reaching out, she ran a slow finger along the line of his cheek, down his jaw, to his lips.

"Sheriff, you make it sound as though you were doing the seducing. Maybe we should clear up that little misconception."

"Oh?" he said, arching a brow. His lips closed around her fingertip, drawing it between his teeth and giving it a small tug. "Is it a misconception?"

She moved up, reversing their positions and smiling down at him. "*I* seduced *you,* not the other way around."

"Is that right," he murmured, running his hands along the sides of her waist. "And what was it—exactly—that I was doing while you were seducing me?"

She leaned down, brushing her lips to his. "You were taking it."

"Yeah," he murmured, laughing deep in his throat. He reached up and pulled her head close. "I guess I was."

The kiss was long and deep, and left him feeling a little light-headed. There was so much he wanted to tell her, so much he wanted to say. But the time wasn't right. There were still too many questions left between them, too much undecided. He'd learned sixteen years ago that a night of passion didn't come with any guarantees. Right now, it was enough that she was in his arms, enough that he could hold her, and touch her and please her.

"Since we've established that it was you who did the seducing the first time around—" in one smooth motion, he sat up, carrying her with him, and swept her up into his arms "—then I guess that means it's my turn now."

"I watched you there."

Marissa turned away from the window and looked back at him. He was propped up against the headboard, the sheet tossed carelessly over him, exposing his broad chest to the faint light of the dawn.

"You watched me?"

Dylan nodded, remembering the night he'd sat in his Jeep and watched her from the street below. He'd been on the outside looking in that night, but he'd wanted her, had wanted to be in her bed. He hadn't thought then it could ever happen, had held out little hope, and yet here he was.

"At the window. I checked on the house one night," he said, his eyes moving over her. His knit polo shirt was too big on her, but she managed to make it look sexy. Maybe it was the way it clung to her soft curves, or maybe it was just that he knew she was naked beneath it. "You pulled the shades and opened the window. I watched."

Marissa leaned back against the windowsill and studied him from across the room. It had happened again—he'd come into her life and changed everything. Only this time she'd gone into it with her eyes wide open. She couldn't blame it on youth or inexperience. The responsibility was all hers. Maybe she should have been more cautious, maybe she should have trod more carefully, but she'd been careful all her life. If this was all there was, if there would be no future, at least she would have this—and for now, that was enough.

"Where is there a cop when you need one?" she said, walking soundly across the room toward him.

He reached for her arm, pulling her onto the bed, and kissing her. "Right where he wants to be."

Marissa's heart caught in her throat, and she let her arms drift up and encircle his neck. "Is it, Dylan? Is this really where you want to be?"

Dylan looked down at her, the smile slowly fading from his lips. "You sound like you don't believe it."

Marissa reached up, brushing his hair back from his forehead. "It's not that. But this thing...it's happened pretty fast for us."

"Fast?" Dylan smiled, stroking long, silky strands of hair back from her face. Her hair spilled around her on the bed like a rich vein from the Mother Lode. How could he tell her how long he'd dreamed of this day, how could he tell her how much it meant to him to be here with her. "I don't call sixteen years between dates fast."

She smiled at his teasing, but the smile faded quickly. "I guess I just want you to know...well, I don't want you to think that I expect anything from you because of tonight."

"What are you trying to say?" Dylan asked, unconsciously working his jaw.

"I guess what I'm trying to say is I wanted tonight to happen," she whispered. "No matter where we go from here."

Dylan brought his lips close, hovering just above hers. "I wanted it, too."

Marissa not only heard the emotion in his voice, she felt it in his body, and she saw it in his face. Her eyes filled with tears. She didn't know if he was every woman's fantasy, but he would always be hers.

"Dylan," she whispered.

But his name was lost somewhere in the silence of the dawn as he lowered his mouth to hers. He'd been kissing her for hours, they had made feverish, passionate love, but this kiss was different—very, very different. It was gentle; it was achingly tender; and it was fraught with all the emotion, all the sentiment, that had gone unsaid.

Marissa felt herself floating. There was nothing teasing about the way he kissed, nothing concealed or hidden away. He might be able to hide what he felt with flippant words and a tough-guy attitude, but he couldn't hide it from the kiss. The urgent, gnawing hunger in her had been sated, clearing the way for a whole new set of needs. She not only wanted his passion and his fire, she also wanted his heart.

"Dylan," she said with a sigh, his name meaning need, and longing, and love to her. "Dylan."

"So long," he murmured, looking down at her. The soft, gentle sound of his name on her lips caused a band of emotion to burst free somewhere inside, and his body stirred with life. "I've waited so long for this—to hold you, to love you again." In one smooth, sure motion, he brought their bodies together, sliding into her warmth and watching desire fill her eyes. A surge of longing had his body moving, had the need in him rising to an uproar. "I don't want it to be just one night, Marissa," he whispered against her lips, kissing, biting. "I don't ever want to let you go."

Marissa gave herself over to the motions of his body, gave over to the inevitable demands of the flesh. It wasn't the first time he'd touched her, wasn't the first time he'd filled her body with his, but it was different just the same. This time there was more than a joining of bodies—hearts were united, minds were linked, and souls were made one.

As the first streaks of the morning sun began to peek over the horizon, they touched and held each other. There had been no formal commitment made between them—not with words, anyway. But hearts were now involved—he knew it, and she knew it—and it gave their lovemaking a whole new dimension. No longer was this just one night of passion, no longer would there be any questions or any doubts. They might not know exactly what direction they were headed, but there was no doubt they were headed there together.

It was a long time before Dylan collapsed beside her on the bed, a long time before they lay wrapped in each other's arms, dozing lightly and resting their weary bodies. Dylan pulled her close, nuzzling his face close into the nape of her neck. The sun shone bright, filtering through the curtain along with a cool morning breeze. Her long hair splayed out on the pillow around them, falling over his shoulder and under his cheek.

"So beautiful," he murmured against her neck, stroking the delicate skin along her waist. "Beautiful, Marissa."

Marissa smiled, too content to open her eyes. It was so quiet and peaceful lying there together—so perfect.

But then, out of nowhere, all that changed. She sprang up suddenly, pushing her hair back from her face and feeling her heart racing in her chest. "Oh, my!" she shrieked. "Oh—oh, my!"

"W-what?" Dylan stammered, alarmed. He sprang up behind her, grabbing her by the shoulders. "Marissa, my God, what is it?"

"My sister," she said, turning to Dylan, whose dazed, confused expression made him look sweet and endearing, and even more like Josh than ever. "I have to call her."

"What?"

"I have to call my sister," she shrieked again, reaching up and kissing him quickly before turning for the phone. "She's going to have a baby!"

"I still think it's weird."

Marissa reached across the small redwood table that separated their patio chairs and gave him a playful swat.

"There's nothing weird about it."

"No? Two sisters living in two different states, separated by hundreds of miles, who read each other's minds?" Dylan pulled his sunglasses down his nose and peered at her over the top of the lenses. "It's weird."

"It's not weird," she insisted, thinking of the telephone call she'd had with her sister earlier in the day. Mallory hadn't thought it *weird* that she had "intercepted" the news about the baby any more than Marissa had found it *weird* that Mallory had known she was with Dylan. "It's just the way things are with us."

"Twilight Zone," Dylan said, shoving his glasses back in place and whistling the familiar theme song. "So, is your sister excited?"

Marissa smiled, feeling Mallory's happiness. "Are you kidding? She can hardly wait. She'll be a great mom."

He shifted around and looked at her. "How about you? Can you wait?"

She turned her head, carefully schooling her features, but a tinge of tension made the muscles at the base of her neck start to tighten. This wasn't exactly a subject she was comfortable with. "For children? You forget, I've got 316 at Sutter to look after."

He nodded his head thoughtfully. "That's true. And of course, there's Josh."

"And Josh," she added, her voice sounding wooden and stiff to her ears.

"How you think he's going to take this—you and me?"

Marissa closed her eyes, feeling a little overwhelmed. "I'm not sure. I hope he'll understand."

"I'll talk to him if you want."

She turned and smiled up at him. "Thanks."

Dylan leaned his head back against the cushion of the chair and closed his eyes to the afternoon sun. "Getting back to children, though. Would you ever want a family of your own?"

"Sure," she said, reminding herself not to read too much into the question. "Someday. When the time is right."

"Twins, maybe?" he asked, turning to look at her again.

Marissa turned and gave him a dubious look. "What do I look like to you, a glutton for punishment?"

Dylan had to laugh. "So, am I to understand that being a twin is a lot better than *having* twins?"

"I'd say that was a safe assumption."

"How about Mallory? Is she going to have twins?"

"Graywolf's the one with second sight," she said, giving him another playful swat. "Not me."

"Oh, yeah, that's right," he said dryly, holding up an arm to deflect the blow. "I forgot, you just read your sister's mind. He reads everybody elses." He turned his head and gave her a smile. "Weird."

"It's not weird," she muttered, shaking her head. The rays from the afternoon sun had become too much for her fair skin, and she pushed herself up out of the chair. She walked around the chairs to a shady spot on the steps leading to the commons. Sitting down, she leaned her head back against the railing post and closed her eyes. "It's not weird at all. It's just a . . . a *twins'* thing."

Dylan's gaze followed her as she moved past, a slow smile spreading across his lips. He enjoyed just sitting there with her, talking and relaxing—enjoyed just about everything about her, in fact. Especially the way she looked. Her long legs were smooth and golden in the breezy little shorts she had on, and his body stirred, remembering them wrapped around him.

They'd talked about twins, he thought as he watched the hot summer breeze blow a lock of hair across her face. The subject of twins had been a sensitive one for him for a very long time, bringing back memories he'd wanted to forget. But all that was different now. After the day they'd had together, after the night they'd shared, the subject didn't seem so unpleasant any longer, those memories so dim he could hardly see them anymore, so far away, it was as if they'd never existed at all. A heavy burden had finally been lifted off his shoulders, and he was free of it at last.

"A twins' thing, huh?" he said, leaning forward in his chair. "Like . . . trading places?"

Despite the summer heat, Marissa went cold all over. Like a baseball through a windowpane, the quiet, lazy afternoon shattered into a million pieces all around her. She sat up, turning to look up at him, and stared the past in the face. "Dylan, I—"

He stood up, walking across the patio to where she sat. It had been stupid to bring it up like that—so flippantly, so lightly. He'd just been feeling so good, so free of the past, he'd wanted to free her of it, too.

He reached down, grabbing her hand and pulling her to her feet. "Don't look so worried," he said quietly, reaching up and running a hand along her cheek. "It was a long time ago."

"But it was a bad time," she confessed, not able to meet his dark gaze. "I—I don't know if I'm ready to talk about it yet."

His dark eyes narrowed, and his hands settled lightly on her hips. "Maybe it's time we did. Maybe it's time we were honest with each other."

Marissa squeezed her eyes tight. Honest? How could she be honest?

He was right, they should be honest with each other. There should be no lies, no secrets, no misunderstandings between them. But there was so much he didn't know.

She looked up at him, searching his face—the anger and the loathing she'd once seen in his eyes sixteen years ago haunted her. But there was no anger in his clear, dark gaze now—no fury or outrage. But if she were to be honest with him now, *really* honest—if she were to tell him about Josh, about everything—what would she see in his eyes then?

"You're right," she admitted, letting her arms drift up and encircle his neck. "It's just been so wonderful today—being with you, being together." She clutched at his shirt, her hand balling into fists as a wave of desperation swept through her. "I don't want anything to spoil it."

The urgency in her voice surprised him, and he felt his heart lurch in his chest. It had been a wonderful day for him, too. And it was because it had been so wonderful between them that he'd felt the need to clean the slate of any remnants of the past, lay them to rest once and for all.

"Nothing's going to spoil this," he said, pulling her close. "Not this time."

"You sound so sure," she whispered as he brushed his lips to hers. She wanted desperately to believe him, wanted to believe that nothing would change the way it was between them right now.

"I am sure," he murmured against her lips, pulling her tighter against him. "Because I love you, and that's never going to change."

Marissa felt her whole world tilt, felt the ringing in her ears become a roar. Tears stung the lids of her eyes, and the air seemed to lose its way to her lungs. He loved her. Dylan James loved Marissa Wakefield.

"Dylan," she murmured, wanting to tell him about the feelings swelling in her heart, wanting to tell him how much she loved him, too, but his mouth had locked on to hers, and she could think of nothing else.

But even as she found herself succumbing to the passion of his kiss, even as she felt herself being swept away by the growing need inside her, a cold spot of dread had begun to form at the core of her heart. She had to tell him the truth about Josh. He had to know about his son.

"Dylan," she said, tearing her mouth free from his. "Dylan, I have to... I have to tell you—"

"Later," he growled, cutting her off with a voice made rough with need.

Marissa felt the words die on her tongue. She couldn't think when he was kissing her, couldn't remember voices or commands—or maybe it was just that she didn't want to. She told herself there would be time later for the truth, consoled herself that there would be time to be honest later. Now she let him sweep her up in one swift motion and carry her through the house.

After that there would only be vague recollections of tangled sheets on the bed, clothes scattered around on the floor and faded sunlight drifting through the shades. The sequence of events were unimportant—the only thing that mattered was that she was with Dylan, and that he loved her.

"Oh, yeah, and you would have noticed me."

"I would have," Dylan insisted, absently running a hand back and forth along the swell of her hip. The setting sun through the window painted the sky a brilliant canvas of soft, rosy hues, casting the entire bedroom into dark, muted shadow and making her skin glow like warm, rich gold. "Eventually."

"Yeah, right," Marissa snorted inelegantly. Two hours ago she never would have believed she could be lying there casually joking about the time in her life—the one time in her life—when she'd wanted to be her sister. But two hours ago she hadn't known that Dylan loved her. She knew it now, and it had changed everything. "The fact is, Mr. Hotshot Quarterback, you wouldn't have given the captain of the debate team the time of day. But a cheerleader with a cute little short skirt..." She purposely let her words fade into the twilight, making her point. "Well, now, that was a different story."

"Are you trying to say I was superficial?"

She made a play of acting bored—checking her nails, polishing them against the sheet. "If the shoe fits."

Dylan slowly pulled her beneath him, framing her face with his hands. "Speaking of shoes fitting."

Marissa smiled as he bent his head low for a kiss. She loved the good-natured ribbing. There had been too little of it in her life—too little of him.

She was beginning to understand why he'd struck out at her all those years ago, how he'd thrown up a smoke screen of flippancy and fury to cover the fact that she'd hurt him. If only she hadn't been so blinded by her own shattered feelings—their lives could have been so different.

But there was no going back. She'd been given a second chance, and she was going to make the most of it. She wanted it all now—Dylan and their son—and she wasn't going to let anything stand in her way of getting it.

"You know, maybe I wasn't the only one who was superficial back then," he murmured, planting small kisses along the line of her jaw to her ear.

"*You're* calling *me* superficial?" she said, lifting her head off the pillow and arching her brows indignantly. "You? With your letterman's jacket and football jersey?"

"*I'm* calling *you* superficial," he repeated, settling back against the pillows.

"How do you figure?" she insisted, rising up on her elbow and cradling her head in her hand.

"Oh, the fact that I was quarterback on the football team didn't make a difference to you?"

"Of course it didn't," she insisted, faltering just a little. "Well, I mean—"

"And I suppose if I had been on the chess team instead," he said, cutting her off, "you would have been just as anxious to meet me, right?"

"Well—" she said with a little laugh, but again he cut her off.

"And I guess if I'd walked around school with a pocket protector instead of a letterman's jacket, you still would have wanted to go out with me."

"Dylan, this is silly—"

"Because none of that other stuff mattered to you." He turned to her and gave her a smug look. "Did it?"

Marissa looked up into his dark, handsome face and started to feel pretty smug herself. "Wrong."

Dylan blinked and laughed. "Wrong?"

"Wrong. It did," she said simply, running her hand slowly down the length of him. "I admit it. You were right. It wasn't your mind I was after."

"No?"

"Of course not," she said simply, sliding her hand down around his bottom and giving him a squeeze. "It was your body. Actually, it was your butt in those tight football pants."

A slow smile crept across his face. "So it was purely physical, then."

"Of course," she said flippantly, moving her body close to his, giving his buns a squeeze again. "It still is."

"For me, too," he laughed, pressing a kiss against her lips. But the kiss became long, and sweet, and when it had

ended, Dylan's breathing was shallow and uneven. "I...
never meant them," he whispered against her lips. "All
those stupid things I said, I never meant them."

"I know," she murmured, her heart swelling. And for
the first time in sixteen years she did.

"All right, look, lady," Dylan said loudly after a moment, breaking the mood for both their sakes. "If you're
going to keep me here and expect me to continue your car-
nal appetites, don't you think you could at least feed me?"

Marissa laughed, realizing just how hungry she was, too.
The meal they fixed turned out to be a collaborative effort, Dylan pulling two frozen trout from the freezer and
defrosting them in the microwave while Marissa cut up
hearts of romaine and shredded fresh Parmesan cheese for
a Caesar salad. They lingered at the table long after their
appetites had been appeased, drinking white wine and
chatting casually—talking about old times, and filling in
the gaps. They'd started the day out as lovers, and were
ending it by making a momentous leap to friends.

"I can't believe it," Dylan said after she'd told him the
whole story of her broken ankle and how she'd injured it
while helping a young, and very pregnant, Navaho woman
and her daughter, and then how all three of them had become stranded in the desolate wilderness of Arizona's Big
Res. He reached across the table and wove his fingers
through hers. "You must have been so scared."

"Getting lost and then outrunning a flash flood didn't
bother me," she said with false bravado. "But when Ruth
went into labor." She stopped and shook her head. "*That*
was scary."

He leaned forward, bringing her fingers to his lips, kissing them. "Promise me you won't go roving the wilderness any longer, okay?"

She smiled, wondering if it was possible to be any happier than she was at that moment. The truth still hung over
her head like a dark cloud on the horizon, and she knew

that someday she would have to go to Dylan with it. But not tonight ... not tonight.

"Dylan," she murmured, leaning forward and pulling his hand to her lips. "I love you."

Dylan looked up at her, feeling his heart stop in his chest, and the air leave his lungs in one long, involuntary sigh. The moment stretched out—defying convention and the limits of time. He wanted to just stay there and absorb it, feel it in his pores and let it seep into his skin. He wanted to preserve and to hold on to as much as he could, for as long as he could.

The telephone warbled quietly, causing them both to jump and bringing the real world back into focus again.

"Talk about a mood breaker," he said, his wry tone covering just how deeply shaken he was.

It warbled again, and Marissa glanced down at the hand he still held. "I should answer it."

Dylan looked at their hands, too. "It would be wrong to just let it ring, wouldn't it?"

His look of regret was very real, and her heart swelled with emotion. "Very wrong."

"I was afraid of that," he mumbled, reluctantly letting her go.

The phone sounded again as Marissa stood and started across the kitchen. She reached for the handset, lifting it from its cradle, and lifted it to her ear.

"Hello?" Marissa felt her throat tighten as she listened to the familiar voice on the other end of the line. She glanced across the kitchen to Dylan, sitting quietly at the table, and felt the feeling of dread grow. "Josh, sweetie, hi, how are you?"

Chapter 13

Marissa waved one last time, watching as the Scalettis'
minivan disappeared around the corner. She turned to Josh
beside her, and put an arm around his sturdy shoulder,
giving it a squeeze. "I missed you."

Josh grinned, the color in his cheeks rising. "I missed
you, too."

"You hungry?" she asked as they started up the walk
together. "I've got some cold cuts and cheese. I could fix
you a sandwich."

Josh shook his head, holding the front door open and
following her in. "Maybe later. We stopped on the way
home for fast food." He tossed his duffel bag down on the
bottom step of the stairs as he followed her through the
house toward the kitchen, patting a hand over his stomach. "I'm still stuffed."

Marissa laughed, knowing that probably wouldn't last
much longer. "Then let's get something cold to drink," she
said, flipping on the kitchen light and opening up the refrigerator. "I want to hear everything about your week-

end. Did you have a good time, what was the beach house like, did you and Nico get along?''

Josh made a play of rolling his eyes, but Marissa knew he was pleased by all her questions. He liked it that she was interested, liked it that what he did mattered to her. He hadn't had enough of that in his life the last few years. Penny had been too caught up in her own problems after Caleb died to give Josh the kind of attention he'd needed, and Marissa was determined to make up to him for that. Besides, she really was interested. She'd missed enough of her son's life already, she didn't want to miss anything more.

And Josh didn't disappoint her. Despite his protestations, he hopped up on the stool at the kitchen counter and started on a full accounting of his weekend away—including picnics on the beach, playing Hacky Sack in the sand, boogie-boarding in the surf, and watching Fourth of July fireworks from the cliffs overlooking the ocean.

Marissa listened, watching his dark eyes flash bright with humor and excitement as he talked, thinking how far he'd come from that scared, troubled kid she'd taken custody of only six weeks ago. It was so good between them, being together had changed both their lives for the better, and she didn't want anything to ever change that.

But having Dylan in her life was a big change, and as she stood there, sipping a cold drink and listening to Josh chatter on, she couldn't help wondering how he was going to react to the news.

Her weekend with Dylan had been wonderful—virtually like a dream come true. She had no second thoughts, no regrets—how could she? She loved Dylan, and it still seemed too good to be true that he loved her back. It felt so good between them, so right, as though fate had lent a hand because they were meant to be together. Still, she couldn't help being apprehensive about the prospect of telling Josh. How many more changes could Josh take in his life? How would he feel about Dylan being a part of her life, and a part of *their* life together?

And yet, telling Josh about her feelings for Dylan was just going to be the beginning. Sooner or later she was going to have to tell them both the truth—the whole truth. They were father and son—they had to know, and somehow find a way to make them understand.

Marissa drew in a deep breath, and rubbed at the tension building at the bridge of her nose. One step at a time, she reminded herself. She could only take one step at a time. First she had to tell Josh how she felt about Dylan— had to help him get used to the idea, get comfortable with it. She'd worry about the rest of it later.

"You okay?"

Marissa abruptly stopped massaging her forehead and glanced across the counter at Josh. "Sure, I'm fine. Why?"

"I don't know," he said, gesturing to her forehead. "I just thought you looked a little worried. Your head ache?"

"No, I'm fine," she insisted, shaking her head and flashing him a bright smile. She waved him on with her hand. "Finish your story."

"Oh, okay. Anyway, the fireworks were really cool. It was really fun, well . . . until Dino and Gina got scared of the dark and the noise from the fireworks," he said, referring to Jill and Dom Scaletti's two youngest children. "And started crying."

"Poor things," Marissa said, taking a sip of her soda. "But you know, I remember being scared of those loud bangs during the fireworks displays on the Fourth when I was little."

"Yeah, me, too," Josh admitted, reaching for the soda can and pouring the rest of it over the ice in his glass. His expression grew wistful. "Dad used to let me sit on his lap, and would cover my ears with his hands."

"Yeah, I remember that, too," Marissa said, reaching out and running her hand along his cheek. "You miss him a lot, don't you."

"Yeah, I do," Josh murmured. "And my mom." He was quiet for a moment, then pushed his feelings aside with a deep breath and went on. "When the kids started crying, Mrs. Scaletti said we were all going to have to go back to the house, but then Nico and I started playing Hacky Sack in the dark. We were falling down and goofing around—it was pretty funny, and the kids got laughing and sort of forgot about the noise and being scared."

Marissa studied him as he talked, watching his expression change. Just like Dylan, Josh had used a tough act and smart attitude to hide how much pain he'd been in after losing Caleb, but that was changing. He was a different kid than he was six weeks ago—happier, freer and a lot better able to deal with life.

"Jill says Nico usually loves to tease the little ones," she said, seeing the affection in his face.

"He calls them the rug rats," Josh pointed out. "They drive him crazy."

Marissa laughed. "Sounds like you got along with them pretty well, though."

Josh looked up and shrugged. "I guess. Oh, they could be a pain sometimes, but they're actually kinda cute." His eyes grew wide as he laughed out loud. "But you should hear Nico describe the new baby coming—he does this thing like a preview for a movie that's coming. It drives his mom crazy." Trying his best not to smile, Josh cleared his throat loudly and made his voice boom. "No one is safe. It knows where you live. It's loud, it doesn't always smell very good. It's—" he made the sound of a drumroll "—Rug Rat Part V—The Final Conflict." He then dropped his voice down an octave. "Coming soon to a theater near you."

Marissa laughed at his crazy joking, but a small band of remorse twisted at her heart. He had so much to give—so much love and humor. He needed people in his life, needed a family—brothers, sisters, mother and father. He would like playing the role of "big brother," he would be loving and protective of a younger sibling, and she regretted once again all the things he'd missed out on.

They talked for a while longer, and Josh continued to make her laugh with his silly stories and joking around.

"Mrs. Scaletti told me how you used to help her baby-sit her little brothers and sisters," Josh said after a while, reaching for his glass of soda and finishing it. "You two must have been pretty good friends back in high school."

"Yeah, we were," Marissa said, remembering the noisy Lawrence house with its endless bedrooms and countless children. "It was rough on them after their mom died."

Josh took a deep breath. "I can relate to that."

"I guess you could," she said, reaching across the kitchen counter and patting his arm affectionately. But she saw him mask his sad eyes with a teasing sparkle.

"She also told me something else," he said with a cryptic smile.

"Oh?" she said warily. "I'm almost afraid to ask."

"She said she always got the idea that you had a secret crush on Sheriff James."

"What?" Marissa gasped, a loud ringing sounding in her ears.

"Yeah," he said, laughing. "That you used to talk about him a lot and watch him all the time."

Marissa groaned, feeling heat pour into her cheeks. She'd hoped to broach the subject of Dylan, but this wasn't exactly the lead-in she'd been looking for. "She said that?"

Josh's smile widened. "Yes, she did."

Marissa quickly picked up their empty glasses and carried them to the sink. "Well, you'll have to remind me to thank Jill next time I see her."

Josh leaned across the counter toward her, his eyes dancing. "Auntie Mar, I think you're blushing."

"Don't be ridiculous."

"Did you get all hot and bothered by Sheriff James back in high school?"

"I'm not talking about this," she said sternly. He only laughed that much harder. She busily placed the glasses on a rack in the dishwasher and carefully wiped her hand on a towel.

"I'll bet he got all hot and bothered over you."

Crossing her arms over her chest, she leaned back against the sink and regarded him for a moment. "Gee, it would be a real shame if I had to discuss with the teachers on my staff the idea of assigning additional homework to *certain* students in their classes."

The smile on Josh's face abruptly stiffened, and the laughter choked in his throat. "Okay, okay," he said, his hands coming up in a gesture of surrender. "You win. I get the message. The subject is closed."

A slow smile spread across her face. "I thought you might see things my way."

"You never told me what you did this weekend," Josh said after a while. "Did you go over to Gram and Gramps for the Fourth?"

She thought of lying in Dylan's arms and how they'd made their own fireworks on the Fourth, and her cheeks went warm. "Uh—no, actually, I didn't."

"No?" Josh's brow furrowed. "You spent the weekend alone?"

"For the most part," she said, hedging. It wasn't really a lie, she told herself. She was *alone* with Dylan. Didn't that count? "I worked a little, but mostly I just stayed around the house."

Josh's frown deepened. "I hope you weren't lonely."

"No, no, I wasn't," she insisted, shaking her head. Her palms were moist and sticky, and she wiped them along the smooth cotton of her shorts. It wasn't that the opportunity hadn't presented itself, because it had—it had practically fallen into her lap. He'd asked her about her weekend, and this was the perfect time to tell him. And she'd been practicing all afternoon various ways she could go about telling him what had happened while he was away....

Well, not *exactly* what had happened while he was away, but how she and Dylan were . . . that they were . . .

Were what? Boyfriend and girlfriend? That sounded ridiculous. Were they an item? Seeing each other? What did she say? What was the tactful way to tell your fifteen-year-old son you'd just taken a lover?

She closed her eyes tight. She felt confused and embarrassed. None of those well-rehearsed speeches were right; she had no idea what to say.

"Actually, Josh," she started again, taking a deep breath. "Actually there's something—"

But the telephone rang and threw her thoughts into chaos. She wasn't sure she was angry or relieved, but she reached quickly for the phone before it had a chance to ring again.

"Have you told him yet?" Dylan's voice over the line sounded anxious.

"Hello," she said in a false voice. "How are you?"

"I take it that means no?" he surmised dryly.

"Right." She nodded, smiling at Josh. "That's right."

"Maybe I should come over?"

"No!" Marissa gasped. She made a dismissive gesture with her hand when Josh looked up, surprised. "No, that's okay. I can take care of it."

"You sure?" Dylan asked.

"Yes," she said, nodding her head again. "Yes, I'm sure."

"Okay," Dylan conceded, sounding disappointed.

"But call me afterward, okay?"

"Okay."

"I miss you," he said in a low voice.

"Yes, well," Marissa said in a businesslike tone. "That certainly goes for me, too."

"And, Marissa?"

"Yes?"

"I love you."

Marissa closed her eyes tight, feeling a soothing warmth spread through her body. "Me, too."

"Who was that?" Josh asked as she hung up the phone.

"Oh, just someone from the district," she lied, feeling guilty. "Business stuff. But there is something I'd like to talk to you about."

"Okay," he said, giving her a half smile. "But first, you said something about a sandwich?"

"Marissa said she talked to you."

Josh finished driving the nail into the two-by-four, pounding it flat, and slipped the wooden handle of the hammer through a leather ring on his carpenter's belt. Turning around, he looked up at Dylan, his frown deepening. "Yeah, she did."

Dylan waited a moment. It made him furious to think he was nervous—and yet he was. A year ago if anyone would have told him he would be asking Josh Wakefield's approval on anything, he'd have laughed in their face. But here he was—practically with hat in hand—waiting with bated breath for what the kid would say next, and feeling a little like he had on that summer night sixteen years ago when he'd shown up at the Wakefield's house on the hill for his first date with Marissa.

He looked into Josh's eyes, trying to decipher an emotion in them, but it was impossible. His dark gaze revealed nothing, and Dylan felt his anxiety level increase a degree.

"Well?" he prompted after a moment, biting back his impatience. "You have a reaction?"

"Yeah," Josh said pointedly, his hands resting at his sides a little like a gunfighter squaring off against an opponent. "Yeah, I have a reaction."

Dylan worked his jaw restlessly. "You want to talk about it?"

"What's to talk about?" Josh asked abruptly, his eyes narrowing. "I don't want her hurt."

"Good," Dylan said, picking up a screwdriver from the ledge of the window frame and handing it to him. Josh loved Marissa, and it was only natural he would be protective of her. But Dylan felt protective, too. "Then we're agreed."

"Are we?" Josh took the screwdriver and slipped it into his belt alongside the hammer.

Dylan heard the hostility in his adolescent voice, and the suspicion. But he also heard the concern, and something in Josh's face flashed vulnerable and open. For an instant it stirred something in Dylan's memory—something familiar and vague, something he recognized and could relate to, but it was there for just an instant—and then it was gone.

"Look, Josh," he said, pushing the thought aside. "I care about your aunt very much. The last thing I'd want to do is hurt her. I hope you believe that."

Josh drew a deep breath, and dropped his gaze to the ground. Letting out the breath in one long sigh, he took a step back. "Yeah, I guess I do."

"I plan to see her as much as she'll let me," Dylan said, laying out his intentions. "I hope you're not going to have a problem with that."

Josh looked up at him and snorted humorlessly. "Would it make a difference if I did?"

Dylan smiled just a little. "Probably not," he said honestly, his voice losing some of its sternness. "But I know it would mean a lot to Marissa if she thought she had..."

"My approval?" Josh said, filling in the blanks after Dylan's words drifted.

Dylan's smile grew wider. "Something like that, I guess."

"And what about you, Sheriff?" Josh asked, kneeling down and picking up a handful of nails from the box on the floor.

There was more wit in his voice than worry, so Dylan didn't take offense. "What about me?"

Josh looked up at him. "You looking for my approval, too?"

Dylan gave him a deliberate look. "Are you offering it?"

Josh stood up, tossing the handful of nails into the pocket of his belt. "I've got nothing against you—except maybe that you hauled my butt into jail a few times too many." He bent down, wedging a small piece of two-by-four into the frame, bracing it. "Aunt Marissa is the best person I've ever met in my life. She's done nothing but good—taking care of everyone else's lives—the kids she teaches, Gram and Gramp, Aunt Mallory, my mom and dad. And now me." He slipped the hammer from his belt and pounded the brace into place. Finishing it, he straightened up again and turned to face Dylan. "She deserves to be happy. If you can do that, you'll have no problem with me."

Dylan looked at Josh, feeling a little as though he were looking at him for the first time. He barely looked like the same young punk who'd created a minor reign of terror in the community for the last two years. Dylan didn't pretend to know anything about kids, but he came across his fair share of troubled ones in his line of work, and there hadn't been one any more troubled than Josh Wakefield. But this wasn't that same smart-talking, cocky youthful offender he'd arrested three months ago. Was that because of Marissa?

He felt a warmth spread through him—a warmth that had nothing to do with the hot afternoon sun. If anyone knew the power of her healing love, it was him. She'd come back to him and breathed life into him again—revived and rejuvenated him in a way he would have thought was impossible.

He looked at Josh again. Marissa had performed this miracle. Her love and understanding had transformed that raw, angry juvenile delinquent into this down-to-earth, caring young man.

Dylan had that feeling again—that curious flash of memory, that peculiar feeling of awareness and recognition. But just as before, it was there for only an instant and then it disappeared.

"Sounds fair," Dylan said with a nod. He really didn't want to think about how relieved he felt, didn't want to think about how maybe this kid was beginning to mean something to him. "And look at it this way, Josh—" he stopped, jerking his thumb in the direction behind him "—it could be worse. She could be seeing Goofus Bug over there."

Josh glanced across the construction site to where Rick Mathers stood instructing Randy with a power saw, and grinned wide. "Be thankful for small favors, I guess."

"Oh, hey, speaking of goofus bugs," Dylan said, searching through his pocket. He pulled out a plastic bag, which held a small fishing fly. "Take a look at this."

Josh took the bag from him and opened it. "What is it?" he asked, holding up the small clump of colorful feathers and string.

"It's a Mother Lode mudder," Dylan announced proudly. "Something I came up with myself."

"I suppose you were sent in here to butter me up."

Dylan stepped up close from behind her and slipped his arms around her waist. "I don't know what you're talking about."

Marissa did her best to finish rinsing the dishes with him nuzzling her neck. It had been the most wonderful two weeks of her life. She was so happy, it almost frightened

her. How much more could she ask from life? She had the
man she loved, and she had the son they shared. Her life
had become very, very good.

Their lives seemed to have meshed remarkably, almost as
though they were meant to be together. They were a family, and together they seemed to be thriving. Summer school
was drawing to a close, construction of the shed was pro-
gressing well, and Dylan had become a permanent fixture
around their house in the evenings. They'd gone to movies
together, on picnics and bicycle rides—she'd even let them
talk her into going fishing with them once. And even with
all of that, she and Dylan had managed to find time to
work on the juvenile work-study proposal, and had presented it, to rave reviews, to their committee. It had been
sent to the board of supervisors for consideration, but
they'd all agreed it would pass with no resistance at all.

Of course, finding time to be alone hadn't always been
easy. She didn't want to do anything that would make Josh
feel awkward or uncomfortable. But there had been occasional evenings alone, and they'd been wonderful.

"I know exactly what you're trying to do," she said,
trying her best to sound stern and disapproving. "But it's
not going to work."

"Isn't it?" he murmured, tightening his hold. He pulled
her close and brushed her bottom against him, making her
aware it was working for him.

"*Dylan,*" she gasped in horror, feeling the indisputable
evidence of his arousal against her. She quickly pulled
away, holding him at arm's length. "Josh is right in the
next room. He'll see us."

Dylan had to smile at the deep color filling her cheeks,
and he took a step closer despite her feeble attempts to stop
him. "You mean you don't think he knows that we've—"

"Will you stop it? He'll hear you," she said in a low
voice, sending a nervous glance in the direction of the living room.

His smile grew wider. "Marissa, you're blushing."

"No, I'm not," she insisted, but embarrassedly felt her cheeks glow hot. "Not really."

"Yes, you are," he said, backing her up against the counter. "Relax, will you? Why are you so uptight? Josh isn't a baby. He knows the score." He bent down, plucking a kiss on the tip of her nose. "Or he's got a pretty good idea. He's not bothered—why should you be?"

"I know," Marissa admitted with a long sigh, relaxing a little. "You're right. It's just, I need a little time, you know, to get comfortable." She slid her hands up the front of his shirt. "I guess I'm a little rusty at having a *boyfriend*."

"Boyfriend, huh?" Dylan made a face and pulled her close. "I like the term *lover* better." He gave her hips a little twist. "And it's certainly a more appropriate description, wouldn't you say?"

Marissa gave him a stern look. "When it comes to Josh, it's boyfriend—got it?"

"I got it," Dylan said with a laugh. He brushed a light kiss along her lips. "And as your boyfriend I'm curious to know when we can get together for another..." He purposely let his words drift, giving his eyebrows a wicked wiggle. "A *date*." He brushed more kisses against her mouth. "Because I've really liked *dating* the last couple of weeks." He kissed lightly along her chin, her cheek, her ear. "And look forward to *dating* again soon." He kissed her full on the mouth this time. "And *dating* many more times in the future."

"I look forward to it, too," Marissa whispered, feeling her cheeks grow warm again. But when she looked up into his dark eyes, the warmth suddenly spread throughout her body.

Dylan groaned and kissed her again. But there was nothing playful or teasing about it this time—his desire was simply too strong. He felt the need building within him—that desperate, urgent need that was always just below the surface whenever he was with her, whenever he touched her, whenever he so much as thought of her. The hold on her hips tensed, and he pressed her to him tight.

"I've missed you," he whispered against her ear. "Missed feeling you, being with you, waking up with you."

"I've missed it, too," she murmured, desire feeling thick and breathless in her throat.

A shudder rumbled through him, and he drew in a shaky breath. He looked down into her eyes, resting their foreheads together. His chest heaved, and he could feel the throb of his heart pulsating at his temples, and inside his brain. Tension arced between them—strong and potent. "Maybe we should...uh..."

"Yes," Marissa agreed, clearing her throat. "Maybe we should."

After several more deep breaths, he set her purposefully away from him. "I don't know about this boyfriend thing," he said, taking a step back and putting distance between them. "I'm not sure I have the temperament or the patience."

He joked, but Marissa recognized the vulnerable look in his eyes—the need—and her heart swelled with love.

"Well, you know what they say," she said, pushing away from the counter. "All things come to those who wait." She gave him a quick peck on the cheek as she passed, pausing just long enough to whisper in his ear. "And Josh goes to bed around ten-thirty."

Instantly Dylan's gaze shifted to the clock on the wall. Seven-fifteen. It would be hours before he could touch her, hours before he could taste her lips, or feel her soft skin against him.

He watched her as she began clearing up the counter again—loading the dishwasher and straightening up. He might be able to wait, but he could never be patient.

"So what about Josh going with me on Friday?" he asked after a moment, desperate to move his thoughts to something else and away from the sight of her beautiful breasts shifting just slightly beneath her cotton shirt every time that she moved.

"See? I knew you were just buttering me up," Marissa teased, slipping the dinner plates into the dishwasher.

"Okay, okay, I admit it. I'm buttering you up." He reached for two glasses from the counter and handed them to her to stack in the dishwasher. "Can he come?"

Marissa slid the glasses into the top rack. "Finals start on Monday. The whole idea of not having classes Thursday and Friday is to give the kids extra time to study. Besides, he still has to report to the construction site by one o'clock."

"But it's just a few hours on one morning. And I promise we'd be back in time for him to report to work."

Marissa reached for a few more dishes and loaded them onto the racks. "I don't know. He really needs the time to study."

Dylan reached across the dishwasher, and ran a finger along the line of her cheek. "We really want to test out this new fly. I even taught Josh how to tie it himself." He gave her a helpless look. "Come on, it's summer vacation. It's just a few hours of fishing. A kid's got to have some fun."

"Two kids, you mean," she corrected him, folding her arms over her chest. She thought for a minute, giving him a stern look. "You'll have him back by one?"

"Cross my heart," Dylan said solemnly, making the gesture across his chest.

"All right," she said reluctantly. "But only if he hits the books tonight."

Dylan reached over the top of the load of dirty dishes that separated them and put a finger beneath her chin, tilting her head up for a kiss. "You're a pushover, you know that, don't you?"

"Only when it comes to certain people," she murmured as he kissed her again.

"We'll bring you back another line of trout," he whispered, his hand slowly moving along her cheek and encircling her neck.

"Don't you dare," she warned. "I can't get rid of the ones I've got now."

Dylan smiled as he kissed her again. "What time did you say Josh went to bed?"

Chapter 14

"You want to talk about it?"

Josh swore again, sucking the spot on his fingertip where the hook had pierced the skin. "Talk about what?"

Dylan slid the top off the clear plastic box that held his various selections of flies, and began searching through the small divided compartments. Josh had been distracted and irritable since he'd stopped by the condo to pick him up, and the teen's moodiness had only gotten worse as the morning sun grew hotter and the fish seemed less and less interested in biting. "Come on, Josh, something's been eating at you all morning. What's going on?"

"It's nothing," Josh insisted carelessly, but his frown deepened. "Just in a bad mood, I guess."

Dylan selected the fly he wanted and carefully slid the lid closed on the box. "Have anything to do with Marissa and me?"

"No," Josh snorted sarcastically, snatching up his pole and standing up. "Why?"

"Just curious." Dylan shrugged. "Thought if you had some second thoughts we could talk about it."

Josh shook his head, swiping at the sweat beading up along his forehead. He adjusted the reel on his pole, and made a few practice casting motions. "You?"

"What? Having second thoughts?"

"Yeah."

Dylan had to smile, thinking they were both pretty good at feeling their way *around* a subject. "Only in wondering if this fishing hole is as good as I remembered it." He gestured with his chin to the two lone trout threaded onto their tie lines. "The only one who seems to be getting hungry around here is me."

Josh released his hook, and started to cast rapidly. "What's the matter, Sheriff? Afraid of being shown up by a juvenile delinquent again?"

Dylan laughed, but he heard the hard edge to Josh's humor. He finished making the last loop to secure the fly to the line and came slowly to his feet. "There's nothing I like better, kid, than a challenge. Stand back and watch a master work." He moved a short distance down the bank and began casting. However, he continued to watch Josh from the corner of his eye. "So," he said after a while. "If you're okay with Marissa and me, what's got you in such a bad mood?"

"Nothing," Josh said as he continued casting. But it was obvious his concentration wasn't there. His normally smooth, fluid motions were stiff and clumsy. "Just... stuff."

"Stuff?" Dylan asked as he stopped casting and lowered his pole to his side. "Or Skip?"

Josh's line tangled in the dense limbs of a scrub oak tree on the far side of the stream. "What do you know?"

"I know he's loaded most of the time," Dylan said, walking carefully along the bank toward him. "I know he's got himself involved in something that's liable to blow up in his face, and that he's in way over his head."

"That's got nothing to do with me," Josh said angrily, yanking on the line, trying to pull it free.

"Maybe," Dylan said purposely. "Maybe not."

Josh yanked harder. The thin test line snapped from the violent jerk and sent tree leaves and the pole flying free. Angry, Josh turned to Dylan, tossing the pole onto the ground near his feet.

"What the hell is that supposed to mean? Is that what all this is about—the fishing trips, the big buddy routine, the little heart-to-hearts? You want to bust Skip?"

Dylan felt the full brunt of Josh's angry words, and they hit him like a hard right to the jaw. Something in Josh's eyes had Dylan hesitating, had him scanning his memory again and searching for something, searching for...

For *what?* Frustrated, Dylan tossed his own pole down, and drew in a deep breath. What was it about the kid that got to him? Was it because he saw so much of himself in the kid, saw so much of his own confusion, his own frustration, his own anger?

"Is that what you really think?" he asked Josh, wondering how the words of this angry teenager could hurt so much.

"What am I supposed to think?" Josh demanded, turning away. "You practically accused me of doing that junk with Skip."

"I wasn't accusing you," Dylan insisted, taking a step closer. "I'm...I'm..." He started to reach out, started to comfort, to console, but his hand stilled in midair and fell back to his side. "I'm worried about you, that's all."

Josh whirled back around. "Worried about *me?* Or interested in impressing my aunt?"

"Josh, come on," Dylan said quietly, taking another step closer. "You know me better than that."

Josh stared at him, his chest heaving with emotion. "Do I?"

Dylan stopped in his tracks. There was no anger in Josh's eyes now—only sadness, and a loneliness that reached out to him on a purely emotional level. He and Josh Wakefield had led very different lives—had faced different hardships and different obstacles. But there was something about this young man, something Dylan identified with, some chord of communion he understood and empathized with.

Dylan knew what it was to be on the outside looking in. He'd grown up poor, on the wrong side of the tracks, wanting more than he could have, and settling for less than he really needed. For him there had never been enough material things in his life—money, clothes, cars. But for Josh, it had been very different. Josh had had all the money he'd wanted, all his material needs taken care of. But what he'd lacked, what he'd needed most, was someone to hang on to.

Dylan finally understood Marissa's devotion to this boy, why she fought so hard and cared so much. He'd cared, too.

"Yes," Dylan said quietly. "I think you do. And I think you know you can trust me. Something's going on with you. You need help."

Josh squeezed his eyes shut tight, and his shoulders slumped in defeat. "No one can help."

"That's not true." Dylan's hand came out again, but this time he didn't back down. He reached for Josh's shoulder, gripping it tight. "If you don't want to talk to me, I'll understand, but Marissa loves you, and you know you can trust her. Talk to her. She would do anything—"

"No!" Josh said adamantly, his eyes flashing open as he cut Dylan off. "I don't want her involved in this. She's done enough for me, she doesn't need anything more to worry about."

Dylan saw that fierce protectiveness again, and understood it. "Then talk to me."

"Talk," Josh snorted, making a helpless gesture with his hands. "Talk's just talk. It doesn't solve anything."

"Sometimes," Dylan sighed. "But sometimes it does." He slid his arm around Josh's shoulder, and walked with him to a fallen tree trunk near the stream's edge and sat him down. "What's going on?"

Josh drew in a deep breath, his hands balling into fists. "You already know most of it. Skip's sort of flipped out."

"I've suspected for a while there's been some drug use," Dylan said. "And burglaries."

Josh's eyes widened. "You know about the burglaries, too?"

"Small town," Dylan said with a shrug. "And snitches aren't called snitches for nothing. That bull about honor among thieves is just that—bull!"

"Then why haven't you arrested him?"

"On what? Suspicion and loose talk?" Dylan leaned back, shaking his head. He hesitated a moment, giving Josh a quick glance from the corner of his eye. "Besides, I bring him in, the D.A.'s going to want you and Randy brought in, too."

Josh's head jerked up, and he swallowed hard. "Then that really could happen?"

"That was the ruling of the judge. Just a way to make sure one of you doesn't lead the others astray. Sounds like you've had some concerns about that."

"Some," Josh conceded with a shrug. "I didn't know if it was really true, if it could actually happen."

"It could," Dylan admitted, feeling a few puzzle pieces slip into place. He understood it was important to be honest, but he also had to acknowledge the fear he saw in Josh's eyes, and the need in himself to reassure him. "At least until we could get things straightened out with the courts." He reached over and gave Josh's arm a reassuring

pat. "But it's nothing you need to worry about right now
We haven't actually caught Skip doing anything, and i
takes more than rumors and hearsay to get a conviction."

"But the way Skip's got it figured," Josh said, taking
resigned breath, "he'll never be convicted, because he'l
never get caught."

Dylan shook his head and laughed. "If I had a dime fo
every time I heard some genius say that, I'd be a rich mai
today."

"Skip believes it."

"I don't doubt he does. What he doesn't know is tha
jails are filled with punks like him who thought the same
thing," Dylan explained, squinting to block out the glare
of the sun off the water. He was glad to see that some of the
color had returned to Josh's cheeks, but he could still see
the fear. "But I will bet Skip is smart enough to want to
press any advantage he can."

Josh gave him a guarded look. "What do you mean?"

Dylan stretched his arms back, cradling his head agains
his hands. "Well, I'm just guessing here, but let me run this
by you. The way I see it, Skip is feeling pretty confiden
about now. I mean, let's say he's aware that my hauling hin
in would mean I'd have to haul you in, too. But with you
and I being . . . *friends,* and your Aunt Marissa and I being . . . *friends.*" He paused, and looked back at Josh. "How
am I doing?"

"Pretty good," Josh mumbled. "How did you know?"

"Just a hunch."

"I tried to tell him," Josh said, looking up. His eyes were
red and watery, and his voice cracked with emotion. "I really did—but you know Skip—thinks he knows everything. And he's just been out of control lately. Figures he's
got his ace in the hole—you won't touch him because that
would mean bringing me down, too. He thinks he's got all
the answers he needs."

Dylan sat listening to Josh, watching the tension drain from his muscles and his voice as the words began flowing out. This was what the kid needed—to get it all out, to release some of the tension that had been bottled up. He told Dylan about heated arguments he'd had with Skip, and about Skip's threats and bragging.

There were things Dylan would have liked to have asked, questions he had—especially after Josh had mentioned Skip's taunting remarks about Marissa, and his resentment of her as both an authority figure and a woman. But he decided to keep them until later. It had been hard enough to get Josh talking; he didn't want to do or say anything that might make him clam up again. Besides, he and Marissa had decided not to mention anything to Josh about Skip's attempt to break into the condo for the time being, and he was glad now that they had. Tensions between the two boys were strained enough, and it only would have made things worse.

"And where does Randy fit in all this?" Dylan asked when Josh had finally run down.

"Randy," Josh snorted, and shook his head. "Skip's got him so scared he doesn't know which end is up. He'll do anything Skip tells him to."

"So where does that leave you—odd man out?"

"Me?" Josh scoffed, turning to him. "Don't worry about me. I'm sure as hell not afraid of Skip." He paused for a moment, punching his fist down hard on the tree, scratching the sensitive skin along his knuckles. "And I'm not afraid of going back to jail. Skip's not going to use that against me any more." He brought his fist up, watching droplets of blood begin to ooze up from the scraped skin. "He's not going to push me around."

Dylan sat for a moment, listening to the quiet rush of the stream. "You know, you could have come to me with this. You didn't need to keep this all bottled up. I would have understood."

"I guess I didn't think..." Josh shook his head. "I mean, you're the sheriff. I'm not really used to talking to you about...you know. It seemed kind of..."

"Awkward. I know," Dylan said after Josh's words faded. "But I guess I'd hoped we'd moved beyond that sheriff thing."

Josh stood up, reaching down to pick up a handful of pebbles, and began tossing them into the stream. "Did you mean what you said back there, about us being friends?"

"Sure," Dylan said, leaning forward and resting his elbows on his knees. He watched as Josh sent a pebble flying into the air. "I'd like to think so."

Josh sent another pebble flying, then turned back to Dylan, giving him a cautious look. "You don't sound so sure about it now."

Dylan came slowly to his feet. He saw the challenge in Josh's eyes, and the question. "Friendship is like a tango, kid—it takes two. I can only speak for myself. I consider you a friend. You've got to fill in the rest yourself."

Josh reached down and picked up another handful of the gravelly rocks. Extending his hand, he offered some to Dylan. "You and Auntie Mar just friends?"

"Oh, no," Dylan said, a smile breaking wide across his face. He held his palm out flat as Josh dropped several of the stones into it. "At least, I hope not." He reached back, sending a small round pebble sailing high into the air. He waited until it landed in the water with a small splash, then turned back to Josh. "I'm crazy about her."

Josh chewed his lower lip, considering this. "Sounds serious."

Dylan tossed another pebble, taking much less time and interest in it this time. "I'm just trying to be honest. I thought you deserved an honest answer." He waited a moment. "Besides, I'm always honest with my friends."

Josh tossed the entire handful of rocks into the water, watching as they showered down in a flurry of splatters.

"I'm crazy about her, too," he said, brushing his hands together. "And I'm always honest with my friends, too."

"Good." Dylan nodded, accepting what it was Josh was saying to him without any fanfare or bother that would only embarrass them both. Still, his heart lurched in his chest, and he felt a little like a one-ton weight had been lifted from his shoulders.

"Oh, and Sheriff?"

"Yeah?"

"What do you say keep this between you and me—about Skip and everything? You know how Auntie Mar is. I don't want her to worry."

"I understand," Dylan said, regarding him for a moment. He looked into Josh's dark eyes, feeling that odd, unexplainable connection again. They shared a love for the same woman and a fierce need to protect her. But neither of them was comfortable with emotional displays—at least not with each other, and so he quickly changed the subject. "Your instincts sending you any messages about where the fish might be biting in this stream—at least those we haven't scared off throwing rocks?"

Josh turned his head and looked at the rushing water next to them. "There are fish in that stream?"

Dylan laughed out loud. "Come on, kid, let's get a few casts in before we pack up. I promised your aunt I'd have you back by one o'clock, and the last thing either one of us needs is a lecture from the principal."

Josh laughed also as he fell into line behind Dylan, stepping carefully along the muddy stream bank. He stopped just long enough to retrieve his fishing pole from the rocks on which he'd tossed it.

"Hey, Dylan," he said as he adjusted his line and slipped the pole over his shoulder.

Dylan stopped as he headed up the rocks to the spot where he'd tossed down his pole. He was surprised to hear Josh call him by name. "Yeah?"

Josh took an uneasy step forward, then shifted his gaze to one side. "Uh, thanks."

Dylan slowly bent down and picked up the pole. "No problem, kid, no problem."

Marissa glanced up at the clock. Five minutes to one and still no sign of them.

She swiveled around in her chair, craning her neck to see what she could of the parking lot from her office, looking for Dylan's Jeep.

She swung her chair back around, gazing out across her cluttered desk, and sighed heavily. She knew she should be angry, knew she should be annoyed at the irresponsibility and the carelessness of them both, but somehow, she couldn't quite get herself in the mood. She was simply too happy, and that happiness had a way of permeating all her other emotions. She tried to hold herself in check, tried not to walk around with a perpetual sappy grin on her face all the time—even though that's exactly what she felt like doing. She'd never thought she would ever feel this way, but she never thought Dylan would be a part of her life again.

She thought of the last several weeks, of stolen moments together, of the telephone calls that stretched out into the wee hours of the morning, and very secret, very quiet, late-night visits. She felt almost like a schoolgirl in the throes of her first crush.

But this was no crush—this was real, and alive, and what she'd waited for her whole life. She loved Dylan. She was wildly, passionately, head over heels in love with him. He was a part of her.

Mallory may be her identical twin, they may share a common link as sisters and as twins, but it was Dylan who was her soul mate, her second self.

She'd spent so many years without him, too afraid to hope there was even a chance they could be together again.

It had seemed too impossible—like dreaming the impossible dream.

Except her impossible dream had come true. She had Dylan, and she had Josh, and she was almost ready to believe anything was possible now. Almost.

Marissa leaned back in her chair, feeling the sting of tears against the lids of her eyes. All three of them had come so far. They'd made it through the pain and the betrayal, and the long years apart. But there was still one big hurdle they had to get over, one huge mountain to scale. The truth.

Fate had played a cold and curious joke in their lives—had allowed time and circumstance to separate them with miles and emotions. But somehow, by some quirk of nature, some act of providence or miracle of faith, they'd managed to find their way back to each other. They'd managed to get beyond so much, but would they be able to get beyond the truth?

She thought of Dylan and Josh together, and of the small miracle that was happening between them. Even without knowing their true relationship, a bond had begun to form between them. But what was going to happen to that bond, that fragile line of communication and caring, once they learned the truth?

"Headache?"

Marissa jumped violently, her eyelids flying open. She stared at Karen, who stood in the doorway of her small office, and tried to pull her thoughts together. "W-what was that? What did you say?"

"Marissa, I'm so sorry, I didn't mean to startle you," Karen apologized, her face filled with regret. "I just thought you might have a headache. You looked a little tired."

"No, just resting my eyes," Marissa lied, pushing away from her desk and coming to her feet. She pointed up at the clock. "Do you know if that's the right time?"

Karen glanced up at the clock on the wall, and checked it against her wristwatch. "Yeah, just a little before one."

Marissa frowned. "You haven't seen Josh around anywhere, have you?"

Karen shook her head. "No, is he coming by?"

Marissa's frown deepened. "Well, he's supposed to report to work by one."·

"Well, he's still got a few minutes," Karen said, walking back toward the door. "Rick's going to be late today, anyway."

"Rick? Why? Where'd he go?" Marissa asked, following her out of the office and to the bank of file cabinets along the wall.

"You remember," Karen said, pulling out a file drawer. "He went to that computer fair in Sacramento. He should be back around two."

Marissa did remember. She'd just filed it away somewhere in the back of her brain and forgotten. "I think I'll wander out to the construction site—just check on the boys, make sure Josh gets there all right."

"Go ahead," Karen said absently, searching the jammed drawer for a file. "I'll hold down the fort."

Marissa smiled as she headed down the corridor and out the door. The blast of hot summer wind that greeted her almost felt good in contrast to the frigid air in her air-conditioned office. And as she headed down the walk toward the maintenance yard, she began to feel better. Still, the truth loomed large in front of her, staring her in the face like a formidable opponent. Soon she would have to find a way to deal with it—for all their sakes, and the sooner, the better.

Marissa walked quickly past the maintenance trailer, slipping through the makeshift chain-link fence that cordoned off the building site from the rest of the yard.

"Josh?" she called out, walking toward the framed structure. "Anyone here?"

She stopped and listened for a moment, then stepped carefully around the littered work yard toward the framed structure. Something didn't feel right—it was too quiet, too deserted. It was obvious Josh wasn't there, and she knew Rick would be late. But where were the other two boys?

"Skip? Randy?" she called, walking around the framed shed. With most of the drywall completed, it was difficult to tell if there was anyone inside. "Hey, anyone in there? Where are you guys?"

Sidestepping several large rolls of insulation material, she grabbed hold of the framed doorjamb and lifted herself up onto the concrete floor, ducking low to avoid a low-hanging beam. She looked around, dusting her hands on her skirt and blinking to help her eyes adjust to the shaded interior.

"Randy?" she called again, carefully making her way farther into the shadows. "Where are you guys? Skip?"

But again there was no answer, no sound of any kind. The place was empty.

Her hands went to her hips, and she pushed her hair back away from her face. The enclosed structure was stifling inside, and beads of sweat began to form along her forehead and upper lip.

"Where *is* everyone?" she murmured to herself, frustrated and hot. She moved an impatient hand along her forehead, swiping at the perspiration, and looked about helplessly. She crinkled her nose, an acrid, pungent odor suddenly filling her airways. "What's that smell?"

But the flash came so suddenly, she had no time left for an answer. There was no time to think, to reason, to understand—it was just there in a flurry of lights and sounds, exploding in her head and against her face. Yet even as her head came down hard onto the concrete floor, she didn't worry. Dylan and Josh would be coming, they would know what to do, they would know the answer. She thought she heard their voices—calling, shouting—but then the darkness came and swallowed everything in its path.

* * *

"What time does your watch say?"

Josh tipped his wrist, checking the LED readout on his sports watch. "One-eleven," he said in a precise voice as he turned and looked across the Jeep to Dylan. "And fifteen seconds."

Dylan groaned and pushed his foot down harder on the accelerator. "Marissa's going to kill me."

"Not only that," Josh added dryly. "You're speeding, Sheriff, and I feel I must point out that it's not exactly the kind of example you should be setting for an impressionable lad such as I."

Dylan shot him a killing look. "Oh, okay. I'll slow down, then, and let you explain to the principal that we're late because your old bones kept encouraging you to give it one more try."

The smile on Josh's face cracked and threatened to crumble. "Away, my good man," he said with a British accent and a sweeping gesture of the hand. "And don't spare the steed."

They were both laughing as they pulled into the school parking lot and brought the Jeep to a stop in the space next to Marissa's car.

"I'm surprised she hasn't called the cops," Josh joked as he jumped out of the Jeep.

"Cops, nothing," Dylan snorted, taking off across the parking lot on a run. "I'm surprised she hasn't called in the National Guard."

They rounded the corner of the building, running along the walk outside Marissa's office. Dylan peered through the window as they passed, seeing no sign of her inside. He shot Josh a helpless look.

"It would be too much to hope that she's just stepped out for lunch, wouldn't it?"

Josh jogged along beside him, nodding his head. "Way too much." He pointed off into the distance, in the direction of the work site. "Let's face it. She's out there waiting for us, and it's not going to be pretty."

They'd followed the walk past the school offices and headed for the maintenance yard. They had just started toward the trailer that housed Rick Mathers's office, when Dylan slowly came to a stop.

"What is it?" Josh asked, coming to a stop beside him. "What's the matter?"

Dylan pointed to the sky above the trailer, squinting against the sun. "Is that smoke?"

Chapter 15

Dylan peered through the break in the curtain, watching the crush of doctors and medical personnel crowd over Marissa. His heart rammed so violently against the hard confines of his rib cage, there was a physical pain in his chest.

He closed his eyes, seeing the hideous scene that had greeted them as they'd run past the maintenance trailer and headed out to the construction site. The entire shed had been engulfed in flames—a huge fireball of heat and fire, and he shuddered to think what would have happened if Karen Hamilton hadn't been there, screaming frantically that Marissa was inside.

The smoke had been so black, the heat so intense—he could still feel it burn against his face as he'd searched frantically through the inferno for her. She'd been so pale when he'd finally found her, her body had been so limp, so lifeless, and that had frightened him even more than the falling structure around them. If they'd been just a minute longer, if they'd caught a red light or had stopped in at her office, he never would have gotten to her in time.

He squeezed his lids tighter, feeling the salty sting of tears and bracing himself against a fierce wave of panic. She had to be okay; she just had to. He couldn't face life without her; he wouldn't want to.

"Sheriff, got a minute?"

Dylan opened his eyes and turned away from the screen. What was left of his fishing vest hung in tatters from his shoulders, its sturdy canvas material having spared him from the heat and flames. "Yeah, what have you got?"

Deputy Ronnie Henders hesitated for a moment, glancing over Dylan's shoulder to the emergency medical team working furiously in the background. "We've got the O'Riley kid down at the station. He's crying like a baby. A unit's still posted at the Carver house, but there's been no sign of Skip yet."

Dylan slowly crossed the waiting area of the Amador County Hospital's emergency room, where Josh sat waiting. "You had a chance to question Randy?"

"Yeah," Ronnie Henders said, nodding, falling into step beside him. "He swears he thought they were just going to scare her. He didn't know anything about the fire."

Dylan saw Josh pop up from the tired, worn-looking sofa where he sat with Marissa's worried parents. With wide, expectant eyes, he rushed toward Dylan, his face eager and hopeful.

"How is she?" he demanded. "Is she awake? Is she going to be all right?"

"There's no news," Dylan said, wishing like hell he had more, and better, news to report. "The doctors are still with her."

"What's taking so long?" Josh yelled, his voice cracking with emotion. "Why isn't someone doing something? Isn't there someone around here who can help her?"

"She is being helped," Dylan said, feeling more helpless than he had in his life. He understood Josh's anger and his frustration. He felt the same way himself. He wanted to stalk into that examination room and demand that she be okay. Disheartened, he turned to Marissa's mother, who now stood beside Josh, and saw the worry and concern in Josh's face mirrored in hers. "All we can do right now is wait."

"I'm sure they're doing all they can," Marie Wakefield said in an attempt to soothe her grandson. She turned her anxious gaze to Dylan. "Were you able to see her?"

Dylan shook his head, feeling tears stinging his eyes again. He thought of Marissa's beautiful face—now streaked and ashen—and the army of medical personnel working to keep her alive. "They wouldn't let me in."

He turned back to Josh, slipping a comforting hand on the teen's shoulder. Josh desperately needed someone to lean on, someone to be strong to look up to and to keep him going. Dylan discovered he wanted very much to be that person. And maybe he needed Josh just a little bit, too.

"Just try and hang in there," he said in a low voice, his hand on Josh's shoulder squeezing tight. "She's going to make it, and she's going to need you. Hang on, okay?"

Josh nodded his head, a tear spilling down each cheek. "I'll try. I—I will."

Dylan gave Josh's shoulder a final pat, then turned to Ronnie Henders. "Has the arson team had a chance to look around?"

"Yeah," Henders said with a long sigh. "It's pretty much as you thought. Looks like he waited until she got inside, then ignited the fire with some kind of remote control device."

"Arson?" Josh's head snapped up, the anger in his face turning to rage. "What are you talking about?"

"Slow down, slow down," Dylan said in a calm voice, putting a hand on Josh's shoulder again. "Let me take care of this. Let me—"

"No," Josh said with a sneer, pushing Dylan's hand away. "You're saying this was done on purpose?"

"We don't know anything for sure yet," Dylan insisted, a whole new type of panic setting in.

"It was Skip," Josh said in a cold, flat voice. "You don't even have to say it. I know. It was Skip."

Dylan stared into Josh's cold, dark gaze. "We've got units out looking for him. We'll pick him up."

Josh started to back away. "Don't bother," he said, turning and starting for the door. "I know exactly where he is."

"Joshua, you come back here," Marie Wakefield cried. "Where are you going? Josh, *please.*"

"Josh," Dylan called after him. "Wait. Let me go with you."

"No, thanks, Sheriff," Josh called over his shoulder, making his way through the noisy emergency room. "I'll take care of this myself."

"Wait up, Josh. Come back," Dylan shouted, running after him. But the crowd was too thick. By the time he got to the doors, Josh was gone.

"Sheriff James?"

Dylan turned back around, swearing under his breath, and looked up at the tall, haggard-looking doctor standing in the crowded corridor. "Yeah? I'm James."

"The fire victim you brought in," he said, holding a shiny stainless-steel clipboard. "She's asking to see you."

"Nurse. *Nurse,*" Dylan called out anxiously as Marissa's lids drifted closed. Dylan wasn't sure he'd ever experienced panic before, but he recognized it immediately—he was experiencing it now. He'd only just gotten there, the doctor has said she'd asked to see him, but there was no response from her—no sign of life. "Could you come here, please? I think . . . I think something's wrong here. There must be something wrong."

The nurse walked around the gurney, glancing down at Marissa and reaching for her wrist. "No, she's fine, Sheriff. She's just sleeping," she said after a moment, gently placing Marissa's hand back down and tucking the sheet around her. "Don't worry, she's going to be fine. She just needs to get some fresh air into her lungs, and let that nasty cut on her arm heal. Before you know it she'll be as good as new," she assured him. She pointed to the clear oxygen mask hanging above the gurney. "If she starts coughing, give her some oxygen. But she's exhausted. What she really needs is her rest." She glanced at Dylan and winked, giving him a reassuring pat on the shoulder. "I'll leave you alone for a little while, but I'll have to boot you out of here soon. We need to get her cleaned up and to her own room."

Dylan could only nod as the nurse slipped past him and disappeared through the curtains that surrounded the small cubicle. There were things he would have liked to ask, questions he'd wanted answered, but he was too drained to speak, too emotional to get the words past his throat.

He reached out, gently stroking Marissa's cheek with the back of his fingers. Her face was still streaked with soot, and beneath it her smooth, golden skin looked pallid and ashen. But to him she'd never looked more beautiful. She was alive, and that was all that mattered.

"Dylan," she murmured drowsily, then began coughing loudly.

Dylan jumped at the sound of her voice and reached for the oxygen mask.

"Breathe deep," he instructed, slipping the mask over her nose and mouth. After several deep breaths, her coughing stopped and she pushed the mask away.

"Where's Josh?" she demanded, grasping at his hand. Her eyes were open now, looking red and tired, and she looked wildly around the small cubicle.

Dylan returned the mask to the hook above the gurney, then gazed down at her. Reaching out to push her hair away from her face, he smiled down at her. "Don't worry about him. He's all right."

Marissa's head shifted back and forth on the pillow. "But he's okay. He's not hurt?"

"He's fine," Dylan said, bending down and brushing a gentle kiss along her cheek. But inside of him, a cold, hard knot of dread began to form. "Just relax. The doctor said you need your rest. I'll be right here."

"I-it was Skip," she stammered, her skin looking pale and white beneath the smudges. "It was Skip. He wanted to hurt me—and Josh, too."

"Don't worry," Dylan said, patting her hands. "I'll take care of it. Please, sweetheart, don't worry."

"But, Dylan," she sobbed, straining to lift her head from the pillow. "You can't tell Josh. You can't tell him about Skip."

Dylan squeezed her hands tight. The look on her face tore at him, and all he wanted was to gather her up in his arms and tell her he would make everything all right. But how could he? Josh had taken off like a bat out of hell— angry and dangerous. There was no telling what the kid would do.

"Don't think about this now. We'll have Skip in custody soon. They might even have him now, so don't worry about it. Josh is fine. And you're going to be all right. That's all that's important."

She sank back onto the pillow. "Promise?"

The knot in his stomach twisted. "I promise."

She smiled up at him—a tired, weak smile. "The doctor told me you saved my life."

Dylan shrugged, relieved to see the worry leave her face. "It was the least I could do. I got Josh back late."

Marissa clutched at his hands again. "Thank God you did, otherwise...otherwise..." She squeezed her eyes tight, tears slipping from beneath her lids.

"We agreed not to think about that now," Dylan reminded her, brushing away her tears.

"I know," she whispered, reaching up and cradling his cheek in her hand. "I love you."

He smiled, leaning down and pressing a kiss against her lips. "Good. I'd hate to think I ruined my lucky fishing vest for nothing."

She smiled and pulled him close for another kiss. "I appreciate the sacrifice."

"Don't worry," he murmured against her lips. "I'll figure out some way you can make it up to me." He squeezed her hand tight. "How are you feeling?"

"My throat's sore," she said, swallowing hard. "And my chest hurts, but other than that..." She shrugged, wincing just a little and glancing down at the bandage on her upper arm. "Oh, yeah, and this cut on my arm."

"Doctor said there were some tools on the floor," Dylan said, hating the thought of her beautiful skin marred. "That you must have fallen on them during the blast."

Marissa looked up into his handsome face, forgetting about the sore throat and singed lungs. "I guess I got lucky."

"We both did," he murmured, bending low and giving her another kiss. He slowly stood up. He felt better, knowing she would be okay, but he was still worried about Josh. "They told me I could only stay a minute, so I'm going to go so you can get some rest. There are some things I want to check on, but I'll be back later this evening, okay?"

"Okay." Marissa watched as he headed toward the curtain, cringing at the sight of the burned vest and saying a silent prayer of thanks that he wasn't hurt. "Oh, and Dylan?"

Dylan stopped and turned around. "Yeah?"

"Would you send Josh in for a moment?"

The request caught him off guard, and sent him scrambling for how to answer. "Uh, I . . . I don't think . . . uh, actually they won't allow any more visitors."

"But I'm fine," she insisted. But there was something about the way he looked at her, something in his expression that had her heartbeat increasing. She rose up on one elbow. "Dylan, what is it?"

"Nothing," he contended, but he could feel the lie contorting his facial features. "Just get some rest. I'll bring Josh in with me this evening."

"But I want to see Josh."

"Marissa, please, just—"

"You told me he was okay," she said, her words sounding more like an accusation.

"He is," he said again. "He's—"

"He's not here, is he," she said, her voice rising with emotion.

"He's fine, he's—"

"Tell me," she demanded, struggling to sit up. "Tell me. Where is he?"

Dylan rushed to the gurney, putting a hand on her shoulders in an effort to calm her down. "Marissa, it's okay. Josh is going to be okay."

"Oh, my God," she gasped, her eyes wide with terror. "Something's happened, hasn't it. Tell me Dylan. *Tell me.*"

"It's just that he's not here—"

Marissa stopped her struggling and stared up at him. "He's gone after him, hasn't he. He's gone after Skip." She clutched at him, wild and desperate. "No, no. You have to stop him. You have to bring him back."

"It's okay, Marissa, he'll be fine." Trying to convince her to lie back down was impossible, and he gave up trying. "Trust me, he'll be fine."

"Fine," she shrieked, clutching at his vest. "Dylan, you have to go after him. You have to stop him before something terrible happens."

"Josh is a good kid, he's smart. He won't do anything foolish."

"But he's angry. He's just like you when he gets angry. He doesn't always think straight when he's angry. You have to listen, you have to believe me. He'll get into trouble again. He'll do something to get himself into trouble again. I can't let that happen. If you don't go after him, I will."

Dylan felt helpless. He'd never seen her like this before. Marissa was always so practical, so cool and calm. But she was nearly hysterical now—completely overwrought, and he was at a loss as to how to console her, how to calm her down. "Marissa, please—"

"I won't give him up again, Dylan," she insisted, tossing the sheet aside. "I won't. I won't lose him again."

"Marissa, you have to stop, you have to calm down."

But she didn't calm down. She pulled at the IV lines at her arm, yanking them free. "I won't give him up," she said again, swinging her legs off the gurney.

But the movement was too much for her; she was too weak, too worked up, and she collapsed to one side. Reaching out, Dylan grabbed her before she could fall, forcing her back down on the gurney.

"You have to stop this," he said in a stern voice. "You're going to hurt yourself."

But Marissa fought against him. "No, I've got to find him. I won't lose him."

"That's silly," Dylan insisted, holding her down. "You won't lose him. He's going to be fine."

"You don't understand," she ranted, her eyes glazed with tears, and terror. "He's mine, Dylan, he's mine. I won't lose him—not again, not again. I won't lose my son again.''

Dylan felt the world stop on its axis. Her son? For a moment, he couldn't move—he could barely think. He sagged back a step, his hold on her shoulders dropping, and the small room seemed to spin around him. The words hung in the air between them like a dark, ominous cloud—dangerous and threatening. Pictures began to flash through his mind—random, scattered images that began to come together, to make sense.

He stared into Marissa's startled gaze, telling himself he must have misunderstood, that he hadn't heard what he had. She was hysterical, emotional, and not making sense. It had to be just a slip of the tongue, a blunder, a stupid mistake.

But there was something in her eyes, something in her expression, in the entire way she held herself that had him believing. He'd heard her correctly. There had been no mistake, no misunderstanding.

"*Your* son?" he asked in a coarse, raw voice.

Marissa saw the expression on his face, heard the shock and disappointment in his voice, and the pain was worse than waking up with lungs full of smoke. How could she have just blurted that out? How could she have gotten so carried away, so out of control? The thought of Josh in danger terrified her, but that was no excuse for being careless. There was too much at stake, she had too much to lose—and from the look on his face, she'd lost a lot already.

How did she tell him the rest? Josh wasn't just *her* son—he was *their* son. How could she tell him that? She needed time to think and to try to find a way to explain, to make him understand.

"Dylan," she whispered, her voice sounding strained and tight with emotion. "I'm . . . I'm sorry, I didn't want it to be this way, I didn't want to tell you like this."

"How did you want to tell me, Marissa?" Dylan demanded. "Or did you plan on telling me at all?"

"Of course I planned to tell you," she said defensively, struggling up. "Just not here, not like this."

Dylan shook his head. "What about Caleb, what about Penny?"

"They couldn't have any children," she said in a low, flat voice. "I was young. I didn't have anything, didn't know what to do, where to go. They were older, settled, they could give him a home and security." She wiped at the tears falling down her cheek, and shook her head. "I...I let them take him."

Dylan felt oddly breathless and weak, almost like he'd taken a fist in the stomach—only it hurt much more. It was so clear to him now—her willingness to take responsibility for the kid, her fervent concern. He remembered thinking how much their eyes were alike, those little bits of resemblance he'd ignored, he'd overlooked. It all made sense, but he couldn't help thinking of how he'd felt all those years ago when she'd kept another secret from him—that feeling of hurt and betrayal. It haunted him now.

"What about his father? Where was he?"

Marissa groaned, an agonizing moan that seemed to come from the very essence of her soul. Her entire world was coming apart. This was a nightmare—a true ordeal she wished desperately she could awaken from. She'd known the truth would have to come out—but not now, not like this. Her strained body and overwrought emotions could take no more, and she sank back on the gurney.

Dylan struggled with his feelings. She'd been through so much—the fire and that awful smoke. She should be resting, recuperating, not arguing with him. He should be holding her, caring for her—not pushing for answers. But something drove him on, something had him pressing for more.

"Where is he, Marissa?" he asked, an odd chill spreading through his veins. Maybe he already knew the answer, maybe he already knew. "Where's Josh's father?"

She turned her head and looked at him, tears streaming down her face. She didn't have to answer, didn't have to say a word. The answer was there in her eyes, written all over her face, and it hit him right between the eyes.

"No," he said in a hoarse groan, staggering back a step. "No, no."

A million random, disjointed, disconnected pieces fell into place, creating a picture of the truth Dylan knew he couldn't turn away from. He thought of Josh—of his young face laughing and joking, or distorted with anger and full of rage. Dylan remembered that curious feeling he'd experienced, that hint of familiarity, that strange sense of awareness. Josh was familiar, he was familiar. Because Josh was *his* son.

"You never told me?" he asked, his question sounding more like an accusation. "Didn't you think I had a right to know?

"Dylan, please," Marissa pleaded, struggling desperately for control. "Things were so different back then. They were so bad between us."

"Bad," Dylan repeated angrily. "Bad? Was it so bad that you had to give away my baby?" Fury had him restless, and he paced back and forth. "Was it so bad you had to lie, to keep me in the dark for fifteen years?" He stopped, and gave her a killing look. "My God, Marissa, you let me arrest my own son?"

"Dylan, it wasn't like that," Marissa said, her voice sounding harsh and desperate even to her own ears. "You have to let me explain. You have to give me a chance—"

"A chance? Like the chance you gave our son?" he asked, cutting her off. He turned and started out, ripping the curtain aside. "What a fool I was to believe you again.

Tell me something, Marissa. Was your sister in on it this time, or did you do it all by yourself?"

"Dylan, wait, please, don't go," she pleaded.

"Oh, I'm going, Marissa," he said. "I'm going to find my son. I'm going to tell him the truth."

"No, Dylan, please. Please, don't," she said, jumping off the gurney. "He won't understand. Dylan, please, don't do this. Let me explain."

"What the hell is going on in here?" the harried nurse demanded as she came around the corner. She pushed past Dylan, glaring up at him as she grabbed for Marissa. "All right, Sheriff, that's enough. Get out. *Now.*"

Marissa's strength gave out, and she could only watch—weak and helpless—as Dylan stepped through the doors and disappeared around a corner. Nothing mattered any longer. She lost Dylan, and she was about to lose her son.

"Thanks for the ride."

"No problem," Dylan said with a careless shrug.

"Sure you don't want to come in?"

Dylan shook his head. "No. You go ahead. I'll catch up with you later."

Dylan sat back in his seat, watching Josh's tall, solid frame silhouetted against the light of the hospital's main entrance. He'd only been a father for a couple of hours—or he'd only been aware of it for the last two hours—yet his heart filled with pride as he watched the handsome young man push one of the hospital doors open and step into the lobby. Josh Wakefield was his son.

His *son.* It seemed impossible. It seemed unreal. He was still having trouble believing, and yet everything in him—every emotion, every sense, every instinct—told him it was true.

Emotion felt thick in his throat. Could he love this kid—the erratic, troubled teen he'd arrested time and time again?

Only the Joshua Wakefield he'd come to know seemed a million light years away from that angry, troubled kid— they were like two different people. He'd come to care about this other Josh. They had shared long talks and good-natured joking—and they'd shared a love of fly-fishing. But were those feelings real? Were they what a father felt for his son? Were they enough?

He'd thought it was because of his feelings for Marissa, had thought it was because Josh mattered to her, that those were the reasons the kid had come to matter to him, too. But now he wasn't so sure. Josh was his son—had something in him sensed that? Had something in him recognized his own and reached out?

Dylan thought back over the last two hours. He'd left the hospital in a state of shock, determined to find Josh and tell him the truth about everything.

Surprisingly, he had managed to find Josh very easily— or rather Josh had managed to find him—at the sheriff's office, of all places.

Dylan had been almost as surprised as he'd been relieved to discover that Josh had brought a surly, but repentant, Skip in on his own. Even though the nasty black eye Skip sported was evidence Josh had exacted a modicum of revenge, it was far less than he feared considering how angry Josh had been earlier.

But as far as telling Josh the truth... he still hadn't decided if he'd had second thoughts, or if he'd just chickened out.

Dylan rubbed at the tension at the base of his neck, hearing Marissa's desperate pleas to him as he'd stormed from the small cubicle in the emergency room. At the time he'd been too angry, too hurt and upset to care how distraught she'd been. He'd just wanted to strike out, to get back at her for having betrayed him, for having played him for a fool again.

But coming face-to-face with Josh, looking at him and recognizing a world of familiarity in those dark eyes, his anger and his courage had deserted him. Somehow he hadn't been so sure he wanted to be the one to tell him, to be the one responsible for taking his world and turning it upside down. Maybe Marissa had been right. Maybe there was a better way to tell him the truth, and maybe—just maybe—he didn't want to be the one telling him.

So Dylan had held his tongue. He and Josh had talked about a lot of things—Skip, the fire and Marissa's condition—but he'd stayed away from the truth. He would give Marissa a chance to do it her way, to go to their son and tell him everything—but it was the last thing he would give to her again.

Marissa. He closed his eyes, seeing her frightened and tear-stained face. His heart twisted painfully in his chest, and he felt his breath falter in his lungs. He'd believed her when she'd said she loved him—just like he'd believed her sixteen years ago. And yet she'd lied to him then, and she'd been lying to him again. How could he have let it happen again?

He opened his eyes, reaching for the keys in the ignition. The quiet rumble of the Jeep's engine sounded dismal and forlorn in the quiet hospital lot, adding to his sense of desolation and despair. Marissa Wakefield held a strange and commanding power over him. He loved her. It was that simple, and it was also that complicated. But it wasn't his feelings that he doubted. How could she love him? She'd kept secrets, she'd lied, and she'd manipulated both him and Josh.

How could she love him, and have denied him his son?

Dylan shifted the Jeep into reverse, backing out of the parking stall and heading through the lot toward the street. He thought of them together in the hospital—mother and son—and the pain that twisted in his heart was almost more than he could bear. It wouldn't take Marissa long to discover that he'd changed his mind, that he'd backed out and elected not to tell Josh the truth. So did that mean that she would do it? Would she tell him the truth, would she ever?

Was it only this morning he thought he had everything he'd ever wanted out of life? How could his heart have been so full then, and be so empty now?

Chapter 16

Marissa leaned back in the patio chair, watching as Josh gathered up the lunch dishes and placed them on a tray.

"I wish you'd let me help with that."

Josh gave her a stern look. "The doctor said you were supposed to rest, so *rest*." He picked up the loaded tray, carefully balancing it. "Otherwise, I'm going to think you have some complaints about my housekeeping."

"No, no." Marissa smiled, shaking her head. "No, complaints here."

She watched as he cautiously made his way across the patio and through the open sliding door. In the five days since she'd been out of the hospital, Josh had been an absolute angel—waiting on her hand and foot, nursing her, nagging her about her rest and her medication. In other words, he'd been perfect.

Of course, that only made her feel that much worse. She didn't deserve such kindness, not after what she had done.

It had been a week since the fire, a week during which she'd been resting and recuperating, and a week since she'd last seen Dylan. She had replayed that awful moment in the emergency room over and over again in her mind. The look on his face when he'd realized Josh was his son would haunt her to her grave. The hurt, the anger, the betrayal in his eyes, had been awful. She would never forget it.

Marissa squeezed her eyes tight. Dylan would never forgive her—never—and she couldn't blame him. She would never forgive herself. She should have told him the truth long ago; she should have been honest. But instead she'd held off, telling herself she'd been waiting for the right moment, the right time. But the right time had come and gone. When was she going to learn? She'd made the same mistake she'd made sixteen years ago—risking her happiness on a secret that she knew would have to come out. And just like before, she'd lost again.

Yet he hadn't told Josh the truth. Why? To force her to, or to spare his son the pain?

Marissa opened her eyes, sitting up straight. Whatever his reasons were, it didn't matter any longer. She'd held off these last few days so Josh could get through his finals. But classes were over now, final grades had been mailed, and the time had come for her to be honest.

"Want some more iced tea?" Josh called from inside.

"No, thanks, I'm fine." She hesitated for just a moment, feeling her heart begin to thud heavily in her chest. "But could you come out here, please? There's something I want to talk to you about."

"Is this about Dylan?" Josh asked quietly, pausing in the open doorway.

Despite the warm summer sun, a cold chill traveled through her. "Why do you ask that?"

Josh stepped down onto the patio, slipping his hands into the pockets of his baggy shorts. "It's pretty obvious something's happened." He shrugged, walking to the steps and sitting down. "I didn't ask 'cause I figured you'd tell me when you were ready."

Marissa felt hot tears sting her eyes. "I appreciate that, and yes, you're right, something has happened."

"You've broken up."

She struggled with the lump of emotion in her throat. "Yes, we have."

Josh looked away, taking a deep breath. "You okay?"

"I'm fine," she whispered, putting her head down and knotting her hands nervously together.

Josh slammed his fist down hard. "He promised me he wasn't going to hurt you."

"Don't blame him," she said quickly, coming to her feet. "It's more complicated than that. That's why we need to talk. I need to tell you something I probably should have told you a long time ago." She walked across the patio, sitting down beside him. "But first just let me say that no matter what, I love you. I've always loved you. If I made mistakes—and believe me, I have—just know that what I did, I did because I loved you, because I thought it was best for you."

The story seemed to spill out of her then. Sixteen years of holding back, sixteen years of keeping up appearances and living a lie, all came rushing out like water over a dam. At times the tears spilled down her cheeks so furiously she had no time to wipe them away, and sometimes the emotion in her throat grew so thick she could hardly speak. But despite all this, she persevered and struggled to get the truth out.

"You mean you and...*Dylan?*" Josh asked, visibly shaken. "You had Dylan's baby?"

Marissa nodded, and closed her eyes. The look on his face was too much; it tore at her heart too painfully. "And the worst part is, I never told him...I never told him about the baby." She drew in a deep breath, opening her eyes. The wave of emotion had passed, and her voice became flat and stoic. "It was a terrible thing to do, I realize that now. But at the time, I was hurt. He'd been so angry when he'd found I'd pretended about being Mallory. He'd said such awful things." She paused again, feeling empty and spent inside. "When I found out about the baby I just couldn't face him. He'd said he never wanted to see me again."

Josh moved close, slipping a comforting arm around her shoulder. "Auntie Mar, don't. You don't have to do this."

"Yes," she insisted dully, turning and looking into his beautiful eyes. "Yes, I do. Josh, that baby—my baby—" A sudden spasm gripped at her, and she closed her eyes again. "Josh, that baby—"

"Is me," Josh said simply, finishing for her.

Marissa's eyes flew open, and she felt a sudden rush of cold through her entire system. "You knew."

Josh slowly nodded his head, the hand at her shoulder tightening just a little. "One night, it was after Dad had died, Mom was drinking and crying, sort of talking crazy—about you and Auntie Mal, how you two were Gram and Gramp's favorites and how they spoiled the two of you, how they gave you everything and ignored Dad." He slipped his arm from her shoulder and caught her hand up in his. "She was especially angry with you—you know how she used to get."

Marissa nodded, remembering her sister-in-law's anger and defensiveness all too well. It had been a stumbling block over the years—sometimes making it difficult for her to see Josh or visit him.

"Then she started laughing," he continued, "and kept talking about how I shouldn't think too much of you, and how she could put you in your place any time she wanted—that no matter how much Gram and Gramp gave you, she had something of yours she was never giving back. I usually didn't pay much attention when she got talking crazy like that, but when I tried to get her to go to bed, she started crying again and made me promise never to leave her, wanting me to say I loved her more than I loved you."

Marissa moaned, reaching out and cradling his cheek in her hand. "She was in a lot of pain then."

"I know," he said, nodding sadly. "Losing Dad just hurt her too much." He paused for a moment, deep in thought. "It was just a lot of little things after that. Things that gradually began to add up. Like how nobody ever wanted to talk about my adoption. And I started thinking about my kindergarten graduation and how you flew in from D.C. just to take me out for pizza afterward, and all the presents you always sent at Christmas and my birthdays, and all those silly drawings of mine you kept . . . and the hundreds of photographs you always took during your visits."

Marissa smiled sadly. "I wanted to take as much of you with me as I could."

"After a while, it just sort of started to make sense." He looked at her, smiling just a little. "And we'd always been so close—you know, like there was a connection or something."

"Why didn't you come to me?" Marissa whispered. "If you suspected, why didn't you say something?"

Josh shrugged. "I didn't want Mom to think that I might know, and I guess, I don't know . . ." He shrugged again, glancing away. "I guess I was a little afraid."

"Afraid? Of what?"

He looked back at her. "That maybe I was wrong."

"Oh, Josh," she cried, pulling him close. "My boy. My son."

Suddenly she was crying again, and Josh was, too, and they both succumbed to a kind of flurry of hugs, kisses, laughter and more tears, as mother and son talked and shared all those things that had been denied for so long. They sat for a long time on the step, arm in arm, just holding each other and letting the emotions of the moment run their course.

"I take it all this has something to do with why Dylan hasn't been around the last week," Josh said finally, after a long silence.

"Oh, Josh." Marissa sighed, feeling tired and defeated. "He'll never forgive me. Never."

"He knows, then? About me?"

She nodded her head slowly. "It all came out so badly there in the emergency room I just sort of blurted it out. He was very hurt."

"Was he . . . upset?"

She looked at him, seeing the question and the doubt in his eyes. "Only at me. Only because I'd lied to him—again. He hates me, Josh, and I don't blame him."

"How'd you find me?"

Josh leapt over the rocks, carefully balancing his tackle box in one hand and his fishing pole in the other. "It wasn't hard. Where else would you be?"

Dylan watched as Josh leapt over the rushing water, making his way across the stream. "Marissa didn't bring you, did she?"

Josh shook his head. "Nope."

Dylan glanced back to his line, left dangling in the water. "You didn't try to drive up here by yourself, did you?"

"Driving without a license is against the law," Josh said with a small smile. He set his tackle box down on the rock and flipped open the lid. "And just for the record, an Officer Young was kind enough to offer me a ride."

"Kim," Dylan murmured, casting out again.

"Yeah, Nico's aunt," he said conversationally as he picked the fly he wanted from the selection in his box. "Having any luck?"

Dylan continued casting. "Not much."

Josh nodded, tying the fly to the end of his line. "Well, good thing I showed up. I can tell you where the fish are hiding."

Dylan reeled his line in, stepping up out of the stream. He looked at Josh, trying to read something in his young face. Had Marissa told him the truth? Was he angry, shocked, disappointed? Had he come to confront the father he never knew he had...or had Marissa decided to continue living the lie?

But Josh's face was like a sphinx, revealing nothing of what might be on his mind. Still, Dylan did see something in the young face that had emotion swelling in his chest—he saw Josh's whole history in his face—the resemblance was unmistakable. Why had he not seen it before? This kid looked just like him; this kid was his son.

Dylan stepped over the rocks, coming to the rock where Josh sat. "Why did you show up?"

Josh smiled, flipping the end of the fishing line through several loops of the fly and tying them tight. "Come on, Sheriff, I'll bet you can figure it out."

Dylan leaned his pole against the rock and sat down. "She told you."

"Yeah, she told me."

Dylan turned and looked at Josh. What were they supposed to do now? How were they suppose to act? They were father and son. Did they hug, shake hands, pretend it never happened? Josh just sat there quietly tying his fly to his line.

"You want to talk about it?"

Josh looked up at him. "If you want."

"If *I* want," Dylan repeated, standing up. "What about you? You're so calm, so laid-back."

"What do you want me to do? Would you feel better if I knocked off a convenience store or torched a toolshed?" He laughed, his smile broadening. "Come on, Sheriff, you should feel good. I've been rehabilitated."

"You're not mad?"

"At what? I knew I was adopted," Josh said simply, setting his fishing pole aside. "I went years wondering who my birth mother was—what she looked like, where she was. She could have been anybody. So I'm supposed to be upset now because the blanks have been filled in? That the aunt I've always adored, who's been there for me my whole life, is really my mother?''

"But she lied to you."

"To hurt me?" Josh asked poignantly. "Or to make my life better?"

Dylan took a deep breath, looking up to the sky. "So you're saying you're okay with it?"

"Look, it's kind of hard to explain." He stood up, pausing for a moment and running a hand though his hair. "You know how Auntie Mar and Auntie Mal have always had this *thing* between them—this way of telling each other stuff without really saying anything?"

"Yeah." Dylan nodded his head, remembering Marissa's special "radar" with her sister, and how he'd teased her about it.

"It isn't exactly like that, but there has always been *something* between Auntie Mar and me, too, something special."

"You're saying you knew?"

"I guess I'm saying I think I might have always known, or at least suspected." His smile faltered and he turned away. "What I didn't know about was you."

Dylan watched Josh scoop up a handful of pebbles from the banks of the stream and begin tossing them into the water. Had it only been a week ago when they'd stood together on this very spot and thrown rocks into the river, when they'd talked about friendship? "How... how do you feel about that?"

"I think the real question is how do *you* feel?" Josh laughed dryly. "I mean, it's got to be a little embarrassing for the sheriff to wake up one morning and find out one of Jackson's most notorious juvenile delinquents is his son."

Dylan began to wonder at that moment if he'd suddenly been endowed with some kind of special insight himself. It was as though he could see beyond Josh's laughter, beyond the flippant remarks and calm facade. He could see so clearly now how Josh used the humor and the jokes to cover up, how he used them to cope with those things that were too tough to take head-on. Dylan saw it, and understood it, because it was exactly what he did himself.

"You think I'm embarrassed?" he asked quietly. This was too important, too significant, for joking.

Josh stopped as he was about to send another pebble sailing into the water, and turned around. "Are you?"

"Yeah, I am," Dylan admitted after a moment, taking a few steps forward. "I am embarrassed. But not because of you. I'm embarrassed because I don't know what to do, I don't know what to say to you, or how to act." He stopped, trying to find the right words. "You had a father—a great dad you loved and looked up to. I mean, you're my son, Josh, but do you want another father?"

"What I want," Josh said, making his way over the rugged stream bank, "what I need, is a friend." He stopped in front of Dylan, slowly extending his hand. "Be my friend?"

"I already am," Dylan whispered, looking down at Josh's outstretched hand. He reached out to shake his son's hand.

But somehow he just couldn't do it—they were father and son, and a safe, staid handshake was too impersonal, too detached. Opening his arms, Dylan embraced his son, feeling his eyes sting and his throat become raw with emotion. And, just as he'd thought it would be, it was awkward and uncomfortable afterward. They both stumbled back a step, looking everywhere but into each other's eyes.

"Okay, kid," Dylan said loudly, bending down and picking up his rod. "You've been bragging about knowing where those fish are. How 'bout putting your money where your mouth is?"

"Sure," Josh murmured thoughtfully, watching as Dylan worked to straighten his line. "Dylan?"

"Yeah?"

"We were almost a family, you know that? Even without knowing the truth, we started to become a family—our own family—you, me, Auntie Mar."

"Josh—" Dylan started, but Josh cut him off.

"She says it's over between the two of you."

Dylan's heart lurched painfully in his chest, and he suddenly understood why he'd felt so empty for the last seven days. "That doesn't mean it has to change anything between you and me."

"It changes everything," Josh said sadly. "She's a part of both of us. She's what links us together." He dropped his gaze to the ground, his hands balling into fists at his side. "And what happens to *our* family? Are we just supposed to forget about it, just let it go?"

"Josh," Dylan said, setting his pole aside again. "You can't let go of something that wasn't there. We weren't a family, not really. It was just an illusion, based on a lie." He drew in a deep breath, struggling through what felt like a sea of emotion. "Marissa lied to me. She lied to you, too. You don't keep the truth from people you care about."

Josh settled his hands on his hips, looking up at his father. "Then why didn't *you* tell me the truth the night I brought Skip in?"

Dylan jerked to a stop, the Jeep's oversize tires screeching against the hot pavement. But before he could push the door open and call out, she'd disappeared through the open doorway of Scaletti's deli.

He leapt up the high curb, making his way down the narrow sidewalk of Jackson's historic main street. He'd been leaving messages on her answering machine for three days, her office had been closed up tight, and no one had answered the door at her condo the few times he'd gathered up enough courage to stop by. Until he'd spotted her just now, he'd almost begun to wonder if she'd taken Josh and left.

He could see her through the store window, smiling and laughing with Dom Scaletti, and felt the muscles in his stomach twist tight. She looked beautiful in the sleeveless blouse and long, flowing skirt cinched tightly at the waist with a silver-and-turquoise belt. Her hair fell loose and free down her back, and her skin glowed rich and golden—a stark contrast to that awful wan, pale way it had had in the hospital ten days ago.

He gave his head a shake, not wanting to think about that terrible day in the emergency room—or the awful things he had said to her. There was too much he had to make up for as it was. It wasn't the first time he'd lashed out at her, that he'd said mean, hurtful things in order to cover up and assuage his own pain. She'd managed to forgive him once, but could she again? The fact that she hadn't answered any of his telephone messages wasn't a good sign.

Dylan's jaw clenched tight. He didn't want to think about that now—he couldn't. He'd made so many mistakes already. It was all so clear to him now, but it hadn't been until his son—their son—had helped him to see what had been right in front of him all along.

There had been something in Josh's eyes that day up at the stream, something wise and insightful, that had demonstrated to Dylan better than anything else just how foolish and self-righteous he had been. He'd been blaming Marissa for everything, holding her responsible for crimes he was guilty of committing himself. He'd accused her of holding back the truth, of covering up, and living a lie. And yet how many times had he done that very thing himself?

He'd spent sixteen years telling himself and everyone else he didn't love Marissa Wakefield and she hadn't really hurt him at all. But that hadn't been how he really felt. He *had* loved her, and he *had* been hurt. Maybe if he'd been honest with her back then, all of this could have been avoided. Instead he'd lashed out and covered up, and he'd ended up living a lie.

So why hadn't he told Josh the truth when he'd found out, why had he held back? To hurt and manipulate his son, or to protect and avoid hurting him? And was what Marissa had done so different?

He walked up the step into the deli, the rich aromas of garlic and spice hanging thickly in the air. But he wasn't thinking about that. He was thinking about the woman who stood with her back to him, and how he was going to convince her to forgive him one more time.

"We're going to talk, and I'm not letting you leave here until we have," he said, taking her by the arm and spinning her around.

She whirled around, the packages of deli meats in her arms falling to the floor and scattering around their feet. "Dylan James. What the hell do you think you're doing?"

Surprise had him unconsciously taking a step back. He stared down at the woman before him, feeling dazed and off-balance. She was so endearingly familiar—the hair, the eyes, the shape of her face—and yet this woman wasn't who he thought she was, this woman was a stranger.

"*Mallory?*" he gasped in a coarse voice. "Mallory, I—I'm sorry. I thought you were—"

"I know what you thought," Mallory muttered, starting to reach for her packages.

"No, please, let me," Dylan insisted quickly, retrieving the packages and meekly handing them to her. "I'm really sorry."

"Forget it, Dylan," she said, slipping the wrapped meats and cheeses into a string bag hanging from her arm. "Oh, I suppose I should call you Sheriff now."

Dylan stared down at Marissa's twin, and saw the anger in her eyes. "I have a feeling there are a few other names you would prefer."

Mallory had to smile. "Sheriff James, I see you've become a mind reader since high school. Interesting."

"Among other things," Dylan muttered, studying her carefully. He was fascinated. She was so much like Marissa—the color of her hair, the slant of her nose, the shape of her mouth. He couldn't find any one feature that was dissimilar. So why, then, was it they looked so different? What was it about them that gave them each such a distinctive look?

And was there really a time when he'd actually mistaken one for the other?

"Hey, Sheriff," Dom called from across the meat counter. "What can I get for you today? I've got some fresh turkey sliced."

"Nothing today, Dom, thanks." While Dom turned to wait on another customer, Dylan's gaze returned to Mallory. He felt awkward, ill at ease, and the anger in her eyes didn't help. "Are you here for a visit?"

"I'm here, Sheriff, because my sister needed me." Mallory's blue gaze narrowed. "She could have died in that fire."

"I know," he said tersely. "I was there."

Mallory faltered just a little. "I know. And I'm grateful for what you did, for getting her out."

"Then tell me where she is."

"Leave her alone, Dylan," Mallory said quietly. "She's been hurt enough already."

"I don't want to hurt her."

"No?" Mallory said skeptically, pushing past him. "Then how come every time she gets near you she ends up hurt?"

Dylan stopped her with a hand on her arm, telling himself what he felt wasn't desperation. "What do you want?

You want me to beg—I'll do it. I'll do anything you want, just *please* tell me where she is. I have to see her. I have to."

"Is there a problem here?"

Dylan glared up at the tall Native American who appeared out of nowhere and stood behind Mallory. But Dylan knew who he was. Only Mallory's husband didn't look at all like he had in the formal wedding photo. He was big and tall, with massive shoulders and long black hair, and he stared at Dylan with cold, menacing eyes.

Not that he blamed him, Dylan thought as he slowly released his hold on Mallory's arm. The man was merely being protective of his wife and unborn child.

"There's no problem," Mallory said, slipping an affectionate arm through her husband's and pulling him close. "Sweetheart, this is Dylan James. Sheriff, this is my husband, Benjamin Graywolf."

"Sheriff James," Graywolf said, extending his hand. His faced had softened, but his eyes remained wary and suspicious. "I've heard Mallory and Marissa speak of you."

"Yes," Dylan mumbled, taking Graywolf's hand and shaking it. "I imagine you have."

"Dylan is interested in talking with Marissa," Mallory said. "I was explaining to him why I thought that wasn't such a good idea."

"I see." Graywolf nodded, his arm moving from his wife's arm to around her waist.

Dylan turned back to Mallory, seeing her stubborn determination, and knew he would never be able to change her mind. "At least tell her for me . . . tell her I . . ." But his words drifted off, and he shook his head. "Never mind," he murmured, feeling awkward and stupid. Giving them both a slight nod, he turned and walked out the door.

He was at his Jeep before he turned around to see Benjamin Graywolf walking up the sidewalk after him.

"We're all staying up at the Wakefield place," he said without preamble. "And I would bet if you wandered up there sometime around two this afternoon, you just might find her alone.''

Dylan stared at this man who was a stranger to him, feeling an immediate kinship, and offered him his hand. "Thanks."

Chapter 17

It was déjà vu. Only this time he knew what he'd had and lost, and what he wanted again—and he wasn't going to leave until he had it.

Dylan glanced at the small doorbell button, his hand perched to press it and call her to the door, but he dropped his hand in hesitation. He drew in a deep breath, feeling his heart pulse thick in his neck and rehearsing again what it was he wanted to say. He realized his work was cut out for him. Just getting her to listen was going to be rough, assuming she would even open the door at all. But he couldn't let that stop him. Taking another deep breath, he reached for the bell again.

Only he never had a chance to make contact with the button. The door suddenly flew open, and he found himself face-to-face with Marissa.

She gasped loudly, the purse in her hand falling to the floor, scattering its contents along the imposing black-and-white tiles of the foyer. "W-what are you doing here?"

His moment had come. She'd given him his cue, and it was time for him to plead his case, to launch into his well-thought-out, well-rehearsed speech . . . except he choked.

"Marissa, I . . ." he stammered in a hoarse voice. "Marissa, please . . ."

Suddenly his mind had gone blank. All those well-planned arguments, all those points he wanted to make and explanations he'd wanted to offer, were gone. All he could think about was that he loved her, and that nothing in his life would mean anything until he got her back.

He looked into her startled blue eyes, seeing the fear, seeing the tears springing up within them, and he died just a little inside. He stepped up into the foyer, causing her to stumble back another step, and said the only thing he could think of, the only thing he knew to be true. "I love you."

"Damn you. How can you say that to me?" Marissa demanded, shaking her head.

"I say it because it's true." He moved across the foyer toward her. "I love you. I always have. I always will."

"Dylan, please," Marissa pleaded, backing away. "Please, just go. Just go."

"Don't send me away. Marissa, please," he said, backing her against the carved newel post at the end of the ornate stairwell. "Don't send me away."

"Dylan," she said, sighing, tears splashing down from her lashes and onto her cheeks. "Just go."

"I love you," he said again, his hands settling at her waist. "Marissa, I love you, and you love me, too."

"No," she said, furiously shaking her head. She pushed his hands away, pushing past him. "I—I don't want to."

"I know, I don't deserve it," he agreed with a whisper, catching her by the arm and pulling her back to him. "I've been a jerk. I've made so many mistakes and I've hurt you so badly. God, I'm so sorry." He pulled her struggling into his arms. "But I love you, and that's never going to change."

"No, Dylan," she said as she struggled. "No, no, please."

But he already had his arms around her, already had pulled her close, and already was pressing his mouth to hers. "I love you," he murmured against her lips. "Don't send me away. I love you."

Marissa grappled, and she tried with everything she had to fight and resist. She couldn't think when he touched her, couldn't make her mind remember all the reasons she wanted him out of her life. She'd spent the last ten days trying desperately to leave it all behind her, trying desperately not to think of all she'd had, and all she'd lost.

And now he was here, holding her, kissing her and saying the words she longed to hear. But she had to be strong; she had to resist.

With one final burst of force, she pulled free of his hold, backing away. "It's not going to work, Dylan. It's too late, it's over."

"No," Dylan insisted, his voice booming loud in the huge entry. "Don't say that, don't even think it."

"But it's true," she said sadly. "We've had chances—two of them—and threw them both away." She took a step toward him. "I don't blame you, I really don't. I know it was me. I never should have kept the truth from you. You deserved to know you had a son. What I did was wrong, and now we all have to pay the price."

"No," Dylan said quietly, walking across the tiles to where she stood. "I'm not going to let you do this again."

"Do what again?"

"Play the martyr."

Anger flashed hot, and she felt it spread through her entire system. "Martyr? You're accusing me of being a martyr?"

"Well, aren't you blaming yourself for everything that's happened, taking all the responsibility, all the guilt?" He grabbed her by the upper arms. "Like it or not, you're not the only one involved here. I'm not going to let you throw all our lives away just because you feel like wearing a hair shirt.''

Marissa yanked her arms free, glaring up at him. ''How dare you say something like that to me?''

''How dare I? I'll tell you—because I love you, because we have something between us, something special, something you only find once in a lifetime if you're lucky, and sometimes not even then. And I'm not going to let you walk away from that—not again.'' He leaned toward her. ''I did and said a lot of stupid things sixteen years ago. I was hurt and embarrassed, and I covered it up by acting like I didn't care, by lashing out and being a jerk. Okay, I was young, and not very smart—maybe that was an excuse. But this time...'' He paused, breathing out a sad little laugh. ''This time I don't have that excuse, but obviously I'm still not very smart—I still lashed out, still covered up because I was hurt, because I was upset.'' He reached out, slipping his arms around her. ''Marissa, we're not kids anymore. Isn't it time we both got smart? I love you. I love Josh. I want us to be together, to be a family. I want a house and a mortgage, and so many kids we'll need one of those silly-looking minivans like Dom and Jill.'' He pulled her close, and she offered no resistance. ''Forgive me. Love me. Marry me.'' He bent close, kissing her long and deep. *''Please.''*

Marissa stared up into his dark eyes, her heart was ready to burst. ''Dylan, I'm...I'm scared. What about next time, what happens then, what happens if it all goes wrong again?''

''It never will,'' he murmured, reaching down and lifting her arms around his neck. ''We're too smart, we'll never let that happen.'' He kissed her with an aching tenderness that left them both trembling. ''I love you. Marry me.''

Marissa surrendered to what she'd wanted her whole life. ''Yes, yes, I will.''

Mallory burst through the door, her eyes wide and excited. She rushed up to Dylan and Marissa, throwing her arms around them both.

"Graywolf says ours are twins," she said excitedly, tears streaming down her face. "And yours will be, too."

* * * * * *

ᵺINTIMATE MOMENTS®

™ *Silhouette®*

COMING NEXT MONTH

#697 THE HEART OF DEVIN MACKADE—Nora Roberts
Heartbreakers/The MacKade Brothers

Though he'd still been a teenager, he'd had a man's heart, and he'd given it. Twelve years later Cassie Connor Dolin was free—but she wouldn't be for long. It was time for Devin MacKade to make his move....

#698 LOVER UNDER COVER—Justine Davis
Trinity Street West

Caitlin Murphy was no naive idealist, but she honestly felt she was making a difference at Trinity Street West. Then Quisto Romero shattered her world. The cocksure detective laid claim to the streets in search of a killer, sparking Caitlin's fury...and an explosive passion.

#699 DANGEROUS—Lee Magner

His reputation had only worsened with time, but Case Malloy wouldn't let idle talk keep him from catching the man who'd framed his father for murder. He would do *anything* to solve the crime— except involve sweet Clare Brown. Because she couldn't possibly imagine the consequences of falling for a man like him.

#700 HOMECOMING—Sally Tyler Hayes

Who was she...really? Foggy images of another life lurked in the recesses of her mind, but A.J. had always suppressed them...until Jack MacAlister began asking questions. The rugged prosecutor somehow worked his way into her heart, causing A.J. to wonder if he wanted *her*—or just the truth.

#701 THE QUIET ONE—Alicia Scott
The Guiness Gang

Cagney Guiness had left the big city seeking peace, but what he found was sheer chaos. A murder mystery had put everyone in his small-town home on edge...particularly acting sheriff Guiness. Because he'd grown way too close for comfort to prime suspect Marina Walden.

#702 THE WEDDING ASSIGNMENT—Cathryn Clare
Assignment: Romance

The bride had been hijacked. Rae-Anne Blackburn should have been walking down the aisle, but instead found herself abducted by her former love, Wiley Cotter. He claimed he was protecting her from her dangerous fiancé, but the only danger Rae-Anne sensed was her own raging desire for the man she'd never stopped loving.

INTIMATE MOMENTS®
Silhouette®

CODE NAME: DANGER

by
Merline Lovelace

Return to Merline Lovelace's world of spies and lovers as
CODE NAME: DANGER, her exciting miniseries, concludes in
February 1996 with Perfect Double, IM #692.

In the assignment of her life, Maggie Sinclair assumed
the identity of an assassin's target—the vice president
of the United States! But impersonating this high-
powered woman was child's play compared to
her pretend love affair with boss Adam Ridgeway.
Because Maggie had done a lot of things
undercover...except fall in love.

Don't miss a single scintillating story in the
CODE NAME: DANGER miniseries—*because
love is a risky business....* Found only in—

INTIMATE MOMENTS
Silhouette®

MAGGIE-4

Alicia Scott's

Elizabeth, Mitch, Cagney, Garret and Jake:

Four brothers and a sister—though miles separated them, they would always be a family.

Don't miss a single, suspenseful—sexy—tale in Alicia Scott's family-based series, which features four rugged, untamable brothers and their spitfire sister:

THE QUIET ONE...IM #701, March 1996

THE ONE WORTH WAITING FOR...IM #713, May 1996

THE ONE WHO ALMOST GOT AWAY...IM #723, July 1996

"The Guiness Gang," found only in—

INTRODUCING...

A collection of award-winning books by award-winning authors! From Harlequin and Silhouette.

Heaven In Texas
by Curtiss Ann Matlock

National Reader's Choice Award Winner— Long Contemporary Romance

Let Curtiss Ann Matlock take you to a place called *Heaven In Texas*, where sexy cowboys in well-worn jeans are the answer to every woman's prayer!

"Curtiss Ann Matlock blends reality with romance to perfection!"
—*Romantic Times*

Available this March wherever Silhouette books are sold.

HEARTBREAKERS

Attention all adventure-seekers:

Have we got the excitement—and the men—for you!

In March—THE HEART OF DEVIN MacKADE,
by *New York Times* bestselling author Nora Roberts:
Devin MacKade had given his heart to a woman
only once, but it hadn't been enough for her. Twelve
years later, Cassie Connor Dolin was free and in
need of a good man's love. It was time for Devin to
make his move....

In April—SURVIVE THE NIGHT, by Marilyn Pappano:
Framed! Dillon Boone needed shelter from some
dangerous enemies, and he had only one option:
take Ashley Benedict hostage. Could he prove his
innocence to his beautiful—if unwilling—savior...and
keep them both alive until morning?

In May—MADDY LAWRENCE'S BIG ADVENTURE,
by Linda Turner: Ace MacKenzie was a storybook
hero, and everything prim-and-proper librarian
Maddy Lawrence wanted in a man. But Ace had a
way of landing in big trouble—and arousing even the
most sheltered of women....

INTIMATE MOMENTS®
Silhouette

TRINITY STREET WEST

where danger lies around every corner—and the
biggest danger of all is falling in love.

Meet the men and women of Trinity Street West in the
new Intimate Moments miniseries by

Justine Davis

beginning in March 1996 with

LOVER UNDER COVER (Intimate Moments #698):

Caitlin Murphy was determined to make a
difference at Trinity Street West. Then cocky detective
Quisto Romero shattered her world. He was willing to
risk everything to catch a young boy's killer—and to
conquer the defenses she had put around her heart.

Don't miss this new series—only from

INTIMATE MOMENTS®
Silhouette®